SCIENCE FICTION
CONSORTIUM

SCIENCE FICTION CONSORTIUM

THE CONSORTIUM

COMPILED BY

JOT RUSSELL

Cover Art by: Ami Hart and A. L. Scott

Edited by A. L. Scott

Acknowledgments

"Temporal Shift" Copyright © 2014 Jot Russell
"The Watch Spring" Copyright © 2014 Allen H. Quintana
"A Shepherd No More" Copyright © 2014 Andy McKell
"Vampirecratic Menace - A Case Study?" Copyright © 2014 Richard Bunning
"Luna-1" Copyright © 2014 James Newman
"The Destroyer of Syn" Copyright © 2014 Ami Hart
"Cold New Planet" Copyright © 2014 Joy V. Smith
"Darklings in the Glow" Copyright © 2014 Sterren
"Host" Copyright © 2014 A. L. Scott
"Consortium" Copyright © 2014 Jot Russell

TABLE OF CONTENTS

FOREWORD

Con sor tium: an agreement, combination, or group (as of companies) formed to undertake an enterprise beyond the resources of any one member

- Merriam-Webster© 11th Collegiate Dictionary

To write is to dream; to look beyond the resources of ourselves of that which we might achieve in this life. This is especially true in science fiction. One need only imagine to travel through time or space, to summon the dead, to create alien species of unrestricted proportions, to awaken intelligence within a machine, or to build a machine that can breathe life into a dead planet. In science fiction, all is possible, except for a void of creation. For without creativity, there is no story, there is no art, there is no imagination.

As with those before, a boy was raised to believe the ancient stories of the Earth being the center of our universe, where all heavenly bodies circled around us. But without the logic (in which math represents) to back up this tale, his studies led him to write a different story. Nicolaus Copernicus placed us in a new realm of what was considered fiction, where the Earth and other planets circled around the Sun. Moreover, by imagining his sight to extend beyond the naked eye, he predicted that a magnified view of Venus would cast a crescent image similar to that of our moon. A theory that Galileo later proved to be correct.

Arthur C. Clark wrote, "Any significantly advanced technology is indistinguishable from magic." We would say that the real magic starts with imagination. Because if we lacked the ability to expand our minds, to reach beyond that which we have yet to achieve, we might still perceive a wheel as magic. For once we learned to draw upon the walls of a cave, our potential became limitless.

Open your mind and allow us to give you a sample of our imagination.

- The Consortium

TEMPORAL SHIFT

By

Jot Russell

TEMPORAL SHIFT

Story and designs by Jot Russell

This is a work of fiction. Aside from the reference to some historic figures and the horrific attacks on 9/11, all characters and events portrayed in this story are fictional, and any resemblance to real people or other incidents is purely coincidental.

Ground Zero

The local blue stopped us at Canal Street. I showed my federal badge to the cop and he waved us through. We parked the van in front of the courthouse and walked the few blocks to Ground Zero. An inch of gray covered the scene that led down Church Street. When I turned the corner, I was immeasurably struck by the sight; a metal skeleton stretching up a hundred feet. Below, an unorganized web of dust covered men and women extending onto the pile. I saw each of them handing buckets of debris to the next on the line, with no visibly present command structure. None asking for special assignments or pushing their weight around as to how to do something. No orders given, but everyone doing exactly what was needed to be done. Driving in, I had only questions about what to do or how to help. In one glance, it made complete sense. I stepped up to the back of a line and handed a bucket to the person who got in line behind me.

Five hours straight working deeper onto the wreckage that was once the south tower of the World Trade Center. A hundred and ten stories reduced to a pile that compressed down to ground level. Across the street, part of the building's skeleton had crashed into and hung fifteen stories above us from a neighboring office tower. I looked over at the hundreds who blindly worked directly below, ignoring the perilous tons of steel that seemed ready to fall down upon us. Someone told me that wasn't the primary concern.

"They have lasers measuring the movement of One Liberty Plaza," he said as he pointed.

I looked over at the forty story tower that loomed above.

"What's wrong? It looks untouched."

"The foundation was hit by the collapse. They're afraid it's going to tip over on us."

"Shit!"

The guy handed me another bucket. I passed it over and waited for the next as I glanced back up at the black office tower. I couldn't discern any such wobble, but I wasn't about to question their measurements. I continued with one eye on the buckets and another on the building. I guess word got around, because we all seemed ready to bolt when someone yelled, "It's coming down!"

Like scurrying rats, we blindly ran for our lives down Washington Street. Instinctively, my arms were extended out, ready to push anyone in the crowd aside if they slowed. A bunch of us turned the corner, hoping the building we ran around would provide some protection from the impact debris. There was none. One Liberty stood strong. I wish I could say the same about our nerves. Not that that had stopped any of us from returning to the pile. In five minutes, the same collection of dust covered men and women were back working feverishly on the site. Back to handing over cement filled buckets and cadaver bags that smelled like bad milk. The latter I carried with honor, each time wondering if I knew the person within. The only other breaks I took were for gulps of water and when there were calls for silence. We'd all stop and watch as those across the rubble listened hopefully for the sound of living souls somewhere within the gaps. As I resumed the mindless process of passing along buckets, a man walked up with a dog that had little protective booties on his paws. The retriever paused, gave the ground a sniff and looked back up at his master. The man looked at me and simply said, "Start digging there."

No please, thank you, nor any pleasantries. Believe me, it wasn't required or expected. I broke from the line and knelled down to start lifting blocks of cement. I didn't even have to look for a bucket, as they appeared in front of me; stacks of buckets that were thrown in to anyone who was ready to catch them. I filled up the first and turned to see a new strand in the web extending from me. The front man took hold of the bucket, handed it over and waited for me to fill another. Each time I pulled up another gray block, I half expected to see my brother's face on the other side. Steve took the job back in 97, loving each day until his last. He and his crew at Rescue-4 called it "The Best Job in the World." I had argued that being a C.I.A. officer was better, but he started to have me believing. Where else can you get overtime working just two days a week? Two twenty-four hour shifts, hanging out with friends, eating, sleeping and getting to do something exciting when a run comes over the wire. Exciting? I picked up another block from my knees, realizing it was anything but.

I paused at another sound of cheers, thinking they found someone. Looking around, there was a fire fighter waving a flag that he had found. I stopped to watch three of them attach it to a leaning pole and contemplate its ascent. Exhausted and hungry, I turned back around and lifted another block into a bucket. Aside from cement, steel, wires and these square rubberized floor tiles, nothing existed on the pile but rescue workers. No chairs, desks, computers, carpet, nor my brother. A month later and they still would have no sign of remains to give me peace.

Under the next block, I saw something: A crystal orb, shattered and burnt, but still somehow intact. Moving my hand over to drop it into a bucket, I hesitated, looking at the writing on the globe: "AON - Insure your vision." I put it aside and got back to work.

The next day, the President came to the site and gave his speech. "I can hear you! The rest of the world hears you! And the people [cheers] and the people who knocked these buildings down will hear all of us soon!"

The chant erupted, "U.S.A.! U.S.A.! U.S.A.! U.S.A.!"

I yelled out my devotion, understanding there was other work to be done. I realized I would serve my brother better by doing my job. And work I did, perhaps more feverishly than that first day on the pile. One by one, we followed the money and intelligence trail that expanded our view of the web they wove. I guess word of my efforts extended up the chain, as a general came down to commend me on my achievements.

"We have another assignment for you."

"Anything sir. You can count on me!"

"Then come with me. We have a suit for you to try on."

I followed him down to a basement facility. It was a part of the Pentagon I had never seen. We passed three security details, and then there was none; just engineers in white suits working in a clean room.

"I'm not an engineer, sir. My training is military."

"That's not the type of suit I was talking about." He pushed a button to reveal some type of advanced combat gear that I thought Batman might wear.

"Battle armor?"

"That's what it was originally intended for, yes. The high-power electromagnetic field it generates was designed to bend light while repelling small arms fire; even rocket propelled grenades."

"Bend light? You mean like a cloaking device?"

"That's right. But it also had an unexpected consequence."

"What's that, sir?"

"It warps time."

"Excuse me?"

"Yeah, I didn't believe it at first either. During testing, they had an overload. The suit's occupant erupted in a fireball within the sphere and disintegrated. At first they didn't know what had happened. But a video recording showed a strange echo, like two transparent spheres occupying the same space at the same time."

"Jeez! Was there anything left of him?"

"No, there was nothing left of her actually. She was our top scientist; the one who came up with the original design."

"Damn!"

"I'll say. It set us back several months. Luckily, the others were able to take over her work and replicate another suit. Afterward, they tested it on a dummy, pulling the thing on a wheeled table."

"Did it explode again?"

"It sure did. The cart stopped after the rope snapped with almost no load. And the rope's breaking strength was rated for ten thousand pounds."

"Great! And you want me to wear that thing?"

"We sure do. It's safe as long as you're occupying a different space when you disengage the system. The third try was built on top of a Segway. Apparently, three is a charm."

"I guess this is going to take a leap of faith on my part. So what's the plan?"

"Well, what would you do with a time machine?" he asked.

"I'd go back a couple months and take out those freaking bastards."

"I was hoping you would say that. Looks like you'll have your chance."

"Yes sir!"

Battle Plan

"Let me introduce you to your new partner. Tric, come on over here."

"Tony Tricarico," was all he said, offering his hand.

"Phil Graseck, nice to meet you."

"Tric will bring you up to speed on the suit."

"So you've worn it?"

"Sure have. Works like a charm as long as you disengage in an empty spot."

"I've heard. So, what's the plan?"

"Walk in the park. We know where these scum bags are and when we can take them out without drawing attention. And being that this project was in the works for a couple years, we have an in with General Gentak."

I looked towards the general. "So you know we're already coming?"

"Nope, but as soon as we realized this was possible, I set up a code phrase to identify shifters as part of my team."

"Wow, good thinking."

"Actually, it was a suggestion from one of the engineers."

"So, what's the password?"

"I'll tell you that once we're ready to send you back. I haven't told anyone else and I'm not about to start until I know you're on your way back."

"So all we have to do is go back and tell you what's going to happen, right?"

"Negative. The government today will stop at nothing to defeat these bastards. However, a couple of months ago is a different story. Our agency does not have assassins and it will take time to convince others that they are needed before such a threat is known. Sorry, but aside from financial, equipment and moral support, you guys will be on your own."

"Understood. So when do we go back?" I asked, rubbing my hands together.

"Patience. Let's make sure you are both properly trained on the suit and the objective. We have all the time in the world, but we need to get it right the first time. There is no telling what type of damage we might cause by altering too much of the past."

The first tests were simple hops. I triggered the temporal shift, took a few steps to the right, and then deactivated the system. The strange thing is that I didn't see myself from the future appear in the spot that I knew I would later...I mean, earlier would occupy. But when I shifted, I saw myself waiting to shift and that man I once was clearly reacted to my presence. The engineers explained that I didn't go back in time to the same reality I was viewing. Once I triggered the shift and returned to the past, it was a completely new reality.

It didn't seem like a new reality to me. I returned back to the same apartment, with the same clothes that I remembered leaving on the floor from the night before. As I cleaned up after my alternate self in my newly acquired time-line, I thought about what would have happened if I decided not to jump when I saw myself appear. Would there now be two of us in this time-line?

I woke up the next morning; only remembering part of how the notion haunted my sleep. I brushed it off and focused on the task at hand; two more weeks of training to prepare for our assault. I almost wanted to shift forward the two weeks just so I could go after them today. These douche bags and their "Big Wedding" won't know what hit them. It was suiting that our operation was dubbed, "Big Funeral."

I was tired from another day of training, looking to unload some of the tension that was building within me. The next morning I woke, thinking about my brother and cursing the bastards that killed him and countless others. The month before, when I was driving towards Ground Zero to help dig, part of me felt better knowing I was occupied towards the cause. So many others, I knew, felt helpless. All they could do was donate money or blood, without getting the chance to directly help or show their devotion to the country. I was about to take a step to alter history, but even though I was preparing to prevent the attacks and save my brother, my feelings were not appeased. I guess revenge is not realized until the dish is served.

I saw that Tric was heading out as well, so talked him into catching a beer.

"What an amazing tool we have." I took a sip of my draft, lifted the glass and asked, "How cool would it be to shake the hand of Arthur Guinness?"

Tric said, "If given a chance, I'd like to meet Jesus."

"Nice one! I think I'd go back to the Kennedy assassination and see what really happened."

"No need, Jim Garrison had it right. It was an inside job."

"Wow, how can you say that?"

"Tell you what. After we take care of our little problem, I'd say the government owes us a little Texas vacation. Heck, they don't even have to know about it!"

I could tell he was serious and I subdued my nod by lifting the pint glass for another gulp. As I sat there enjoying the bitter perfection of the liquid, something hit me.

Tric must have noticed, because he looked over and asked, "What?"

"It just occurred to me that we know where bin Laden has been after the fact and could just take him out ten years back instead of going through the trouble of killing twenty."

He gave me a serious look. "I got a better idea. How about we go back and take out Mohammad? We could wipe away their whole religion."

I coughed out my beer. "That's crazy man! Even if we change something a decade back, the risk of negatively impacting the future is extremely likely. Perhaps we could take some steps to lessen the blow, but if we go back centuries, all bets are off. Even if we didn't change anything, our presence there would likely be enough to affect at least the weather today."

"So, what's wrong with altering the weather a little?"

"Think about it man. Events are planned and changed on account of the weather. Even an election can be altered due to the impact of a storm. Battles won or lost. I'm sure there are plenty of examples like this in history."

"Yeah, I guess you're right. Hey, did you see that game last night?" he asked, clearly changing the subject.

I dropped the argument and went along with the conversation, "Hell yeah. That guy Brady sure can throw."

"If this technology got out, it sure would make things hard for the bookies."

"I'd say it would take the fun out gambling," I interjected.

"Since when isn't it fun to win?"

"Winning doesn't suck, but it's not gambling if you know who's going to win."

"Fair enough."

Flight School

The powerful hum kicked in and was quickly silenced by the masking system. I looked up towards the mirror to verify Tric and myself turning transparent in the room. The light from behind bent around the energy spheres surrounding us, bringing a distorted image of the general into view. I saw him salute and returned the gesture, even though I knew he couldn't see it.

I stepped forward, swinging my arm down to engage the shift. Ahead was a wall, but I ignore the false barrier and walked through towards the exterior of the building. The fire had long since been put out and the crew was working to repair the damage. As I watched, they pulled down a support element that they had just assembled and would, in forward time, assemble again. I increased the power, hastening my temporal shift into the past. Smoke collected down from the sky and into the building. As my clock ran back to 9:37am on September 11th, I rolled the shift down to a tenth of a second back for every second I felt. A huge thick cloud of black smoke sank down and turned into a massive fireball that imploded past me. Even with the flames around me, I felt neither the heat nor shock wave as it was sucked into the building and was gone. Replaced was the massive aircraft rising out of the building and up from the ground. I stood for a minute, watching it escape back into the past.

All this time, I had no sight of Tric. Not that I would. As long as he continued to shift, his presence would not be seen because he wouldn't completely be there. For all I knew, he was standing next to me taking in his own personal view of the accounts on that tragic day. I brushed it off and increased the shift rate. I looked up to see the sun flash around the world. I let it cycle a couple hundred times before decreasing the rate back closer to real-time.

I turned towards the building and decided to walk in through the entrance that I had just seen destroyed. I smiled at the heavily armed security personal, who were oblivious to my presence as they tended to others who were walking backward towards the exit. I continued ahead and over towards the general's office. I stepped through the door to see him behind his desk, scribbling something. I verified the time on my clock and lifted my arm to disengage the system. Surprisingly, he put down his pen and sat up, staring directly at where I was to appear. I disengaged the shift and powered down the suit.

The general looked at me and asked, "Nice of you to stop by. Can I get you something?"

"How about a cup of Earl Gray?" I answered using the code phrase.

Instead of picking up his pen, as I had seen him do, he got up and shook my hand. My mind immediately started to wonder; did I just stop him from writing some type of order that would affect the future? I guess I was already rewriting history in this newly created time-line.

"How can I help you?" he asked.

"We need to stop a wedding," I replied.

"Confirmed! Tric already shifted back and said you would be coming. Phil, we'll have you set up with a vehicle and a driver. Tric said you'd be heading to Florida."

"Affirmative."

When I saw the two of them exit from flight school, my blood began to boil. It's amazing we didn't put two and two together to bring in a couple Middle Eastern students after they blatantly told their flight instructor that they weren't interested in learning how to land. Well, they say that everyone's a genius in hindsight. If so, call me a genius. My driver and I watched, as the two men made it to their van and drove away.

"Should we go after them?" my driver asked.

"You can, because I'll be the one driving the van."

I got out, triggered the suit and walked right up alongside of where the van had been parked. In position, I looked back around to see my echo still within the car waiting to shift. I turned towards the entrance and stood ready. There down the road, I saw the vehicle back into the parking lot and stop alongside me. I pulled out my weapon and waited for the driver's door to open. He gave a surprised look of fear as I disengaged and appeared before him. He sat there hypnotized as I lifted the silenced 38 and put one shot in his heart. His partner panicked, turning to open the other door. One small ping and the deed was done; two of the four pilots out of the picture. I ignored the feelings rushing through me and climbed in. Quickly, I laid the bodies on the floor, grabbed the keys and set off to let the driver catch up with me. He would, as long as my echo also told him to do so before shifting back to repeat the task that I had just performed. Would his echo also have to do the same? How many echoes of reality can there be? Again, I shook the notion out of my head and waited for the driver to catch up with me a quarter mile down the road. Together, we set off to clean away the evidence and prepare for the next phase.

The rendezvous was critical. Without meeting back up to marry the time-lines, we might separately return to two alternate futures; each incomplete from the mission objectives. I walked up to the 13th green of the East Potomac Golf Course at 10pm on July 4th and disengaged my suit. I stood alone, watching the fireworks with a proud feeling of hope and accomplishment. "God, it's good to be an American."

"You got that right!"

I looked behind to see Tric standing there.

"Mission accomplished?" I asked, knowing the answer.

"Just as I said; walk in the park."

"Nice. I can't wait to see my brother again."

"What's the rush? We have all the time in the world."

The words struck a nerve. "I need this, man. I need to see my brother."

He continued looking out at the fireworks. "Just a minute, here's the finale."

I took a breath and patiently watched the colorful explosions in the dark night. The patterns gave me a feeling of déjà vu. I looked over towards the Washington Mall, knowing my brother and I were there together watching the scene. I thought to myself, next year, we will again.

Consequence

We stood on the green and engaged our suits. As the spheres around Tric and I grew transparent to the world, the world itself suddenly changed. Instead of the city lights and fireworks illuminating the grass and trees on this small golf-course island, the only light I saw was from the billion stars that shone above. A fireworks display far grander than that we had just seen. My pupils expanded to take in the Milky Way and all the constellations in spectacular view. But there, in the corner of my eye, something else was out of place. I looked down from the heavens towards the shattered remains of a large structure. As I turned to take in the scene, I realized I was no longer on a golf-course, but the charred relic of a destroyed city. I walked over towards the water's edge and stared across the Potomac. The place I knew that housed the airport, Pentagon and surrounding buildings was also replaced by that of a massive and broken metropolis.

My being shook from the scene, as I helplessly wandered through the rubble. I had seen such destruction just a few weeks before, but now it was all-encompassing. I only half realized that I was still shifting forward in time, because there was no person or animal to give movement to this still life.

The dawn came quickly. The sun rose and sped across the sky ten times faster than normal. It cast the clear and endless view of what must have been a monumental civilization; matched only to its monumental failure. I continued my gut wrenching survey of the destruction. Over beyond towards where the White House should stand, lay the remains of a flattened pyramid. "Who were they? Egyptian? But how?" I asked myself.

I looked over and saw it. "No!" There on the pile lay a large block that displayed the sideways image of an eagle. But not just any eagle. It was a double-headed Heraldic Eagle. "These were Romans!"

I blindly walked through the destruction asking myself, "How?"

As my eyes opened wide, I spoke his name, "Tricarico!"

Tric had done it. He had done exactly what he had suggested. By going after one man, he wiped out a complete religion. But instead of just the genocide of a people, he took out the whole human race. It all made sense. The Arab unification that Mohammad initiated through the installation of a common language, religion and enemy, saw to the balance of power that held the Roman Empire in check and eventually help to lead to its demise. Without this unifying force, the empire rose in power and technology. Control over the land, sea, air and atom. But as with many things in life, control can also be an illusion.

I pushed myself to ignore this illusion, realizing the only real change was to my mission. As I engaged a change in the shift, the sun slowed down and reversed its direction. I hastened its apparent orbit until there was a bright band of light that spanned the sky. I watched the band rise and fall with the seasons. Suddenly, the majestic city appeared back before me; no longer an urban wasteland, but a forest of towers in glass and steel. I looked at the years ticking down on my wrist screen. Nineteen-hundred came and went, but still the towers persisted. One-by-one, they reduced towards the ground and were replaced by smaller structures. In time, these structures disappeared into the woods and were gone. In the distance, I saw an Indian village that shifted in orientation for each year that passed. For thousands of years, these people lived as one with the land. I watched and wondered, allowing myself to question the morality of one society over another. But that wasn't my question to answer, nor was it Tric's. We were not gods, set here to change the course of humanity. We were only here to prevent a single attack. Apparently, that wasn't enough for him. His deep seated anger fueled a rage of bigotry against Muslims, not unlike how many Americans felt for the Japanese after Pearl Harbor. If he lived during that period, would he choose such destruction against their race? Perhaps so, because most did not understand that they would later become one of our strongest allies. Maybe that Great War was needed to grow our race out of adolescence and the limited use of our nuclear weapons to paint the awareness of their capabilities on everyone's mind.

My mother once told me, "Sometimes making an enemy is unavoidable, but that does not mean that two foes cannot later become friends." But now, the man that I had become friends with had changed my view of him to that of an enemy; an enemy of humanity. I had no luxury to view him in any other light. He had to be stopped and I was the only one who could stop him.

I reversed the time-line back towards the future, realizing the natives from this period provided no means for me to cross the ocean and travel to Mecca. Nor could I rendezvous here with Tric, even if I knew the date he decided to first appear back from the future. That future no longer exists, nor does the original English-speaking American colony he had returned back to. The Roman aberration that I found myself within was a direct consequence of the new reality that he created.

What I needed was a means to pay for such transport. For Tric, he could have walked right into the Fort Knox of the time, grab a couple bars of gold and be on his merry way. For me, not only was the city foreign, but the language as well.

I walked down a street of wooden homes and found my first required item. I disengaged the shift, grabbed the white, Roman garb, and used it to cover over the mechanical suit that was as foreign to these people as they were to me.

"Chi sei?!"

I turned to see a man who appeared from the next room. Damn, I should have checked to make sure the house was clear before disengaging.

"Si, si," I said for delay as I fumbled within the cloak for my weapon. When I looked up, he was gone, but reappeared a few moments later through the doorway with some type of rifle in hand. He saw my gun and lowered his to shoot.

The poor guy was in the wrong place at the wrong time, leaving me no choice but to shoot. I tried to discount the feelings. Did his life matter? I was currently employed to wipe away not just him, but his entire Roman civilization. In the time-line that I sought to restore, he wouldn't even exist. I realized that I should be drawing more concern over the loss of a bullet. I could steal whatever I wanted here, but ammunition for my pistol didn't exist in this world. I collected the man's gun and shifted slowly back in time to find some type of short-term wealth.

I left the city of Washington (what they called Halacotania) on a fifty foot yacht. With the proper coins and some work over translating my desired destination, we set off for Alexandria. Conversation was difficult at best, but I welcomed the forty day sail to brush up on my Latin and better understand this culture. There is something to be said about "when in Rome, do like the Romans," because the crew seemed very interested in my presence and origin. I wasn't about to inform them. I guess you could say, "what happens in Vegas stays in Vegas." Not that I had been there, but the notion is a big part of our culture.

The ship's captain set me up with a transport to the Red Sea and I made sure to show the generous tip he received in front my new escort. In any society, good customers can be hard to find. And since my means were without limit, it felt good to splurge a little. Besides, anything that I shifted around here would have no impact back home.

I guess it left an impression because my new host offered me to be carried in a plush, eight-man coach. I pointed towards a horse and then myself. He gave little argument once I agreed to his price. I found out later that was the purchase price of the animal. Again, he happily accepted the animal back as a tip for his service.

Mecca was a bustling city, with the same presence of Roman Catholic rule all around. I was still five-hundred years out from Tric's contamination of this time-line, but I decided to settle in for the night before drawing up my battle plans. Tric and I had weapons from the future and perhaps he expected my return, but would he expect hostilities between us? I had to assume he would. Why else would I leave the memory of my brother and go through the pains of this journey unless it was for drastic reasons. The one thing I had was history on my side. He had killed a child that had long since been forgotten by the overwhelmed collection of censuses. A drop in the bucket now, but I knew once I got closer and found the location of the uncle, I'd be able to obtain an account of when and how the child died. With this information, it was just a matter of shifting back to just before the event to take out Tric before he takes out the child. I guess I could try to reason with him, describing the Armageddon that was to come once he completed the deed. Could I take that chance? Tric also had no family, which led me to question why? Why would they send someone who had nothing to lose from the loss of our time-line? Would he even go back to see the destruction of our species, or was he using the device to live like a King in this time? I knew if I stayed much longer, the intoxication of such power could certainly lead me towards corruption. I kept reminding myself this wealth was just Monopoly money. Instead of selfish desires, I held onto my ideals and goals for the mission. Tric hadn't, and that suggested to me that he was already corrupt. He wanted this power, and like a drug, it likely became more important than the consequence of its usage.

Termination

Tric appeared outside the house just minutes before the child was said to have choked on a date. I disengaged, and pointed my weapon.

To my surprise, he made no sudden reaction to my presence. Just smiled and said, "Are you here to help me Phil?"

"Yes, help you from destroying our world."

"Is it that hard? With our suits, we could easily prevent any such holocaust."

"So you've seen it?"

"Yes, quite a fireworks display. Like I said, it'll be easy to correct."

"Even if you did, without the child you are here to kill, we would be serving the United Empire of Rome."

"Serve? Why would we be servants? They would serve us."

"You gave an oath to the flag."

"That flag no longer exists."

"It will again!"

As I slowly extended my weapon, Tric's voice echoed from behind, "Freeze!"

I glanced around to see Tric's echo standing behind me. I lifted my hands and asked, "Which Tric are you?"

"The one here to take care of our little problem."

"If you kill Mohammed, you'll create a far larger problem; the destruction of humanity."

"Bull shit!"

I continued, "It's true, Tric. Your echo here already did it once. Without the unification of the Arabs, the Roman Empire will grow to rule the world."

"And we will be its Emperor!" said the first Tric.

"Both of you?" I asked.

"Why not? There are countless time-lines that we can control together."

"No! If you do this, the world will be destroyed."

"Is this true?" asked the Tric from behind.

"Nothing we can't fix, starting with Phil." said the first, drawing his gun.

I ducked, flipping the gun that hung from my finger to get it back into my grasp. The first shot went past my head as I extended my aim to shoot. I squeezed the trigger, hitting the Tric in front of me in the head. The sound of my weapon masked the other, but the exit wound that appeared from my chest took over all my senses.

"That wasn't part of the plan," I spoke, dropping to the floor from the pain and sudden weakness. I rolled towards my back to see the other Tric still pointing his gun at me.

He stepped close. "You were a good partner. Sorry it has to end like this."

I watched as he pointed the gun at my head.

The muffled ping shot out, and I lay there confused as to why I was still around to recognize the sound. I opened my eyes to see Tric's smile sink as he dropped to the ground. Behind him was the echo of myself that I had introduced into this time-line with a gun in his hand.

I lay there, holding my hand on the wound, with blood continuing to flow from my chest. My echo ran over and knelt down beside me. "We gotta get you to a doctor. Can you stand and trigger the suit?"

"It's too late for that."

"Then I'll shift back earlier and take them both out."

"No, you'll risk a new time-line with a Tric from the future potentially seeing something and deciding to shift back earlier than you."

I saw myself nodding. "I'm sorry; I should have come in at the right time."

"You did good and together we restored the time-line."

"Nothing is set until we get rid of these suits."

I followed his gaze. "Place the other Tric on top of himself and leave the rest to me."

Again, he nodded his agreement and pulled the two of them on top of each other.

Oblivion

I watched my dying echo engage his suit, become transparent and then disappear into thin air. Backing away, a ball of bright light erupted from the floor, shrunk to a pin point, and was gone. I looked up to see the child looking at me in disbelief. Quickly, I triggered my suit and shifted forward in time.

The expression of the boy's face stayed in my memory. Did I create a new time-line, or was I just restoring that which was laid out before me? Did this child independently grow to believe himself a prophet, or did his vision of me and the bright light influence his path?

The real question I needed to answer was, "What should I do about the future?" As I shifted forward, I knew the time-line I was riding would be preserved. But any step I jumped back could potentially introduce a thread of time that leads to darkness. It took the loss of my partner and friend to understand this. The intoxication from the absolute power that I wielded had brought my will close to the point of self-justifiable corruption. If I truly crossed that line, I knew that there would be no coming back. I was so easily able to write off the Roman man that I shot in his home once I knew his time-line would be erased. Perhaps Tric felt that anyone was expendable as long as the future was in flux.

Taking small steps, I stood witness as the historic events I learned in school unfolded before me. With my present drawing near, I continued to question my mission. In my mind, the primary target had changed. Instead of the natural events that shape humanity based on its struggles, it was the unnatural manipulation of these struggles that presented the real danger. If I notified Pearl Harbor Command that the Japanese were on the way, it might have prevented death and destruction to the American Navy, but perhaps it would have also prevented us from entering World War II. Even though I could use my suit to see what the future will bring, it wasn't my place to play God and take guesses towards what I feel would be a rosier outcome. I had to step back and trust humanity to direct its own future.

I saw my target leave Langley in a Mazda Rx-8. I cycled the time-shift to less than half that of normal time to easily follow the car by foot. It took a few hours to pace her back to her apartment, but I welcomed the time to consider my thoughts. Without my interference, she would be dead in a year anyway. If I did nothing, the man I am from this time would cycle back from the future only to return here contemplating the same course of action. I had no choice but to kill her.

Still, I hesitated. In the dark, it would have been easy to take her out next to the car and leave her as a mugging victim. I increased the shift to near normal time and stood there watching her walk towards the building. Somehow, I was struck by her presence. She walked around as if the world was in her hand, and I guess in some way, it was. There had been women in my life, but I always found myself married to my work. How is it that I would draw such feelings for the woman that I knew I had to kill?

I followed her up to see which apartment she lived in, and stood outside her door for a few minutes trying to muster the energy to complete the task. Rehearsing, I pulled out my gun and walked through the door. She was in the kitchen, making herself a cup of coffee. I stood in her way and pointed the gun. Suddenly, she turned and walked right through me. She paused for a moment, looking back with a strange expression. With a simple shake of her head, she turned and walked into her bedroom.

I followed her in and watched, somehow hypnotized by her. She took a sip, put down the coffee and started to get undressed. My heart raced as I gazed at her perfect form. She folded the clothes before placing them into the hamper, walked to her bathroom and ran a shower. I felt powerless to act, standing there shaking in my skin. Increasing the shift, I hastened her exit of the shower and waited for her to put something on. I turned, exited the apartment and disengaged the shift.

Knock, knock.

I heard her come towards the door. "Who is it?"

I displayed my badge to the peep hole. "C.I.A. ma'am. Sorry, but I need to ask you a few questions."

She opened the door as far as the bar-lock would let her and gave me a confused expression. "What are you wearing?"

I looked down at my Roman cloak. "It's a long story."

She remained suspicious. "Let me see your badge again."

I handed it to her and she looked it over. "I'm going to have to call this in. Give me a minute," she said, closing the door.

I appeared behind her and knelt down on the floor of her hall. "Please don't."

She let out a quick scream and jumped around to see me kneeling. She took a few moments to calm her breath. "How did you get in?"

"Again, it's a long story. But it's a story I need to tell you."

"Why should I trust you?"

"Because I don't want to kill you." I pulled out my gun and placed it on the ground.

"Why would anyone want to kill me?"

"You're working on a suit and although you don't know it, are on the verge of a breakthrough."

She grew angry and actually took a step towards me. "That's top secret! Who told you? Who's your source?"

"General Gentak."

"The general wants me dead?"

"No, it doesn't have anything to do with the general. It only has to do with the battle armor you're working on."

"What about the suit?"

I removed the cloak to reveal her work. "Can we talk now?"

She stepped closer. "That's different from our latest design."

"That's because you haven't created it yet."

"What the hell are you talking about?!"

"I think it's easier if I show you." I got up and engaged the suit. Her eyes bulged as the sphere grew transparent. I disengaged without shifting time.

"Oh my God, it works!"

"A little too well, I'm afraid."

"What do you mean?" she asked and looked behind me at the door. "And how did you get in here?"

"That will take another demonstration. This time, I'm going to disappear completely and reappear in your living room in ten seconds." I engaged the suit, triggered the shift and walked past her. At two-times speed, I quickly walked over to the other room and disengaged. As I turned around, I saw that she held the gun that I had left on the floor and was pointing it at me.

"You were in here before you knocked, weren't you?"

"Yes."

"I felt something, just as I did then."

"I thought you did."

"Did you watch me?" She used her free hand to pull her pajama shirt further together.

"I saw you, but that's not why I was here."

"Why were you here?"

"To kill you."

"Why didn't you?"

"Because I don't want to. I just want to talk and let you decide what to do."

"Okay, talk."

"I'd rather you point that elsewhere."

She hesitated a moment, then lowered the weapon.

"Thank you. As you can see, the suit does more than just bend light, it bends time."

I could see that she had a sudden realization. "Bends time? Space-time? Oh my God, that's it! I can use overlapping gravity wells to spawn the chain-reaction." She moved to a table, put the gun down and started writing on a piece of paper."

"Please don't. It could be very bad if anyone learns of this."

"Why, it's just a cloaking device."

"It's a bit more than that. It allows the occupant to go back in time."

"What? That's impossible!"

"I'm here, ain't I?"

She nodded slowly. "Okay, let's say that it does. Why would you go back in time to kill me?"

"That's not why I came back. The general had us go back in time to prevent Muslim extremists from flying commercial airliners into the World Trade Center and Pentagon."

"No!" she gasped.

"In a few years from now, yes."

"What happened?"

"We stopped them, but my partner had other plans." I sat down and explained what had happened, leading me back to this day.

"So this is a new time-line, meaning you would have to stop them again?"

"That's correct."

"So you're going to stop them, right?"

"Negative."

"What?! You have to!"

"No, I can't. I won't."

"You call yourself an American? You would stand by to watch all those innocent people die?"

"I understand the loss, my brother died on 9/11."

"9/11? September 11th? What year?"

"2001."

"Oh my God!" She picked up the gun and pointed it at me. "Take off the suit!"

"I can't do that."

"You can and you will, or I'll put a bullet in your head and take it off your dead body."

I could see the determination in her eyes and knew she meant it. And since I was stupid enough to let her see how I engaged the system, I knew she would easily shoot me before I had a chance to shift. Still, I drew a glimmer of hope thinking about how history has a way of repeating itself. Slowly, I pulled off the gear and set it on the floor.

"Step over there," she pointed.

"Please listen to me."

She pushed the gun towards me as a way to demand my silence. I didn't comply.

"After the attacks, we initiated a war against these extremists. And we're winning. If we waited for them to get nuclear weapons, they could kill much more than a few thousand, they could kill millions."

"And if they did, we would go back and stop them. Don't you see?"

"Yes, I do see," I said, knowing there was no way to bring her back. Just as with Tric, she would never find her way back from the line that she didn't know she had already crossed.

"On the ground; face down!" she demanded.

I complied with her request, watching powerlessly from the floor as she donned the suit. She wasted no time. With the look of excitement on her face, she engaged the system. It happened sooner than I thought it would. For once, the sphere grew transparent; it spontaneously erupted in a ball of fire and evaporated into oblivion.

Forgiveness

I was wrong about the weather. On the morning of September 11th, it was again beautiful, calm and clear. But for those in the skies and in the buildings, it would be anything but.

I couldn't sleep for weeks, haunted by my own indecision on the matter. Do I tell the feds or even myself from this time-line? Do I call in a fire alarm on the building to try to evacuate those before the planes strike? For whatever reason, I had decided not to play God with the world and instead give to man that which God had already given: free will. I tried every argument to work against the logic that seemed so clear. Even the unknown souls of three thousand couldn't measure in my mind against what I had seen Tric's interference provide. And that was from the loss of just one man. But what is the measure of a man? If I saved but one, might it also see to the destruction of our race? Perhaps if I did save one, I might earn some part of forgiveness for the sin that I bore for the rest.

My brother was not a poet, priest or politician, he was a fire fighter. But not on this day. On this day, I made sure that he and the person that I was were far out on the Atlantic. The cruise tickets were each sent anonymously within a card that simply said, "Brothers forever!"

I prayed they would make those lives mean something.

THE WATCH SPRING

Copyright © 2014 by Allen H. Quintana

THE WATCH SPRING

By

Allen H. Quintana

The Watch Spring

It moved with a precision unmatched.

Every quaking moment and movement – synchronous with the steady rhythmic beat of its hands that hovered over a glittering constellation of gold and precious stones – bedazzled anyone privileged to see them. Its beautiful mechanizations cycled through tight orbits, never tangling in its micro universe, keeping time with its infinitely larger counterpart, matching the heavenly bodies in cyclical cadence.

Just a few external twists at the right time confirmed its day-to-day reliability and precision. This it had proven over thousands of times during lifetimes, from one to the next.

Decades would pass like scudding clouds across vast skies before time would edge ahead in slight instants. Then it was time for change in its micro universe. Like all things man-made, there was a limit to how long they lasted. Some more than others.

Its coil, not as looped as it once was, lost its old taut. Countless tugs to its spring started to tell and wear on its flex, and in its many years of reliable, precise timekeeping, it missed a beat. It was felt in unexplained ways.

It was time.

Bert Walker wasn't feeling his old self. *Must have been something he picked up at the office.* There was always something going around. That was the way of it; someone went on vacation, visited a sick aunt or other loved one they were forced mingle with at another distant family function, then shook a hand, inhaled somebody's half stifled sneeze, or grabbed a well-handled doorknob. It was easy to spread a bug. *That must be it. Great.*

Bert took care of himself; he jogged a mile or two after work most nights, more on weekends, and watched his diet. With a kid off in college and a marriage that didn't take, he had plenty of time to mind himself. So there was no reason why he should be less than the usual 100 percent he knew he should be. He knew what made him tick.

"Hiyo, Silver! What's with the long face?" Portly POR Bob smacked Bert on the back and laughed out loud at his unoriginal joke. His other hand clamped on the pastrami-on-rye Bob had every morning which earned him the nickname 'Pastrami On Rye Bob', or 'POR Bob' for short. Sometimes Bert called him 'PORB', alluding to Bob's shockingly bad breath, but Bert never said it out loud.

"Hey, POR Bob," Bert forced a smile. "You need to upgrade your material. Better come up with something funny, say from Bennett Cerf, or you'll be cross-examined at a McCarthy hearing for that puke you call humor."

"Commies – all of 'em!" POR Bob sniffed and tore a chunk out of his sandwich. "They should find 'em all guilty and ship 'em all off to Stalinland and be done with 'em," Bert inwardly grimaced at his colleague's mouthful of food, with drool on the side. The Senator McCarthy Hearings were big talk around the water cooler when voluptuous Irma was within earshot. When she was, then Irma was the subject for POR Bob, and the other big mouths had to act like adults and loudly fake their way through current events to try to impress the ladies. "Hey, you don't look so good, Bert," he said suddenly going back to his original observation. "You feeling okay?"

"Must be your aftershave, or your breakfast. Or both," Bert waved off the comment. "Better try a new Automat. Maybe you can find one that uses just two-day old sandwiches for a change."

"Hey, nothing wrong with my pastramis," POR Bob said in drippy defense. "They're the best in town." He held the remaining half under Bert's nose. "Wanna bite?" Its strong aroma curled Bert's nostrils, but he forced yet another smile just the same.

"I'll pass this time 'round," Bert put up a hand. "Thanks just the same."

"Missin' out, I tell ya'. Your loss." He stuck the remainder in his mouth like a dog with an old stuffed toy and looked off after Irma. "Hey, Irma!" he muffled. "How's tricks?"

"See you, PORB," Bert said shaking his head as he returned to his office under his breath. *Stalinland.*

Bert felt a sudden wave of light-headedness. *What time was it?* He reached into his jacket pocket and pulled out a beautiful, engraved pocket watch. The silver inlaid filigrees and carefully hand-painted numbering on its face noted the time. The swinging second hand was perfectly tuned to the minute hand. When the second crossed the twelve, the minute hand eclipsed whatever notch represented that minute on its face. It was the same thing when the short hand shadowed the hours of the day.

He looked at the precious timepiece, turning it over. How many times had he been offered vast sums to part with it? More than he cared to remember. No, this had been passed down from generation to generation. How old was it? A hundred, a hundred fifty years? No one was quite sure. Bert had tried to place its origins with the help of professionals. The face didn't note a manufacturer; neither did the inner workings betray its designers who, apparently, chose to remain anonymous. Bert spent a considerable amount of time on phone calls and correspondence to a world-renowned Swiss watchmaker to track down the origins of this particular watch. His digging amounted to nothing, but he did come close to parting with the heirloom once when the Swiss made more than a generous offer for it.

Bert inherited the timepiece more than 30 years ago on the death of Uncle Clay, his then closest relative. He hadn't thought much of the watch at the time until he took a good look at it and realized its true value. Out of respect for his good uncle and with the help of some other generous inheritance – along with the watch – Bert replaced the watch spring that had lost its tight coil.

"It's run like a top for years." Bert remembered Aunt Jessie's words. He had gone back home to attend his uncle's funeral. "Clay wanted you to have it." She had said with a slight tremor. Bert had taken a few days off from the university to attend Clay's service.

"It's beautiful." He cradled the heirloom with both hands, and then handed it back. "I can't accept this. It's too—"

"You *must* take it!" Aunt Jessie's insistence startled Bert. "It's my gift to you. Take it, Bertram Ross Walker!"

"Thank you." He said, somewhat embarrassed. There was no argument when Aunt Jessie resorted to using full names.

"It needs servicing," added Aunt Jessie, "Clay should have gotten around to it. See how it skips?" Her words started to tumble over each other. "There… you see? Look at it when it crosses the top!"

He looked at the watch. The second hand swung in a perfect arc, but just before the top of the swing – just before the twelve – it stopped and fell back half a tick for just an instant, and then returned to its normal orbit as if without interruption.

"You see that?" she pointed almost accusingly. "It stopped. That's not right. Clay was going to get it fixed. He meant too, but he took sick. It completely stopped on the day… well, you know."

"That's understandable," sympathized Bert. "Fixing the watch is nothing compared to Uncle Clay's health. Why make time for that?"

Then Aunt Jessie eyes bore straight into Bert's, serving him with a look he had never seen. "This is yours now." She said, handing him back the watch and wrapping her hands around his.

"Thank you."

"Promise me you'll get it fixed."

"Sure, Aunt Jessie—"

"Promise me—TODAY!"

"I promise. If it's that important." Bert was startled at the look in her eyes. *Was that fright?*

"And never, *ever*, let that watch run down, as long as you live."

"Yes, ma'am," he said. *That look in her eyes.*

"Clay ran out of time..." murmured Aunt Jessie with eyes downcast, "... ran out of time."

How long had he been staring at the timepiece? Bert shook himself back to the present. *Guess I lost track.* Still, it was something to admire and he was glad to have it. He followed the second hand as it cycled in its orbit. *Tick, tick, tick.* Round and round it went, keeping time as it arced to the top of the face.

Then just for an instant, before the last notch of the number twelve, the hand caught and reversed itself half a tick.

Time stopped for that moment and Bert felt as if his heart did the same.

"May I help you, sir?"

The jewelry store was abuzz with shoppers. There were several patrons admiring the sparkling baubles that they could only dream of buying. A young couple with the giddiness of a man-and-wife-to-be huddled about the ring section with big dreams and ambitions of their future together.

"Is there a watchmaker on duty?" inquired Bert as he wiped sweat from his brow with a handkerchief.

"That would be me, sir," Replied the man in the dapper black suit and hairline mustache. "I am Mr. Jasper. How may I be of service?"

"My, uh, pocket watch needs a new watch spring," Explained Bert. "It's been running slow. I thought it was time to bring it in."

"Ah, you made a pun. Very amusing sir." Bert wasn't in a joking mood and he could see the man really wasn't amused, just humoring him. *Well, that was funny.* Bert was feeling anything but himself.

"It just needs a new part."

"Of course sir," grinned Mr. Jasper, reaching for the watch in Bert's hand. "If I may, please…"

"What?" Replied Bert absently.

"The watch, sir," said the man with a tinge of polite annoyance in his clipped voice. "If I may look at it…"

"Oh, uh, yes. I'm sorry. Not myself today." Bert said gently handing the watch over.

"Perhaps you would care to sit down, sir? It *is* a warm day."

"I think I will. Thank you," Bert said tiredly. He shuffled over to a large, comfortable chair that only a jewelry store could afford.

"Very nice," said Mr. Jasper, admiring the timepiece. "May I ask where you acquired such a unique find?"

"It's been in the family for ages," Bert answered breathlessly. "I heard tell one of my great, great, greats or greater, picked it up somewhere in the Himalayas, or Timbuktu, or from some Carpathian gypsy. *I don't know.*"

"Very unique and exquisite," aired Mr. Jasper. "I would have to consult my books, but I'm certain I could come up with its origin. Odd that there is no name or maker of it that I can find." He turned the watch over and inspected the back.

"Please be careful," Bert said in a nearly-begging tone.

"Of course, sir. Nothing but the best from Brock's Jewelers. Now where is…" He looked for the stud to the back cover. "Here it is." The cover popped open with hardly a sound.

Bert let in a sharp gasp and jumped out of his chair. He wasn't sure the intake of air or the man handling the treasured item was why he felt the way he did.

"Oh, my, my, *my!"* Mr. Jasper's eyes rose to impressive proportions, almost losing the magnifying eyepiece as he took in the workings of the watch. "Sir, this is a truly beautiful find! The jewels, the gold inlay, the craftsmanship… I cannot recall seeing anything made to such perfection. I must congratulate you, sir!"

More beads of sweat glistened on Bert's forehead. He dabbed at them with a dampening handkerchief.

The watch smith produced a tiny tool in his hand as if by magic, holding it near the watch's gears. "It seems to be in working order, however, if you haven't replaced the watch spring in…"

"…about thirty years."

"I see. Then it certainly is time." Mr. Jasper displayed a wide grin as if he had made a very funny joke, which did nothing for Bert's fatigue. "Ah, here we are."

Bert could only see the face of the watch as it ticked on. He could only guess what was happening behind.

Mr. Jasper gingerly took the tiny probe and touched the watch spring.

The watch's owner saw the second hand stop dead.

"Uh!"

Bert's knees gave way under him. Reflexes caused his hands to grasp for the counter in front of him as light faded all around. His heart felt as if it was in his head, a base drum pounding, then stop, freezing the moment. *Is this it?* He asked himself, as a blanket of darkness enclosed him.

"Sir!" A startled Jasper exclaimed. A professional to the last, the man didn't drop the timepiece as most would have done, dashing the precious instrument in a hundred pieces on the tile floor. Rather, Mr. Jasper, cool and in control, crisply and economically, snapped shut the back cover of the watch, setting it on the counter. The actions jarred the jeweled mechanism back to life, even advancing the hands back to perfect time, humming in the rhythm for what it was made.

A cross between a yell and a grunt came out of Bert's mouth. He noisily sucked in a lungful of air as he steadied himself at the counter. The veil of darkness that was around him had gone, leaving Bert wide-eyed and scared.

"Are you all right, sir?" queried Mr. Jasper, concern in his voice.

Bert stared at his hands, firmly gripped on the edge of the counter. He closed his eyes absorbing just what had happened. Was that his heart? Did it just stop and start again as if someone had just flipped a light switch?

"Sir?"

His eyes snapped open. Just for a moment, Bert couldn't focus.

"Are you all right, sir?"

He took another breath, and relaxed his hold on the counter. He could feel his heart beating a steady cadence in his chest. He then realized how quiet it had to be to hear his own heartbeat. A desperate look about the jewelry store revealed that all business had stopped with personnel and patrons alike, staring at Bert.

"I, uh…" Bert didn't know which he felt more: embarrassed or frightened. "Sorry. I'm, uh, fine…." Then he said abruptly, "I have to go." He reached for the watch near his left hand and pocketed the timepiece.

"Quite all right, sir," said Mr. Jasper. "If you like, I would be happy to fix your watch right away. You can pick it up later."

Whether it was the frightful moment that clouded Bert's thinking or the idea of parting with his precious keepsake for a short time, getting it fixed then and there. *Not now.*

"No. I'll just have to come back," he said. "I just need a little rest."

"Of course, sir," said Mr. Jasper. "Please do return," he said with concern again, then added, "If you would, please consider selling that wonderful timepiece. I'm sure we could come to a mutual figure that would be satisfactory." The watch smith handed Bert his business card. "Please call me any time."

"I'll think about it," said Bert taking the card.

"Any time," Mr. Jasper repeated as Bert left the shop, the door closing behind him to the cheery sounds of a small bell hanging from the doorknob.

"You look fine to me."

"What?" said Bert, not believing what he'd heard. "I almost died right there in some jewelry store! Are you telling me you found nothing wrong?"

"You're in perfect health," said Dr. Samuels. "You have the health of someone twenty years younger."

Bert was sitting at the edge of the examining table in the doctor's office, buttoning his shirt. He couldn't believe what his physician was telling him. "How do you explain what happened?"

"The body is a strange thing, Bert," Dr. Samuels said calmly. "You've taken care of yourself pretty good. I'm sure it was just a muscle spasm. You know you have plenty of musculature around your rib cage. It's easy to make that mistake in thinking that it's your heart acting up. In reality, it is muscle cramps on the chest wall."

"It was more than just achy ribs, doc," countered Bert. He then wondered about Dr. Samuels' credentials. Bert preferred his original general practitioner, and he kicked himself for that. It had been years since he had reason to see his original physician. Between Bert's infrequent doctor visits, a new office policy had come into play there: if a patient was not seen after three years from the last visit, then the patient's medical records would go into storage and the old patient would then be classified as a 'new patient' for that next appointment. It was bad enough to have the office retrieve your medical records for a fee, let alone the patient having to give an account of ailments on numerous new forms. In the case of

Bert, who needed to be treated for a sprained ankle due to stepping into a gopher hole during a jog, he found out to his displeasure that his old physician had deemed Bert a 'new patient' two and a half weeks earlier. Even worse, his doctor was no longer seeing new patients. Enter Samuels.

"Must be stress," Dr. Samuels opined. "Take a few days off; do you a world of good. I'll prescribe a muscle relaxant for you. That should cover it."

"'Should cover it'," repeated Bert believing it little.

"Chin up, Bert!" piped Dr. Samuels. "You're in tip-top shape! Even your pulse is perfect: sixty beats a minute. You can set a clock to that."

Bert said nothing.

"You get some rest," said the doctor. "And take good care of that ticker of yours, you hear?"

He didn't bother calling the office; he wouldn't be going back for the rest of the day. Bert had a lot to ponder during his walk back to his flat. He held his hat absently in his hand, caring not a whit of the beating sun on his head.

It couldn't be, he denied inwardly. What power did this mysterious watch have over me? Bert asked himself as he trudged home.

"It's just a stupid watch!"

The doorknob rattled against the key as Bert let himself in.

His apartment was unremarkable; a few books on shelves, table and chairs and other necessary furniture, the minimal amount for its lone tenant, a few of the expected photos of family summed it up. Utility... nothing more, nothing less.

But in the corner – its perfect position always drawing his attention to it whenever he came home – Bert took a long look at a photo of himself, his son at about age ten, and his wife. It was a happy snapshot of a time when things were perfect. They didn't have much at the time, but it didn't matter.

How it had changed. How they had changed. How *he* had changed.

Maybe he should have taken her back, forgiven her weak moment with a coworker on that business trip. It hurt him badly, and he told her to stay away despite her attempts at reconciliation. This only forced her back into the arms of the man who caused the rift that Bert was now certain could have been closed.

And the boy, too young to understand, only remembered his dad's refusal to take his mother back. That father-son relationship turned a corner as well and to this day, he and Bert had been only cordial acquaintances, no longer close. Bert had lost much.

But he had to think of the now. Bert was dealing with a new crisis. What? *His life?* How could that be? It was just a stupid watch! What did it have over him? *Come on!*

"It's just a stupid watch!" he yelled.

Bert reached in his jacket pocket and stared at the timepiece. The face of it stared back. There were no features to offer any expression, just numbers, notches and hands. Somehow, it mocked him, and for some unexplainable reason, he suddenly felt hate for the thing.

How long had he owned it? Over thirty years – he was certain of that. Why not put the blame on it for his lonesome life? It had been there. It had witnessed more sadness than gladness. He lost more than he had gained. Forget his successful job and his other material things; many would say Bert had no room to complain. *You're doing great, Bert. Wish I was so lucky.*

Would they think so if they really knew? Bert had a watch that was considered precious and nearly priceless as it was one of a kind. He recalled at least a dozen or so prospective buyers who made more than generous offers to take ownership of the thing.

"I'm more stupid than you!" Bert said to the watch face. I should have let you go and there would have been something in my pocket besides you!" A new thought made him laugh out loud.

"*Hey, buddy. Wanna buy a watch?*" The memory of the street vendor some months ago selling cheap and questionably-running timepieces made him laugh again. He acted out the scene. "*I'll make you a fair deal. Hey, cheap at that price. There ain't nuthin' better 'n these babies.*"

Then Bert played the part of himself in the exchange. He overly acted out the part reaching in his jacket breast pocket in a flourish, pulling out his watch and showing the street vendor his inherited clock. "*Beat that, buddy.*" He remembered the vendor stare at him for a moment, then walk away.

"Jokes on me," said Bert to no one. "If you were here right now, I'd do a straight trade for a $5 El Tiempo Cheapo. *You-hear-that?*" he yelled at his watch.

"I hate you!" Bert shouted. "You're a waste of my time—ha!" He bellowed at the ironic line. He held the watch over his head as if on a stage, actor to audience.

"*Alas poor timepiece, I knew it well,*" he ad-libbed.

"*This is the time that tries men's souls!* No—*my* soul!" Bert got louder and more manic at every oratory.

"*My clock runneth over!*" Louder still.

"*It was the best of times—no it wasn't.*" His voice could be heard through the wall. He held the watch aloft as if he was about to smash it to the floor. Then he started on Poe.

"*But anything was better than this agony! Anything was more tolerable than this derision! I could bear those hypocritical smiles no longer! I felt that I must scream or die! – - And now – again – hark! Louder! Louder! Louder! LOUDER!*"

Bert's voice was a high-pitched, horrifying shriek. He glared with total rage at the face of the watch.

"*Villains!*" I shrieked, dissemble no more! I admit the deed! – tear up the planks! – here, here! – it is the beating of his hideous heart!*"

Whether it was a direct reply to Bert's tirade, some surreal, sentient vengeance from a supposedly inanimate object, or just, ironically, innocent perfect timing? The second hand stopped in its incessant arc and vibrated in place.

An electric shock does the same thing to the body. All the muscles spasm and contract in on themselves. Among the many tendons, sinew and the rest, Bert's hand holding the watch gripped it in a vice as he slammed onto the hardwood floor. The grip on the timepiece saved it from shattering to smithereens. The jolt put the mechanism back on course.

It felt as if there was fist-sized, red-hot coal searing Bert's chest cavity. Nothing mattered but the pain. A deep-throated howl did its best to put Bert's agony to voice.

The second hand swung on its face, instants slower on each tick. Bert's heart did the same.

"Help!" It was a weak cry through gritted teeth. Bert managed to get his knees under him and started to edge across the room.

The humming of the watch began to flag, its mechanism's speed not as fast.

His movements were slowing. *The phone—just a few more feet.*

Within its jewel-encrusted mechanism, the watch spring began to vibrate along its center pin.

"Operator."

"I need an ambulance," Bert hissed, breaths coming in spurts. "Please hurry!"

"Please state the nature of the emergency, sir." The operator said in emotionless tone.

The watch spring began to resonate against the pin. Micro-fractures began to form along a weak spot on its coil.

"It's my heart" he squeaked. "It hurts."

"Address please."

"I'm at… I'm at…" The room around him spun, starting to fade. "527 North Vista Road… room three-C… Hurry!" Bert's voice was no more than a rasp.

He could hear it. The tick of the watch in his fist, within earshot. Tick. Tick. Tick. Each beat a little slower than the last. The pulse in his head, in perfect unison, synchronized with the dying clock. *Boom.*

"Please state your name, sir."

Boom. Boom. Boom Boom. Boom.

"Please state your name, sir."

Boom. Boom. Boom Boom. Boom.

"Hello?"

***

It has been said by few that when someone departs to a higher plane, or crosses over, or moves on to that 'great beyond', that all the reserves left in his or her body are released in one last burst of energy, whether that is in the form of physical exertion or mental.

Bert saw it in his mind.

The human brain is capable of much more than the estimated 10 percent that experts calculate are used by humans. It wouldn't be just 10 times as much, rather an exponential explosion of mental ability, far beyond the computations of a room-sized difference engine, rudimentary and stone-aged, in comparison to the thought-processor made of synapses, neurons, and the incomparable dura-matter with which life is blessed.

Bert saw it all. Everything made sense when his brain fired up to full capacity—even the calculus class in his senior year in high school. Problematic equations escaped him then, but now he could see everything as elementary concepts that were as simple as child's play. The universe seemed much simpler now as his mind brought it all together with a beautiful clarity. The dim of the room wasn't there; in its place were colors that he had never seen before. Each shade glowed from within as if alive, despite his energies pouring away.

Was it a long running passage of his life in front of him or did it take an instant? There was no telling. It was like running his thumb over the pages of a photo album of memories flipping by: a skinned knee after a fall from his tricycle; a mother's hug; his first catch on a fishing trip with dad; the base hit that won the ball game; graduation; the funeral of his parents after the accident; college and the nervous asking for a date; their vows; cradling his newborn son; the break up....

Boom... boom... boom...

And somewhere in that mental photo album of memories was the watch he inherited, handed to him as it had been to family before him upon the passing of a previous generation.

Boom... boom... boom...

As it had *always* been.

Boom.

And then to the next.

"No!" Bert gasped.

Boom.

"NO! Not Steven! I won't!"

That mocking face did nothing in front of his. What energy was left to smash it onto the floor where he lay and end this curse? Hardly was there any strength to raise his arm. Somewhere, beyond his care, an approaching wail of a siren...

"Forgive me, Steven," Bert said to an empty room. *"Forgive—"*

He felt more than heard the thrum of the watch.

And within its workings, the watch spring pulled on itself, the banging against its center pin, fracturing a weak point on its coil.

Sproing! The watch spring parted in two, halting its gears, hands—and much more around it.

"You got a time on that, Jeff?" The police officer asked, notepad out.

"I'm going along with his watch, Frank," said the coroner. "Must have stopped when he hit the floor." He scribbled some notes down.

"Place looks clean," said a second cop walking into the living room from the kitchen. "I talked to the neighbors. They said a lot of shouting was coming from the apartment. No sign of mischief, though. Looks like the guy's number was up."

"Knock it off, Mickey!" scolded Officer Frank. "I knew this guy. A good egg all around."

"Well, I'm done here, gents," informed the coroner. "Too bad. He looked in pretty good shape, but that's how it happens sometimes. Let's go, boys."

Two orderlies maneuvered a stretcher, body and sheet covered over it. The wheels produced creaks on the floorboards as it was rolled out the door.

"I'll let you know the cause," Jeff the coroner called back. "Won't know for sure until I open him up, but it has all the signs that his heart gave out."

"'Preciate it, Jeff. See 'ya 'round." He took another look at the place. "Okay, Mickey, let's lock it up."

"Hey, Sarge," said Mickey, "nice watch." Frank looked over his shoulder. Mickey was eyeing the timepiece. "Doesn't work but it sure is a nice piece of junk."

"Don't even think it, Mickey. All of this goes to next of kin. Gimme that!"

Mickey handed the heirloom over with a grumble. Frank opened the back. "Yeah, needs a new watch spring. This one's snapped." He had an idea. "The news is gonna be a blow to his kid. Least I can do is to get the thing ticking again. Here's a business card for a watch smith." Then he asked, "What's the kid's name?"

Mickey looked at his notes. "Uh—here it is. Name's Steven. College kid. "

"Okay," said Officer Frank. "Time to get started."

A SHEPHERD NO MORE

Copyright © 2014 by Andy McKell

A SHEPHERD NO MORE

By

Andy McKell

A Shepherd No More

Somewhere in my cramped, tin can of a spaceship, the incoming message tone sounded. My eyes opened slowly on yet another lonely day shift. *Joy of joys!*

I stank. My three-month beard itched. The incessant engine rumbling remained incessant – my ship's gloomy lighting revealed the same slab of dull metal barely a foot from my nose, as ever. And the straps of the bunk restraints had chafed me where they always chafed me every last damn sleep shift of every last run. *Again, joy of joys.*

I am not a morning person. And I long for gravity.

Incoming message? The alarm still sounded. Not a dream. Panic got me moving. *Jacqui? The baby?* Whatever it was, it could only be trouble. I started multi-tasking, calling for message playback as I hit the bunk restraint's snap-release and called-up the overnight status displays.

I recognised Ahmed's perpetually-calm, relaxing voice through the static and punched up heavier filters.

#Crackle! NEO Lunabase Mission Control to Shepherd-4. Crackle! Priority One Mission update despatched. Hzz-pop! Crackle! Read carefully.#

The message was fractured by solar flare interference. I rolled-in stronger filters until his voice was almost unrecognisable. The next part would be the important part.

#On the domestic front, splashdown ETA remains unchanged and the crew is doing well. Expect a one, repeat, one day window! Crackle! How's your weather, today? Crackle! Enjoy your flyby. Hzzzz! NEO Lunabase, out!#

Yes! Jacqui was fine and the birth, the 'splashdown', was on schedule.

But a 'one-day window' meant a three-day mission extension. The birth was due in four days, I should have been

home, should have been there. A three-day diversion is the last
thing I wanted.

A flyby? Three days to eyeball an incoming asteroid. Hell, I
wanted to be home! Jacqui hated these long runs; I hated these
long runs. And now another diversion. This had better only
take three days or that rock could just do its own flyby for all I
cared.

I pushed off from the bunk and floated to the adjacent
command deck; that's the part of the cabin I don't sleep in. A
NEO-Shepherd craft was a single-chambered, windowless box
fitted with manipulators and gravity tractor spare parts,
everything needed for herding asteroids on near-final approach
to the orbital factory platforms. When NASA's 'Near-Earth
Objects Observation' program added 'intervention' to its
functions, it sounded glamorous. *Space-guard? Huh!* Rock-
shepherds, is all we are. I punched up my first cafsub bulb and
sucked hard as I stabbed a finger at the secure-chief reader –
any finger – the damn machine could work out which of my
fingerprints it was reading today. Who else is going to read my
mail, out here? I leaned back in the command seat and belted-
up, feeling the straps chafe again. *The romance of space
travel? Keep it.*

He'd asked, "How's your weather, today?" *Huh? Damn
comedian.* But I couldn't resist a quick glance at the nose-view
screen. No surprises there. Like there was ever anything to look
at except stars and blackness or maybe blackness and stars.
Any surprises out here and I was already dead. My weather?
Dark. Very dark. But, bright side shining, this was my last run
ever and my baby was on the launch pad.

Weather? He meant more solar flare fronts headed my way.
I'd checked already, automatically on waking. The magnetic
shielding was holding; the indicators all glowed a steady green.
A flash of concern hit me about Jacqui and the baby, but the
bases were super-shielded these days. They were safer than I
was. I turned away from that thought and drained the cafsub. I
lobbed the bulb into the catchall, watching it sail, arrow-

straight towards its target. My aim was good, even in zero-G. It always was. Lots of practice.

I punched in the new flight co-ordinates as I read the rest of the briefing. The directional thrusters juddered as we swung to nominal starboard. The straps chafed again as my body was pulled in a new direction. Thank you, Newton, for inventing momentum and inertia.

There was no piloting to do for a while. I called Lunabase as I scrolled through the briefing.

"Shepherd-4 to NEO Lunabase. Briefing received. Message integrity confirmed, after two reloads. Otherwise, weather is optimal." I glanced again at the view of space outside, just to be sure. "Shepherd-4 out."

What was so important to extend my contract by another three days? It looked like just another standard swing past another standard hunk of rock to check for and fix minor trajectory anomalies. Routine, routine... Then I looked a little harder. This was different. Telemetry checks indicated approach trajectory discrepancies.

So what was this rock, this asteroid, NEA-9753? A standard, water-mineral rock-ball, behaving itself millions of kilometres from Earth for maybe four billion years. Then ten months ago, some rock-jockey team straps a set of thrusters on it and fires them up as computed. They wait a few days then launch a gravity tractor alongside it to make automatic adjustments to its route all the long, long way to Earth orbit and recover the thrusters. Rock-jockey team wipes its collective hands on its pants and sails off, presumably, to partners and homes and to collect prospector bonuses. No problems. Not until now.

Now it's three days out from the orbital factory platforms and it's in trouble. I'm the nearest craft by a good twenty hours. "*Me, boss. You, rock-herder. Go see. Go fix.*" Huh!

NEA-9753: 500 metres average diameter, 550 million tonnes of mixed rock, minerals, stunningly-valuable gem-stuff and ice worth maybe 200 billion to the AstroMining Consortium.
Sweet!

I read on and reality took a small holiday... the damn thing was travelling way too fast and wasn't ever going to be reined in to a manageable harvesting orbit. Not by a Shepherd-class craft. We didn't carry heavy-duty gear or atomics. We tweak, we don't aim. It wasn't even going anywhere near the factory platforms. It would miss them by... I stopped breathing. I read it again and again, my brain refusing to accept what my eyes were telling it. But no matter how many times I read it, the result was the same... by enough to impact Luna!

I snapped on the comlink and yelled. "Ahmed! What the-"

#Crackle! NEO Lunabase to Shepherd-4. Switch to secure channels as directed. Crackle! Out!#

I'd missed that big red flag in the briefing. Burning, I flipped encryption on, dampening the remaining static. "Ahmed, gimme details, now!"

#NEO Lunabase to Shepherd-4. Need-to-know only. Just get eyes on and report.# He was being formal. That would be for other ears listening and for the recording.

"Forget it! I got a damn good need to know. I got a wife and kid down there. Gimme everything, now, or I'm turning 'round and coming home!"

#NEO Lunabase to Shepherd-4, please hold.#

Nothing changed visibly in the starfield as we travelled a tiny fraction of the distance to the target. I chewed off the ends off my moustache as I tried over and over to read something different in the briefing.

#Mike...# So I was no longer Shepherd-4; it was me, Mike, a human being. They were as rattled as I was. *#I'm authorised to provide a fuller briefing.#* I waited while he gathered his thoughts to make it as reassuring as he could.

It was hijackers, he told me. Hijackers, pirates, terrorists – call them what you will. A separatist group from the Mars Colonial Territories and the Belts were claiming sovereignty over the entire Belt, accusing AstroMining Consortium of piracy, of stealing their rocks. "Stealing their rocks"? *Insanity.*

Like we were all cavemen or apes or... Hell! I didn't care why it happened. I got the technical details eventually.

They'd tried to steal the gravity tractor, for their own harvesting operations. They'd made a grab for the tractor. Something went wrong. They'd crashed into the rock. Result? A runaway, monster asteroid.

"Why the hell didn't someone notice their ship?" This was irrelevant, but I was angry.

#Solar flares, Mike. Lunanet and Marsnet both went down. Maybe the flares affected their own navigation, causing the crash. The group's press releases are vague about that.#

They'd approached during the last bout of solar flares, then hid in the rock's own radar shadow.

#It had been 100% on target until then... so it was a low priority for Tracking when the nets came back online.# He didn't sound impressed with Tracking.

"Survivors? Armed?"

#No-one is expected to be alive by the time you arrive." He changed tack. *"We are evacuating Lunabase...#*

I didn't like the way he left that sentence dangling. "Jacqui's safe?"

#Mike... she's too near term for even a lunar lift-off.#

Kick me in the teeth as you watch me burn. I raged, impotent, helpless, too far away... *My wife! My child!*

I remember screaming. I don't remember much else for a while. It was the pain in my hand that started to bring me back. I gazed at the pain. My hand, my sleeve, red. I gazed around. I became fascinated by the ruby droplets floating in the air, slowly being drawn towards the recycler vent. At some point, I'd slammed my fist against the console. I ripped away a strip of uniform and bound my damaged hand slowly, letting my anger drain away.

I was calmer when I spoke to Ahmed. A cold, emotion-drained calm. "I am coming home."

#Negative, Mike. You have a twenty-hour lead on the others. You are the only one who can do this. You must go see.#

I must go see. I nodded. Slowly. They couldn't see, no video-link was open. But they took my silence and my unchanged route as acceptance.

I sweated out the dark hours as the distance to the monster closed, so painfully slowly. I didn't eat or sleep, just kept sucking cafsub until my supply was gone. I recalculated obsessively, hoping to find an error the dome-heads had missed. *Me – rock-shepherd Mike. Fat chance.* I wasn't thinking clearly. I was a zombie. What good would *"eyes on"* do? *Stupid Mike, rock-shepherd Mike.* I really hadn't caught on yet – didn't catch on for a long time...

Rubbing the grit in my eyes and making them burn redder, I saw the featureless grey blur I'd been watching for hours slowly begin to transform into a grey blur with lumps and hollows. I patched all camera signals through to Lunabase. They had kept silent; they remained silent, for now.

Let the man do his job. For now...

At first, all I could see was grey upon grey, darker and lighter. Then the craters emerged, the shadows at their rims as black as my thoughts. White plumes from the aft end were the signal. I manoeuvred for a better view. The wreck inched into the field of view. It lay in its own crater, the centre of a spider's web of impact cracks venting off water vapour and dust.

It looked like a decrepit mining transporter, probably long overdue for the scrap yards. No signs of life. I hailed them. Only unbroken static on the radio. There could be no survivors after so long.

I didn't need fancy telemetry or high-ticket computing to know that this rock was unstoppable in the time available. Too late for a gravity tractor to slow its Luna-bound rush, or to steer it back on target. A nuke on the nose might divert it, but I had no nukes on board.

I spoke at last, in a dry rasp. No formalities. Just man-to-man, stating the obvious. "Listen, get the dome-heads to explain to the suits that Shepherds do final nudges, not major re-routing on final approach.

#They know.# Ahmed had been waiting. Waiting for my call and waiting for my inevitable assessment.

"So why am I here? Just to get eyes on? Gimme a plan, Ahmed."

#I hear you, Mike - zzzz...# All protocol was gone; this was the Mike and Ahmed show, two buddies sharing the pain. *#AstroMining are considering their response. Wait for orders. Please confirm.#*

"Damnit!" I tried to yell, but couldn't pull it off. "Every minute loses us hundreds of kilometres. We have no time for Shareholder Meetings."

I heard Ahmed sighing deeply from so damn far away and slowly repeat his previous message.

I had to get busy, had to DO something. "I'm sending a drone down. Just in case."

#Fine, Mike. But you don't have much time.#

I missed the import of those words. I was busy launching the coffin-like drone. *Coffin-like!* Appropriate, if coincidental.

I patched its cam-view into the Lunabase feed. Through static flashes I saw the torn hull, the crushed nose. I felt the deadly, cold stillness down there and turned up the ship's heating without thinking. I was used to the stillness of space, darkness, silence. But this craft had been a bubble of life for human beings, however crazy. And now it lay broken and shattered for a cause I barely understood. I became one with the drone as it drifted – as *we* drifted – down, down towards the crumpled mess that was once a space-faring vessel. The wreckage that had not spread itself into the vacuum lay scattered around the impact crater, bits and pieces drawn back by the tiny gravity field of the leviathan rock.

I felt an even deeper silence about this graveyard. Lunabase shared my experience and kept its own silence.

We cruised among the larger chunks of hull and bulkheads, an engine here, a cabin frame there. My brain automatically identified the occasional part; most were not big enough to label. I told my eyes to not see, but I could not stop myself looking for survivors. Even body parts that I could bring back for their families would be something to bury... I saw nothing, no-one, no part of anyone.

Somehow, the rear airlock had survived almost intact. *Maybe a more sturdy construction?*

Then I felt a physical blow to my chest. I saw dismembered body parts strewn in and around the airlock. Parts of arms and legs and heads and torsos, scattered, discarded. I stared, horrified, transfixed – unable to look away. I spun the cam angle and tuned a close-up. I slid my hands into the remote control gloves that turned the drone's extensibles – its arms and fingers – into extensions of my own. I wanted to be ready, *just in case, just in case...* Then I saw clearly what my brain had shut out.

Spacesuit parts. Empty. No body parts, anywhere.

I closed my eyes to shut out the horror. Behind my eyelids, visions of real body parts floated.

I swore. I swore again. I longed for a hard shot of something. We all knew there would not, could not be any survivors. But still, the chill shook me aware and I turned the drone's cam away. There was nothing to collect. Bodies would have been instantly compressed by the impact, then scattered by the explosion. Any fluids had long ago boiled away into eternity.

And I knew there was no-one below waiting for rescue. Anyone surviving the impact would have died long ago when their spacesuit ran out of oxygen. Eight hours maximum. That would have been over two days ago.

I felt the oppression of the hard vacuum just inches away from my own fragile body. *Another chill. Another shaking to alertness.*

"Let's move on. It's over. We tried. We were just too damn late."

#Please wait for Mission briefing.#

"Again, Ahmed, what am I supposed to do?"

I carried no nukes, because that's a crazy move, blowing up a heavy rock on near approach to Earth orbit. Crazy. Okay, this far out, it might have reduced the risk; let the others blast and shepherd the bits and pieces. If they were lucky, they could minimise the damage. Not prevent disaster, though. I had no time to tweak its trajectory with the tools available. All I had was the Shepherd. And I needed that to get home. *Stop this monster with the Shepherd itself?* I laughed.

Then I stopped laughing.

I left the drone on the surface. I didn't need it any more. I had worked it out. *Finally.* Worked out why I was here; what the mission actually was.

I swore at the screens, the walls, the chafed skin, the insanity of the activists and of the suits playing board games safe at home. Light had dawned in my little brain.

"Okay, Lunabase. I think I see why I am here."

Ahmed's silence rode on waves of static and flare noise. Finally, it came. *#Confirmed, Mike.#*

"Bastards!"

More hiss and crackles and no word spoken. I understood. What could he say?

Dammit, I'm a Shepherd not a hero! Bitter humour out of bleak despair.

"Ahmed," I was speaking to a sole person, not a conglomerate. I needed to think about living people, that personal touch. "As I see it, my only plan is to crash the NEO into its leading edge at full speed, try to divert it. Agreed?"

#Our projections confirm that as the mission objective. We are sending optimal co-ordinates, approach angle and thrust required.#

Oh, Ahmed, give me emotion! But his coldness showed how much pain he was swallowing.

I found myself screaming into the mike, hearing the overload rattling. "I am gonna hold my baby in my arms, I tell ya!"

#Mike, we suggest you evacuate the NEO before impact.#

Thanks for nothing! Sure, I could attach a "buddy" set of tanks to my suit, doubling my O_2 allowance. But this was a one-man ship. No buddy, no buddy-pack. If I jumped, I'd have eight hours' oxygen. There was no way to take along all that lovely, sweet, scrubbed and re-scrubbed oxygen filling the ship, which still stank of Mike-sweat. Eight hours in which to torture myself with imaginings of how it would feel to asphyxiate. I'd rather go in a sudden, brief, impact flare. *A flash of glory? Huh!*

"Gimme a confirmed ETA for the other NEOs."

#Confirming twenty hours.# Ahmed's voice sounded weary. How many times had he checked and rechecked and gotten back the same answer? How big a cafsub high was he coming down off?

"Twenty? Two-zero? Five-sixths of a day?" I couldn't hold back my anger. "Twelve hours after my O_2 runs out?" I didn't deserve a reply. It wasn't his fault.

I tried to calm down. There had to be a way. Could I jump hard in the right direction, use the suit's tiny manoeuvrability jets to boost my velocity? I added-in the asteroid's own velocity; I was matching that already, reversing towards Jacqui, I would have that starting bonus. I ran some fast calculations; they were not enough, not enough thrust, not enough fuel... I need something to accelerate me; I'll move at that velocity forever.

Damnation! Deduct the asteroid's motion – that was already built into the twenty hour rendezvous estimate.

I ambitiously added in an Olympic jumper's upward thrust. Yeah, I'm no athlete, but this was a gravity-free environment... I still could not make the numbers work. No matter how I tried and how much I lied to myself.

Was there something I could salvage from the airlock wreckage? I spun the drone around, set its cam lens to wide angle, I leaned closer, my eyes scanning for something, anything...

#Mike, we need to begin repositioning for final approach.#

Euphemisms! He meant it was time for me to prepare to die. Through the strain of total concentration, I could feel the sweat prickling, stinging my eyes, floating off towards the vents.

Something sparkled; I nearly missed it. We floated closer. A set of tanks. A single set of apparently undamaged tanks. Four beautiful, silvery tanks, still hanging on the shelf. If they were intact, if they were full, if I could hook them up to the buddy nozzle, they would give me sixteen hours total. That's a lot of "ifs". And I still needed another four hours. I could breathe slow, use less oxygen. The eight hours calculation was based on an active space-walk. Maybe I could squeeze another hour out of the eight tanks? Another two hours? If I held my breath? Another three?

I gazed at the drone below me. It was my only hope. My exhaustion and desperation fed me an impossible solution. I chose to believe it because it was all that I had.

I slipped my hands back into the drone gloves and lifted those cylinders as gently as if they were my own unborn.

"My wonderful drone, I love you, drone, love you. Bring me my baby, gently, now, ever so gently...!" I was more than a little crazy, on the edge looking down – and "down" is a long, long way in space.

#Calm down, Mike. Breathe slow and deep. Slow and deep...# Ahmed sounded rattled. He depended on me to complete the mission. Earth, Lunabase depended on it. Most of all, Jacqui and the baby depended on it.

What the hell did they know back at Luna? I was here, I was on the spot, I was in control. It was my flyby, my mission, my baby, my wife, my life...

I ran and re-ran all the calculations; the drone lifted and matched my velocity; I drew her closer; a little nudge of a jet and she slid home into the docking bay like it was made for her.

Hell, it *was* made for her. I sobbed, choking on my laughter as I watched her bringing home my salvation.

The slam of the bay doors trembled through the entire ship. I punched in the mission coordinates.

I punched-in some more commands, set the timers. My sweet Shepherd-4 ship turned as slow and elegant as a ballet dancer and headed for zero point. She was ready for suicide. I was not. *Not yet.*

My NEO would do as she was told. I suited-up and ran numbers in my head and out loud. I no longer cared what Lunabase thought. I had to fill my brain with something other than the mission.

"Twenty hours 'til the others rendezvous, less the hour I've been here, that's nineteen hours..."

I flooded the drone dock with breathable air.

"Must stay alive, close the gap, get ahead of the rock..."

I cracked the drone bay airlock. No room to manoeuvre the extensibles. Had to lower myself into the bay, squeeze in the cramped space, reach out for the cylinders...

"Got them!"

I struggled getting them up into the cabin.

"... starting with the asteroid's own velocity..."

The cylinders looked good on an eyeball check.

"...need to test 'em for punctures..."

#Mike? How's it going? Remember the window's tight...#

I hooked up the pressure outlet and checked the gauges.

".. jump real hard... maybe down to eighteen hours..."

Solid! All tanks full and leak-free.

"... double tanks, double duration, down to nine hours... hold my breath..."

#Mike? Are you okay, Mike?#

"Not now, Ahmed. Later. Grab a cafsub. Say 'hi' to Jacqui. Down to nine hours... minus the suit's jet thrusters, and I'll hold my breath...yes, hold my breath... thrusters gonna be empty, but time saved, distance... Did I mention the boost from the impact shock-wave?"

#Mike, you're looking good. Slow and steady, now...#

I could tell from his voice, the poor guy was trying to transmit calm down the tight comms beam. I laughed out loud. "No! I'm not crazy, Ahmed, not crazy!"

#Almost in position. Hold onto it, now... just a little longer... stay with us... Okay, keep working on those numbers if it helps, stay focused...#

"Shush! Listen! I can squeeze the air, I know how!"

#Okay, Mike. That's good. Whatever you say is okay. Keep going. We see you're almost there. Don't lose it now...#

I heard background murmurs on the link. They sounded scared.

"Trust, me, boys, trust me."

I strapped the spare cylinders on my back; secured the buddy breather link; crawled again into the drone bay. No time for a final look around the Shepherd.

#Mike...# His pause stretched out forever. *#We'll make sure Jacqui and the baby are okay, don't worry.#*

"Who's worried? Not me. I'm coming home. Gonna hold my baby boy and kiss his sweet mother."

#Okay, Mike, if you say so. That's good. Just get the Shepherd in position...#

Shepherd? Forget it! I'm a shepherd no more.

"Ahmed? You there? Tell those boys I'm a shepherd no more!" I heard some maniac laughing somewhere nearby. Must have been me. Lunabase would think I had really had gone under. I imagined them praying, praying I was doing what they needed.

But I had the answer, I had the answer...

* * *

Those final moments burn in my soul... over and over as if it's happening now...

"Final check." I'm talking to myself, but it's by the book, always by the book.

"Shepherd-4 in position: Check."

"She's aimed and primed and pointed and the timer's ticking down: Check."

"Suit: Check." Nothing I could do now, if it wasn't.

"Grab the extensibles. Got 'em! Another Check!"

Buzzer sounds. Five seconds. Time's up.

Drone bay doors open: one push and I'm falling. Falling through hard vacuum into infinity.

Falling towards home. Falling towards Jacqui.

A sudden flare. Shepherd leaps towards destruction. Engines ramped up to full power. A raging wall of flame nearby – too damn near. Cooling unit whirs into overtime. Anti-glare visor kicks-in... I'm blind...

Something slams me in the back. *Shock-wave. Clinging on, clinging on...*

#We see flares, Mike. Goodbye, old friend. And thank you...#

"Get the champagne on ice, Ahmed. I'm coming home!"

Counting seconds. Bracing myself. Still blinded. Did it work? Another vast, appalling kick from another silent shock-wave. The pain...

Shepherd-4 is no more. I whisper into space, "Goodbye, old friend."

Now, to kick-in the final boost, the magic extra thrust that makes the whole damn thing possible...

Ohmygod!

Whiplash! Neck broken? No. Taste blood. God, oh God, oh God... my back, my arms, my fingers...

I'm screaming one vast, primal scream of terror and pain on the galaxy's greatest white-knuckle ride into eternity...

$$* * *$$

No-one talks any more about my precision piloting. No-one compliments me on impacting at just the right speed and angle and the explosion diverting the rogue 'up' and out of the plane of the Earth's orbit.

Sure, I got a medal for that, and a very nice pension. But everyone remembers something else. And sometimes, I sit and watch the recording with little Jason on my knee. The view from the leading rescue NEO. Lump-in-the-throat stuff. I wait for the moment when I come into focus, no longer a blur, but *me*; really me, festooned with O_2 tanks. And Jason always asks, pointing, eyes wide, "Is that really you, daddy? Is that really you riding that drone like a cowboy?"

A shepherd no more, I came home a cowboy.

And my tears flow.

Vampirecratic Menace- A case Study?

Copyright © 2014 by Richard Bunning

VAMPIRECRATIC MENACE- A CASE STUDY?

By

Richard Bunning

VAMPIRECRATIC MENACE-

NOWNATION MONTHLY
October 2052, London.

Full Transcript of a Lecture Given by James Pickles, Director of Legacy Information Inc.)

Westminster Theatre, Keele University, Staffs.

Will Science Turn the Rich into Body-Snatching Vampires

Back in the second decade of this century, George Church and Sri Kosuri were involved in their pioneering work on data storage using DNA. Few foresaw how comprehensively this technology would integrate our minds and engineered memory. As we all now know, our civilisation was soon to take a huge man-made, evolution distorting leap, massively expanding our intellectual potential. As yet this wild and accelerating launch seems to have had no clear landing place, as integrated biological and artificial 'thought' systems become ever more complex. This technology, as we are all now increasingly aware, hasn't just astronomically expanded 'intelligence' capabilities; it is set to make a mockery of nature's strict cycle of birth and death. On the foundation science that Church, Kosuri and others laid down we have suddenly taken a course that most must have thought could only ever be very improbable, future, science fiction.

Until very recently, we had only seen this technology used to advance the mental capacities of the very rich. Enhanced intellect has rapidly widened the power balance between the already dominant elites and the masses. The growing dominance of the few mustn't be allowed to go unchecked any longer. What is more, augmentation mustn't be allowed to just slowly filter down through a few more levels of wealthy society; it needs to be made available to everyone. The march of cold progress can probably stand the empowerment of only a minority, but humanitarianism certainly can't be trusted to elites. DNA data storage technology is so empowering that it needs to either be made available to all, or else be rigidly, emphatically, and forever, outlawed. There is a grave danger that this mind blowing science will prove to be an overwhelming weapon of control, forever suppressing the Commonwealth of Mankind. The longer the technology remains the toy of the rich and powerful, the less the chances of human society retaining even our institutional nods to equality.

Life can never be one of truly equal opportunities, but most states and cultures have gone a long way towards that goal since the days of the all powerful Machiavellian princes. We need to guard the "democratisations" that our nations have achieved.

In the second half of this piece I will focus on recent history of just one influential family, the one that I have married into. This allows me to shine a narrow beam of penetrating light on the core social dangers in a far more intimate way. This will help the cause of brevity. However, that can't negate the need for background, for a broad understanding, before the pinpointed case has a chance of acting as a catalyst for concern. I try for further intimate connection with you, the reader, by writing the second part as drama. Rest assured that the detail is factual. The case I use is old and well entrenched in the public domain. A newer one would only elicit yet more litigation against this publication. 'Nownation' simply hasn't got the bottomless pockets needed to fight the legal challenges of less historic and well documented cases.

The satisfactory ending to my story certainly isn't typical of most others that I could theoretically tell. Perhaps that is as well, because along with a realisation of the danger, we also need hope. We are fortunate to still have the press freedom in this country to publish on this topic at all, as the wealthy powerbrokers in their gated communities have already closed down the decaying embers of democracy in so many territories. The spotlight at the end reveals a very intimate story painted with partially remembered, partly reinvented, past conversations, giving life to the cold facts. I write with the help of those principles that are living and were willing.

As early as 2012, Church was reported as saying, "A device the size of your thumb could store as much information as the whole internet." These devices can now be passed literally from one mind to another, down the generations. He was actually over-estimating space requirements for data storage, but even this claim seemed extraordinary at the time, especially considering the capacity of silicon-based memory that people were then familiar with. We now have 'enhanced beings', each with more data storage and analytical power than the fastest and biggest computers that existed at the dawn of this millennium. This science has advanced so rapidly that now 40 years on the rich can keep manmade copies of their minds alive, indefinitely. As we are all only too aware, the manipulation of synthetic DNA and its subsequent introduction into the living has allowed individuals to not just gain intelligence but to increasingly escape death.

We can best understand the threats to society by understanding the problem on a personal level. Our imaginations work in brighter colours when we look at the pain of identified individual, than when we distantly study the miseries of populations. My extended family's story, from 2033, has been repeated many times with a thousand permutations. Not even the strongest of repressive governments can control stories provided they are deeply enough entrenched in public knowledge and widely dispersed physical records. This lecture is just one small but vital part of that record.

The science has moved on a long way since '33 when the main part of this study took place, but all the major dangers were already apparent. It was already possible for the rich to have their recorded knowledge transposed indirectly into the next generation through DNA. Recently direct transfer from one living person to another has become feasible. In '33, the rich still couldn't keep their true 'selves' alive, their true personalities, but they could already 'pass on' very good likenesses.

Of course people have always passed on not just genetic information, by reproducing, but also something of their private history. There has always been transferred knowledge from one generation to the next. Humanity has depended on the old teaching the young since the dawn of our species. So in a sense, we have all always been able to live on after death. We can say that Shakespeare still lives in that his words are still very much within our culture. This millennium has seen a massive explosion in information that could be passed on from generation to generation. Of course, the ignition of the process goes back to the dawn of mankind, to the birth of language. The accumulation of information soon started to accelerate, first with writing and then with the rapid development of books, to eventually soar exponentially in the Digital Age. The ever increasing speed of accumulation, which even the youngest of you listening to this lecture must recognise as dramatic, looks capable of continuing indefinitely with further developments in DNA data storage.

The process started to exponentially feed on itself from the '30s when scientists learnt how to seamlessly connect the biological brain and synthetic data storage. 'The Age of

Scientific Intelligence' as sociologists call the present, had its foundations in the 19th Century, though its start date is usually taken as day one of this millennium. The day when computers finally proved their veracity by not malfunctioning because the early programmers hadn't coded for year number 2000. The predicted chaos, the revenge of the then 'luddites' never happened. We forget now, but total chaos had been so widely predicted. As it turned out, there was hardly a hiccup. Man didn't have to seize back control of life-support systems from the silicon chip. I think that was the day when it dawned on the world that the computer might not inherit the Earth but that it was certainly going to order it.

We will briefly skim over the ground that DNA data storage technology has covered since about 2010. That will make it easier to put the case history into the context of its time. As said, by '33 indirect data transfer from one human mind into another was already a possibility. Though this was a million times less holistic than up-to-date direct brain-to-brain transfer, for the first time, one's exact recorded memories could be surgically implanted in another. A synthetic DNA record could be physically added to augment a living brain. Theoretically, if illegally, the same data could also be transferred into any number of individuals. There are all sorts of ethical issues that still haven't been systematically tackled despite the years that have passed since the initial crude methodologies were established. None of these is bigger than the possibility of transferring the same data into countless people. Such a robotic transfer, especially of what might well be deviant ideas, is potentially a terrifying prospect. Imagine an army of similarly-programmed political or military storm-troopers being used to enforce an autocratic control. North Korea in the early decades of this century was proof of what is possible with the control of the mind, and that autocratic power was achieved without any biological or chemical interventions. Starvation and indoctrination were sufficient strong weapons.

At this time, rather than legislators having really bitten the bullet by tackling the details of the issue, we have a system of crude blunderbuss like laws. All multiple transfers of artificially encoded data, human-to-human, or machine-to-human, are outlawed by a strongly worded, but unenforceable, United Nations convention signed by over 190 member states.

In the early days, the data was digitally saved by building binary code into single strands of artificial deoxyribonucleic acid. These strands are just tiny fragments compared with what goes to make up the long double helix of biologically-useful DNA. The building blocks of these units that enable life's genetic coding and which are now our primary means of long-term data storage are the chemicals, thymine, guanine, adenine and cytosine. We abbreviate these as T, G, A and C. In those early days, the bases T and G represented one, with A and C representing zero, allowing the on/off, yes/no, stop/go type signalling of familiar digital coding. This artificial DNA was then and is now stored in 'dry-skin cell DNA capacitors' matching the recipient's own tissue. At first the introduced data could only be analysed slowly, in minutes rather than microseconds, but the scientists have become increasingly good at chemically-manipulating the cell stores, so that now accurate and ever faster data retrieval is possible.

Two inventions were needed for a living recipient to make use of a DNA Data Store. The first of these to become a reality was the 'Nucleotide Shuffler', which was followed a year later by the 'Search and Replicate Worm'. The first enables the strands of DNA data to be mixed and sorted, and the second is the device that allows the selection and copying of precise snips of information in the required order. In the Thirties, this sorting and retrieval process was extremely slow when compared to the speed that silicon chips have since achieved. However, even then, inside of a single minute any information from the implanted memory could be accessed to influence the thinking of the host individual.

Both our natural wish to pass on what we know to those we love and the normal expectations of our culture, mean that the recipient is usually a younger member of the knowledge provider's family. As already touched on, it is currently illegal to transfer memory to any more than one other individual. I possibly need to say even more about this.

For individuals, the major moral and ethical implication of having two or more minds sharing the same memories is the possibility of creating a deep identity conflict between them. We could easily end up with more than one almost identical personalities struggling against others to be recognised as the same desired persona. Biological twins tolerate each other. In fact, they are normally extremely close. However, twins are not two independently nurtured individuals who suddenly find themselves face-to-face with another, actually dissimilar-looking, individual that happen to have exactly the same memories. Anyway, twins often have very different slants on the memories they share, while between copied minds there will be precise memory and tagged attitude. Twins have built their memories independently, copied brains haven't.

It seems inevitable that at some stage, somewhere, multiple copied personalities will create dangerous conflicts. Inevitably, these struggles will threaten not just the individuals immediately involved, but also the wider social order. International law in this area is now universally strong, but variations in practice and application are sure to emerge. There is never any shortage of dangerously-corrupted institution attempting to subvert any approved practice for their advantage. Even were criminality doesn't win out there is always plenty of scope for individual states to interpret established laws differently. For now, the worst case

Frankensteinesque scenarios that science suggests as plausible, if controls aren't vigorously enforced, seem to be incentive enough to ensure that most territories attempt to uphold unsatisfactory international regulations.

Perhaps there is some flawed logic in our very consistent and insistent worries. We must hope that is the case. Whatever, burying our heads in the sand is unlikely to yield any answers. The risks involved in losing focus on the hypothesis that 'the cloning of minds is always dangerous' are so great that we are best served by assuming the very worst of postulated outcomes. As with climate change, the very worst outcomes are unlikely, but it is short-sighted to not plan for them.

If there are real flaws in the 'bad-outcome hypothesis', what may they be? The first possible counter is that any two identical lives would immediately diverge to become increasingly different as a result of individual experience. Individuality will thus always be in the process of emerging. Secondly, at least in the case of simple data transfer into an already-established mind, it is clear that the original biological self will play its part in modifying and interpreting the shared data differently. Obviously, the uniquely original biological minds of all individuals must play a huge part in directing what the enhanced being becomes. This is all provided, of course, that the original brain is left intact. In any transport of knowledge there is going to be a blending of influences between the host and the introduced persona, unless the host's mind has been removed. It is clear that we have much greater worries to think about than even mind extension and duplication. Complete replacement is the start of even more frightening outcomes.

Nowadays, we have the technology to completely replace one brain in any skull with another. Additionally, when the old brain is showing signs of decay it is possible to refill 'scrubbed' grey matter with every synaptic connection from the unit which is facing decline. Techniques have been found to biologically reproduce and or chemically reformat living grey matter. For permanent record, let it be known that I actually wrote the first draft of this lecture on Tuesday the 3rd September 2052.

Scientific advances are making things ever more complicated. The black-market trade in young bodies is a rapidly growing and terrifying new concern. In some unstable territories, those families that can afford it are having bodyguards follow their children night and day, while most parents, everywhere, have to live in a perpetual state of fear from body-snatchers. Macabre though the idea may be, the wealthy are having complete genetic profiles of their children made. Would they really use this information to make copies of lost family members? What a terrifying prospect. Kidnapping followed by brain evisceration, and subsequent body reuse is already a big and well-established business. Of course, the networks on which this new trade are built have a very long history. Children have been the victims of criminal slave and sex industry trade since the day Hell froze over. In reality, it is the poorest of people who have the real fears, not the wealthy and their pampered and well-guarded offspring. I digress too far. Enough to state the obvious, International Law, well codified as it is through the UN, is often going unenforced.

*

Even in 2033, the relatively crude transfer of personal knowledge could include emotional tags relating to particular snippets of information. In other words, at least some sense of personality and particular sensibilities could already be written into the synthetic DNA. Now there are interphase engines which 'copy' straight from the brain and then 'paste' information into the Dry-Skin Cell DNA Capacitor of the recipient. There is no longer any need to have technicians and computers laboriously checking the digitalisation and encodment of all information. Unfortunately, this also means that the beautiful subversion of the information flow seen in the satisfying conclusion to our case study is no longer feasible. Remember that the satisfying conclusion is just an out-of-date sugar cube used to sweeten this lecture's bitter pill. The ending is an example of just one of many cracks in the industry's armour that is no longer available to guardians of humanity. We must hope that new ways of subverting recent and apparently more robust technologies will be found when the people need them to defend themselves against the ruling elites.

Even though in '33, only vague tags indicating the emotional content could be passed on, such as this fact sequence made me angry, sad, happy or whatever, this still relatively crude technology was nevertheless considered to be absolutely amazing. Of course, the importance of DNA storage was already far wider than enabling one generation to pass person information onto the next. This was the first time in history that a young brain could be filled with an almost limitless quantity of information about anything. Better still, this information once implanted is totally recoverable, never forgotten, never subject to constant decay like information stored in the natural cell. We now understand the massively-increased potential of 'enhanced humans' as being very much due to the mix of 'wet-store brain' and 'dry-store brain' information used in any decision. We still need what biology gives us, our instincts and individual personality; as well as what science can add, in order to be a fully-rounded enhanced beings. We just can't over-emphasise the difference that modern DNA technologies have made to human development, by literally enhancing the job of evolution. Humans with enhanced memories really are totally superior creatures.

What used to take a lifetime to learn, and still does for the vast majority of the population, can now be integrated into another living human almost instantly. At present, most countries outlaw transfer to children under 18 because of the possible dangers in arresting normal childhood development. Who knows what sort of deviant minds could be created? In theory we could give a baby the knowledge of a thousand Einsteins. Further research is needed before we can understand what can and can't be safely transferred to the juvenile mind. Beyond that, long-term equal treatment of all young populations is vital to our progress as a single, egalitarian, species.

The ethical issue of using DNA technology in robots is another of the many thorny areas of the new industry that has so far been largely avoided. Research in this field has been outlawed by yet another typically toothless United Nations mandate. It merely masks the very worrying concerns that such technology raises. We may well ponder just what frightening things are being done behind many secretive scientific doors. For now, the dangers of creating a robotic life-form superior in every way to humans, by using dry-store DNA, is thankfully still very much the stuff of Science Fiction. However, it would be naive in the extreme to think that research in this area isn't being done. There have been plenty of 'leaks' suggesting that illegal research is already yielding terrifying results. Cyborgs are on their way.

As in-body memory storage gets cheaper, more and more traditional information storage becomes obsolete. Of course, electronic data storage will still be required, especially for the analysis of current-time data flow, and for making good data-crunching predictions about the future. Computers that can slave at any speed indefinitely will always be needed to complement our human capacities. The enhanced human's synthetic DNA mind is subject to the same fatigues and emotional hiccups as the biological body in which it resides. There are certain human frailties that a robotic DNA computer will always triumph over. Humans will always have animal frailties. Nothing can change that other than robotic and synthetic replacement of the whole genetic being, God forbid.

Strong democratic institutions are going to be needed over the following decades, to ensure that this empowering technology continues to be rolled out evenly. The idea of there being any long-term elites of enhanced individuals lording over the rest of humanity is intolerable. There was far more than a thousand years between the ending of a crude democratisation in Greece and Rome, and the first glimpses of true democracy in the modern state. We can do without another millennium-long Dark Age. In fact, if the enhanced humans ever came to view themselves as especially unique, truly a superior species, then the masses of 'backward' mankind could become the harvested cattle of all future time. Humans could truly become the calorific nourishment of a species of body snatching synthetic DNA-based vampires.

We must all guard against subversion by the new elites. Our history is evidence enough of that. By the end of the first decade of the 21st century, there was better health and a better quality of life among the populations of most countries than there had ever been at any other time in history. Societies had been transformed in 300 years from nothing much more advanced than rule by birthright and brute strength, to a brief flowering of democracy. For the first time there was even equality between the sexes. Our golden age of political equality, of the rights of the individual, is in as great a peril as ever. Democracy has peaked; now we must guard against its fall. Indeed, some previously 'free' countries are already experiencing almost totalitarian control from enhanced elites. We must do what we can to ensure that these fortunately still-rare dominions are only temporary, and this can best be achieved by making enhancement a basic right of every citizen. The fight for our 'commonwealth' is a never-ending story. It is an ongoing battle against the desire of the over-powerful few to dictate to the many; a battle against the evil creatures like Jonah Jesuorobo Senior. Modern science has just made the eternal battle harder.

We must all hope that we never see the birth of a truly immortal subspecies. It should be clear by now that I believe the identity of each born individual must be maintained. Further, I maintain that the biological identity of any person must always be master or mistress of any enhancement to the body. Brain evisceration and replacement and brain scrubbing must be forever outlawed. The facts are summarised on the A4 sheet that I hope each of you has in front of you.

***

(The Case Study)

Everywhere, powerful, rich families are transferring all knowledge directly from one diabolical generation to the next, while threatening to control the science which gave them this edge. The easiest way for the general population to keep control of this technology is to never let the strongest dominate in the first place. All of us, ordinary citizens everywhere, have to stand up for our rights. Democracy can give no ground to the power of the elites without risking annihilation. Where democratic institutions are already losing, the fight back needs to be through millions of small individual actions that steadily weaken the status quo. The elites won't often be defeated by frontal assault; at least not once military institutions become their playthings. Then they will only be beaten by a million tiny cuts that steadily sap their reserves. Actions need not be violent; but they must be in overwhelming numbers. Few cuts will be as effective as Emma Postlethwaite's, which I now focus on, but every action counts. We must all be part of the fight for humanity.

Worldwide, the degree of control established by the first wave of enhanced specimens has been very variable. Some countries that were already run by strong minorities are now completely dominated by enhanced subjects and others are as free and as democratically run as any have ever been. This story addresses all, calling some to action and the rest to be vigilant. Those who are 'au fait' with the problems may still enjoy my personal dramatisation.

I must state, for the record, that however much I would have liked this story to be based on more recent case history, the legal jeopardy that such a pursuit would create isn't the only risk. In addition, there are safety issues for those people directly involved in recent events. There have been many direct threats to both the proprietors and employees of The Nownation Press in recent times for supporting free speech. I thank them for kindly sponsoring this lecture in return for printing rights.

I can talk fairly freely about the Jesuorobo case of twenty years ago, a story that so well demonstrates the basic characteristics of the exponentially-growing danger that we all face. Indeed, it is not solely the passing of time that protects all involved but also the brave actions of Emma Postlethwaite and even to a small degree, my own weak active contribution.

In '33, the loss of his mind, of a lifetime of thought and planning, was no longer inevitability for Jonah Jesuorobo, despite the fact that his physical body was certainly doomed. When health care, organ harvesting and laboratory-grown organs eventually failed, the very wealthy still inevitably died. Even today, just as always, the hearse still calls for an occasional rich cadaver.

By '33, Jonah had run the family business for 25 years. Profits had nearly always been good, even though the legalisation of some narcotics had for a time undermined his business model. Now he was making most of his money running health farms for the idle, supposedly helping the rich trim their fat girths. Jonas called them his 'Fat Estates', so mocking his poorer clients. But the truth is that Jonah was whale-sized himself. Even after having received the gift of a donor heart, he had insufficient will to follow the doctor's dietary advice. He was sure his new ticker, from a suitably arranged young donor, would give him a couple of good years, but what then? Of course he basked in the glow of the gratitude his financial support gave to one previously destitute village. The home of the donor now had clean running water and Jonah had been made an honorary citizen. But the fact was that he didn't care a brass-farthing about relieving the suffering of those impoverished people. That was just the price of buying a living heart, without risking a low quality purchase by going through the black markets or sourcing from road-kill. Determination to get the best implant that money could buy had resulted in Jonah making one of his very rare forays into legitimate business. The rapid failure of his heart had given insufficient time in which to grow one in the lab from his own tissues.

Jonah dreamt of living on as himself in a younger body. At the time of his demise this wasn't yet possible. He had to settle for the technology of his day, even though he knew that great advances were just around the corner. What was then possible was for his memories, his knowledge, even a crude imitation of his personality, to live on in a new being, a future generation. As I have said, Jonah had often toyed with the idea of having a heart grown for when the donated one gave up the ghost, but in the end he simply left things to late to pursue that avenue. He had felt that as much as he appreciated life, there was a limit to how much he was prepared to suffer. Radical surgery every few years, rendering him vulnerable to his enemies for weeks was not a fun prospect. He had terrible nightmares whenever incapacitated in a hospital bed. He was terrified that some wronged individual from his past could theoretically slip by his bodyguards, approach his supine form, and administer agonising summary justice.

As is the way with such autocratic men, he didn't even really like the idea of relinquishing power to his son, which is why he was determined to make full use of available human-to-human DNA memory transfer. He couldn't hope to have a re-built, perfect, copy of himself established inside his offspring and yet he was determined to get as close to that as then-current technology would allow.

In order to make this story really live in your minds, so allowing you to build a real emotional connection, I am now going to reinvent a dialogue surrounding the known events. The balance of opinion is presently very much with pushing boundaries. The government has the media and the weight of the establishment, the elites, on its side. We the people need all the help we can get, including the powerful opiate of dramatic art. I hope you will enjoy my divergence from the pure facts, from the dry and academic, into something a bit more creative. There is an aspirational novelist in even this old fossil of an academic. We need to feel the affects of this technology on real lives so as to understand why we should try to find the courage to forgo personal enhancement that isn't available to all.

***

(An imaginary conversation: Jonah Jesuorobo talking to himself)

"I have an appointment with 'Legacy Information Incorporated' tomorrow. They are going to start the process of recording every factual detail, every surviving picture and all the background that I can conjure up. Scientists tell me that one day soon, direct mind-to-computer download will be a reality, but for now we have to do everything through speech, written records and stored electronic data transfer. I am so frustrated that, just because I can't live a few more years waiting for technology to advance, I have to pass on such an incomplete version of me. Nevertheless, I will do my best to see that the technicians record details as accurately as possible. What a future is in store for those younger than I am, with the possibility of recreating themselves inside another human shell.

In order to pass on an accurate version of me, I need to talk through as much intimate detail as I can stand. I have to record my true feelings about everything, big and small, good and bad. Of course, I will let some stuff go to the grave with my carcase. How I killed his mother, for example. That bitch, I so enjoyed having her removed. I don't think I should let my son learn the fact that, to help make him strong, I arranged for him to find his mother – newly dead and still coupled. The slut was 'in flagrante delicto' with one of my boy's female schoolteachers. I'm sure that sight helped toughen up Jonah; made him more like me. On reflection, it is probably just as well that we haven't got direct and complete brain to artificial memory transfer yet. I can be selective about my inheritance; trim the excesses. I may even consider adding a few false niceties. Pretending to have loved the boy's mother would be an intelligent start.

I will also take a punt on a more personal future. I may not be dependent on my son in the long-term at all. Kept dry, and in good condition, DNA can remain intact almost indefinitely, so I will make sure a copy of my thoughts is also recorded in cells to be stored in a vault. After all, that useless boy may well die young. That vaulted record can be far more complete, truthful. Then of course, I will make quite sure my actual brain is well preserved. Cryogenic suspension is certainly a good long shot at immortality. Who knows, but in another 50 years, when technology has improved, perhaps I will be able to come back for real. Imagine that! My exact self being brought back to life, an outcome that is far more appealing than just passing my memory on. How great that would be, having my mind literally sewn into a perfect young body that has had its skull eviscerated. That is a nice thought. I must make a recorded of exactly what sort of body I would like to inhabit.

Perhaps I will be able to return and even take back control of the company from my son. Of course I am arranging cryogenic preservation, hopefully, without risking the boy finding out. After all, would he allow me back if he knew I was coming? Would I have let my father back? Not bloody likely! Would my son allow me to regain the reins, rather than see them be handed to Jonah III or his renewed self? Would he Hell?"

***

(A plausible dialogue with Dr. Brownlow)

"It is nice to meet you, Mr. Jesuorobo. Come in and take a seat. As I believe you know, I'm Doctor Alexis Brownlow. It is an honour to meet you sir!"

"Have you got the papers back from my son? Has he agreed to the implant; is he fully committed? I mean, he has been in private, but I know we need his signature."

"Well yes, and yes and no. Yes we have the signed papers back. And a guarded yes, as even though he has agreed to being implanted, he can actually refuse on a wide range of medical and psychological grounds when the time comes. I can't do anything about that."

"He would be a fool not to go ahead. You see, I have a lot of business information that he needs if he wishes to stay alive. Not all our business is done with nice people."

"Right, then! The recording of data can start today. I have given a technician the go ahead on your profile, as I know how time presses. I'm aware from talking to your private physician that you have health issues. As I'm sure you know, the more honest you are and the more detail you provide, the more of you that will be accurately saved and passed on to influence the next generation. The collection of data is the easy part of the job. The second process requires a lot of expensive equipment and many laboratory hours. That is the binary encoding of everything you give us. The code is then transferred to synthetic DNA. We have to create the sequencing framework for a personalised 'Nucleotide Shuffler', so that data opens in a balanced way. The project won't work well unless we get an appropriate relationship between the factual knowledge and, shall we call it, the more spontaneous. A real sense of you, your character, is a crucial component of the overall picture. For a good result it is vital that as you tell your story you give an importance rating to all the information. You do this by literally giving us a score of 1 to 10 with 10 being given to the most crucial information and strongest emotions.

"Tell us literally everything. It doesn't matter how much you repeat yourself. That actually helps us to give data the right priority. There is no problem with storage. We put about 1000 terabytes of data into a single gram of DNA. This is nothing like the theoretical potential; this technology is still in its infancy. It is known that each double helix molecule could theoretically store 455 exabytes of data. We leave plenty of space, within which your thoughts can be constantly reordered.

"Of course, at this stage we need to talk about our special arrangement, don't we sir? Your son won't ever know anything about the personality transfer, provided you give us all the help you can towards building a really rounded profile. As you instructed, we are using new techniques that will allow your DNA mass to be the dominant deep influence. Surgically, we can do this by putting in a secondary connection between the shuffler and the hippocampus. This is strictly illegal, which is one reason for our high fees. I have also had to pay a lot of money for the right staff. We are as concerned as you are that all parties be extremely discreet.

"You will be the driving force, the main influence. Only your son's most basic instincts and short-term assessments will be truly his. The women he fancies, the music, even to some degree the food he likes, will be more yours than his. When it comes to subtle control, difficult decision making, your DNA sequences will be completely dominant. Is there anything you wish to ask, at this point?"

"No Doc, I've been over most of this several times. Please go on."

"As stated, short and medium-term memory and crude instincts will be your son's. Even the very best current switching and data recovery systems, shufflers and worms, aren't fast enough to control these processes. However the really important brain activity, the analytical, the sophisticated workings of the mind, the deep storage, will work by reference to the DNA strands we'll create from your information. If the wrong people ever get wind of what exactly we are about to do, then not only could I lose my licence and almost certainly spend the rest of my life in prison, but the courts would strip your son of all decision making powers. Both our businesses would end up under state control. We both depend completely on each other to keep our secrets safe. I'm sure we see eye-to-eye on this, don't we sir? We live in a paranoid society, but as it happens we both know that it's nowhere near paranoid enough to guess as to just how close I've got to transferring entire personalities to different bodies."

"Don't you worry Doc, I'm not going to tell, and who else would? You umm... you do have the technology don't you? Just to help you get it right, I have a pre-payment on having you silenced if, I, or rather, my son doesn't report a particular code word to the exterminator within 30 days of the implant. I'm sure you understand why I find this insurance necessary. You will be a very rich doctor, provided you are as good as your word. I would be dishonest if I pretended that I hadn't found a way of protecting my investment. The code will not be obvious to your technician, so there is no point thinking you can cut out the critical piece of data being transferred to my son. We have done exhaustive background checks. Your wife is most attractive, by the way."

"You have a nerve! You threaten me and my family, though it is on me you depend. I just spent five minutes telling you how careful we are going to be."

"Absolutely! I'm sure we fully appreciate each other's needs. Even if you find a way of guarding your family without me, and you won't, research can only continue with my funding. You see we both know that the government, under pressure from the left, would be only too happy to have an excuse to close you down."

"I wouldn't be doing the work if I didn't think I was competent. I can assure you of the fact that my techniques work. We have to push boundaries though; I'm sure you understand that we can't eliminate all risk. We are both in this up to our necks. Just for what we have done with the subjects is enough to get us incarcerated, or worse. Remember, sir, you provided the street-kids for the research I needed to do. Dead kids take a lot of explaining away, whatever their backgrounds."

"Calm down, doctor. I have only survived for so long by covering all eventualities. Your family is in safe hands, the safest hands in the land, provided we continue to be friends."

"I have practiced all the surgical procedures many times. I can almost completely alter the thinking of a subject brain by making introduced DNA dominant. What we are planning to do in your case is less radical than I have already achieved, but far safer because of it. Unfortunately, when we force complete dominance over the host by swamping signals from the brain stem, things generally go wrong. For reasons we don't yet understand, complete take over seems to almost invariably result in severe psychoneurosis and sometimes psychosis and eventual suicide. Somehow the dominated personality tries to fight back; having recognised that it has been subjugated to a foreign will. I guess that the host mind can cope with what it judges, though wrongly, to be mere influence, and not so well with what it recognises as dominion. I relish the day when we will have the capacity to simply replace one thought system with another, but we are not yet there. And anyway, that would be far more than you simply becoming a permanent influence on your son; it would be tantamount to killing him off. Scientists are going to be forced to take even greater moral responsibility for what they do in the future. I don't want to risk any lives, not yours, and certainly not those of my family. I am very upset that..."

"Shut it! There is no point gassing on. If I have to go elsewhere then you are already dead, so bear in mind your contrived indignation at my generous warning hasn't gone unnoticed. You knew what you were getting yourself into. Do I make myself clear?"

"Yes... of course. My research is dependent on your money, I am well aware of our mutual interests. I will do whatever I need to do to keep my family safe. None of my staff have any clue about just how far I am taking our collaboration. The only one that will have any usable knowledge is Emma Postlethwaite, and I understand that she will have to be disposed of. I knew the conditions of our contract well enough to know I live by them or die."

"There's a good man. I'm so glad we understand each other. Umm... back to business. Will my enhanced son have any sense of me, will he feel he has grown to be more like me, or will he still have some of his bloody mother's personality? I prefer to think that I'm fully rid of her."

"That is hard to say. He is only volunteering to be connected to DNA memory of yours that has to do with the business. But of course he will be expecting to at least take on some of your private views in that area. We will reinforce the concept that taking on some of your reasoning is normal, so as to cut down on subsequent surprises as much as possible. As we are giving your memories a dominant role, one might intuitively think he will be more or less just you. However, to be quite frank, you will be dead – gone. He will have lost his acute fear of you, but doing things the way you would do them needs to be very strongly ingrained. I know that you wouldn't be showing such faith in him, family or not, if you felt he would ever really turn against you.

Hopefully your son will not really be aware of being any different from the person he has always been. In the future it may be possible to transfer the knowledge of a conscious brain straight into another whilst at the same time slowly closing down the old host memory. One mind would be sort of faded into another. In that way, it might be possible to create an illusion of continuity. For now, that sort of stuff is all theoretical. Of course, we could – if we had all the techniques – put your brain in an empty head, but that is very different to passing knowledge from on living organ to another. We are a few years away from that as well, and too many for you I'm afraid, Jonah.

Remember, what we have agreed. As a part of making all this work you need to be out of the picture. I am not going to risk everything we have done by having you meet what is almost yourself. The psychological fallout could be highly unpredictable, especially as the host won't have been party to the plan to transfer so much of you. Your son will be you in many profound ways; a son that, faced with meeting his new self head-on, might suffer psychological damage. Imagine the sudden surge of information that could well up into his consciousness. One might assume that as he already has all the information, what difference would a meeting make? Lots I'm afraid.

We are not aware of what we know until the information is needed, called up into short-term memory. So it is one thing having individual snippets of information about you brought to mind, but quite another being faced with a surge of information about stuff he might then realise he couldn't possibly have truly witnessed.

Whatever happens, your son will still get a sense that he has changed in some way, that can't really be avoided. As I said earlier, he won't have any awareness of having turned into his father, but that doesn't mean he wouldn't be damaged by a physical encounter. Let's face it, your early memories will, of course, predate and sometimes seem more significant than those that were uniquely his. We can tone down and fragment historic memories, especially the huge parcel of stuff dating back to before your son was even born. But sometimes his balance of thought will feel strangely detached from the person he once felt himself to be. We will endeavour to instil the emotions of early experiences whilst keeping the facts vague. Like stories he has been told rather than directly experienced and then stored away a long time ago. We aim to place your history, a crucial driver of who you are, without leaving him feeling he somehow actually lived it. Your son could get very angry if he came to feel that we had subverted his own life and personality. As you can see, this transfer is an art form as much as it is a science.

Let's give a banal example to explain what we are up against, and to explain why it will take him a while to feel settled. Imagine that you really like lemon ice-tea. He recalls that snippet of information as he looks at the drinks in a store. On the basis of this thought, he buys the ice-tea only to discover that his taste buds register it as unpleasant. That will cause minor and temporary confusion that should be quickly rationalised away. But at the same time he doesn't want to be faced by many such issues at one time, otherwise he might well start to feel that he must be psychologically ill. The long and short of it is that you two should never meet again. We must arrange a fake car crash or something, and get you out of the country. I'm sure you will be very comfortable in Switzerland.

As you must see there is going to need to be a lot of subtlety about how we handle the information, how we effectively label it. Do you ever or have you ever had long meaning of life conversations with your son? Have you ever talked to him about yourself? You need to be brutally honest here."

"Not really, I guess. I haven't ever been one for touchy feely."

"That is what I suspected. We are going to have to invent quite a bit of stuff. We need to instil fictitious meetings and events, during which you got together and talked a lot of detail through. We have to find a way of making the enhanced being, your son, feel that what he has always known a great deal about his father. It is necessary to create a lot of shared space between the two of you, to allow for your son to have reasonably assimilated the greater part of the history we are going to transfer. Only the business data can be just dropped in. Some information we imprint will never surface, as your son won't ever have cause to consider it. As luck would have it the technician you will be using, Emma, is very discreet. She is also – as you demanded – easy to lose, having no living family and few local friends. She has very quickly fitted herself into my business and as an illegally-working foreigner, she is particularly dependent. As you may have guessed, she doesn't even use her true family name. Just to play extra safe, she has been told that we are encoding more of you than the law allows out of moral kindness. She believes your son suffered profound memory loss during the trauma of dealing with his mother's murder. Make sure you remember that. Unless you have anything else you wish to discuss, I think we may as well get you both acquainted straight away."

"No, everything seems clear. We seem to have an understanding don't we, doctor?"

"Very good! If you go back through the waiting room, my receptionist will point you in the right direction. It is time for you to get started on total recall."

***

(A possible conversation between Jonah and Emma)

As soon as she steps through the door, Jonah has a strange feeling he has seen Emma Postlethwaite before. But it soon passes. She's such exciting eye candy that he feels assured that he would have remembered better if they had actually met. Before the thought completely deserts him, he asks the question anyway.

"Do I know you from somewhere?"

"I don't believe so. I'm Emma, Emma Postlethwaite. But I do know your name, Mr. Jesuorobo, from news broadcasts and things. You are really quite famous. I know you run one of the biggest health farm businesses anywhere, but that is hardly like knowing you, is it? I suppose you might have been my mother's boss at some time. She often worked in hospitality areas."

"Yes, I get your point. My age is, after all, the reason we are here. If your mother was as attractive as you are, I might well remember her. Anyway this isn't getting the job done, where would you like me to start?"

"Well, how about your earliest memories and we will see how we get on from there."

"Umm... that isn't easy."

"Don't be self-conscious; pretend like you're talking to a pet dog or something. I can even sit behind a screen if it helps. I'm used to being out of sight and very discreet. I used to do legal aid work for women in abusive relationships. I was often screened off from the courts, as were the defendants, for safety reasons. I know very well how to keep secrets. I've done lots of training, and would never dream of disclosing information I've heard professionally."

"I've had people killed for double crossing me. That is perhaps the first thing you need to know, Ms. Postlethwaite."

"Well then, would you like to start there? Perhaps with a list of bodies we can work through."

"Haha! I think we are going to get on just fine. You aren't easily intimidated are you?"

"I'm of no relevance. All you need to know is that I'm aware we will be crossing ethical boundaries, and that I may be seen by authorities as complicit in the breaking of the law. I have no intention of doing anything that might bring about outside interest. I can assure you that the doctor is paying me well, with your money, to ensure my loyalty.

We need to take great care in building the facts into a solid story as we are going to be embedding them in such a way that they will dominate the mind of your son, short of leaving him feeling he has a bipolar condition. It is sad that your child lost so much in the car accident and that what is left traumatised him so. We don't usually wish to encode nearly so much information.

Umm.... just before you start, let me give you some pointers. There are all sorts of inherent dangers to the host mind, especially if he starts to think that he can remember personal stuff about you that he couldn't have ever been told. As for you, the person that you are now, you must understand that dead is dead – your life will end as God always intended it to. The you that is having this conversation will be as dead as anyone has ever been... when the time eventually comes that your mortal body gives up. What that means to you now probably depends upon your religion. This will always be the case until – God forbid – technology allows us to put old brains into young bodies. It is vital that you understand that we cannot give you any personal sense of continuity beyond the grave. A lot of people somehow assume we already have the technology to be able to do that. Not so, this is all solely about your son. It is also important that you realise that you aren't going to find any of this easy. How much time do we have to build a comprehensive picture?"

"You needn't worry. The doctor has already made all these issues quite clear. In fact, I've heard them a bit too often.

I should be able to spend two or three days a week here without raising difficulties. I'll just need to sacrifice my golf. That new ticker will just have to go short of its exercise."

"Okay, away you go."

***

(Imagining Emma's thoughts)

So that is Jonah Jesuorobo. What a right son of a bitch. I am not surprised that MI5 went to the trouble of approaching me to take the job at 'Legacy Information'. They must have known for some time that Jonah was likely to try and live beyond the grave, and that he had shown an interest in this particular company. And of course they knew that there was no way that I was going to turn down this particular job. I should be unhappy that I am being manipulated, but I'm not. All I want is to see justice done for Jessica. Oh God, I miss you so Jesse...

The truth is that that the intelligence service had me on strings from the very beginning. I know now why I passed the entry exams, having done so little, when so many worked so hard only to fail. I always put my success down to them mixing up the papers, but they didn't, did they? They had my number right from the start. It was just good fortune that having majored in psychology, I looked just about qualified enough to be recruited, or would they have found a way of getting me whatever?

Am I going to be able to hold my shit together if he starts talking about Jessica? I don't suppose he will remember her name, but I can't believe he fails to remember what he did. She was still at school when she was drawn into his world. First of all, it was just selling a bit of weed, then slowly hard stuff. By the time she was 16, she had left home, was a heavy user, and eventually nothing more than traded meat to the bastard's less savoury clients. Even I, her big sister, had no idea what a mess she was in until it was too late. We all blame ourselves, thinking that we could have done something more to get her out of trouble, but I still don't know what. At least some revenge is now possible, provided I don't screw up. I have got to get him to really talk about the really shitty stuff. It isn't like it should be difficult as he knows he is completely dependent on us to pass on his 'legacy'. I am already aware of some of his weaknesses as well, aren't I? Thanks to the little that Jessica did talk about. I wonder at what point Robo learnt that Jessica and his wife had more than a friendly relationship. Probably not immediately, as I'm sure that arrogant prick didn't know what Mrs. Jesuorobo, Elaine, really felt about him. Robo didn't even know his wife was never attracted to him physically. But he must have realised that Elaine had done more than scoop up and temporarily mend the broken child that was Jessica. What I plan isn't only for my dear sister, it is also for Elaine and for all the others, for all the lives the bastard has destroyed.

I must be patient drawing out the information. My impatience, too much pressure, could well mean him clamming up and so weakening the case Intelligence are building. More than that, haste might well cause a slip-up that gets me killed. Actually, I know that whatever I do, or don't do, that my life will be in jeopardy as soon as we have finished the digital conversion. I will just know too much for him to risk leaving me alive. I'm quite sure I will have the sort of accident that my sister had. Perhaps I could end up in the concrete foundations of one of his new 'Health Farms'. MI5 are going to be pissed as hell if I manage to finish him off without bringing him in, but sod them. Cold revenge is far better than waiting for the often derailed, slow-engines, of justice. Besides, I really do feel that either I kill him or he kills me.

To get control of the bastard and not give myself away, I need him to be looking between my legs, not into my eyes. I have never worn over-short skirts, but I will now. And what could be more appropriate than borrowing from Jessica's wardrobe, the clothes that poor mother still can't find the will to clear out. Yes. I may even choose a skirt he has groped up before, that would be most appropriate. I have no intention of hiding behind any screen, not for my safety and certainly not to spare his embarrassment. Anyway, I'm sure he only ever goes red in the face when administering some physical excesses, never through social sensitivities. No, I have got to let him think I am eating out of his hand... let him think that he controls me. I must make him believe I am a slave to his wishes. Then he will open up and tell me all.

***

(A possible following interview, some days later)

"You are looking nice today Emma, those clothes bring out the best in you. Here, bring your chair a little closer... now that's better isn't it. You feel cold dear... Now where were we?"

"You were telling me about your wife. About how she spent more and more time gaming in virtual life, in 'Xanadutu Reality'. You were saying how you found out late on that she was bisexual, how she cheated on you all along and spent too much money."

"Yes, I remember now. You must be hot in that jacket, why don't you slip it off?"

"I'm not sure I'm decent without it, you know, my top's quit tight."

"No one is watching dear. Here, let me help you... Perhaps you should come to dinner tonight, so that we can have a longer chat. Not being in work hours, I could pay a rate appropriate for a private consultation."

"That is very generous, Jonah. Tonight isn't possible, but at the weekend."

"To then, then! Now, we had better get on. Arh..."

"Elaine was cheating on you."

"Oh yes. I was told she was, but I only half-believed it, I mean I knew from having her followed that she hadn't been playing with any pricks. Then I caught her myself, in our bed, with a young slut that worked for me. Thinking about it, as I remember, she looked a lot like you. If I had been invited to join them it might have been different. I guess I lost it a bit. You see, I had already overheard the bitch being, shall we say, less than flattering about me. I didn't let on that I knew, just watched, angry and, well, I can't deny I was aroused. She died the next day with her young lover. One of my men shot the brace of them and made a good job of making it look a hunting accident. I decided to pin the crime on my 'gamekeeper', just to be sure of covering my tracks. So I made it obvious that he had murdered them both. That made a much more convincing story to take to the police. The shooter was taken into custody and then tragically 'passed away' an hour later in a police holding cell. It sounds complicated, but it all went like clockwork. My son had just happened to find the lovers naked together...Dead, but you know, naked. But even that wasn't all bad, because rather nicely, I arranged for Jonah Junior to see the shooter sitting in his car cleaning his shotgun."

"That must have been terrible for your poor boy, how old was he at the time? Surely he could only have been twelve or thirteen."

"I believe so. Yes, that changed him. In a strange way, it was the making of him. The experience, seeing what his mother was really like, certainly helped toughen Jonah up. He had been such a mother's boy. . . Haha! After that I made sure he became an interest of the right sort of nanny. She did a fine job of getting his orientation right. With his mother being into girls, I worried he might turn out to bat for the other side as well."

–"You mean his caregiver did..."

–"Did some practical educating. Exactly! Made sure he knew the right place to stick his action man."

–"I understand, sort of. It almost sounds as though you were pleased the poor boy saw his mother like that. Sorry, I find that hard to... Didn't the boy need a lot of help after that?"

"He had to see the psycho nurses a few times. I can't remember more than that. But yes, I needed to know sometime, whether he had it in him to be strong enough to one day run my business. He is a tough cookie now; far more like me than his mother. He has had the best education money can buy. Not like me, the victim of liberal leaning state schools."

–"What about the girl, can you tell me about her working for you?"

–"She helping me get product shifted, street sales, but like so many she got addicted to the shit. I tried to sort her out, to give her a bit of private attention. She had an accident in the house. Elaine found her and rather than just apply bandages and kicking her out, she persuaded me that there were benefits to keeping her on. She was supposed to be a good cook, though I never saw much evidence of it. I guess they must have started a regular thing right from there. It was probably Elaine's intention from the very beginning to get into her knickers."

–"It was an accident when this girl got hurt?"

–"An accident just waiting to happen... she claimed to be pregnant. Next we knew of it, she'd had a fall. I thought she fell deliberately, to get rid of the kid. The butler said he saw her tumble right down the stairs. Anyway, she didn't quite break her neck. He put her to bed and called me. The doctor decided she would be okay kept out of hospital, seeing as how Elaine was taking proper care of her. Elaine was a nurse once, you know. They put the tart on one of them fancy monitors, so that the hospital could keep tabs on her vitals from a distance. I mean, who the hell stays in hospital unless they're dying nowadays?"

***

(Speculating on Emma's thoughts)

God, I'm cold. How did I hold myself together through that? I just hope he thought I was tense, excited or something, because of where his hand was. How could he have missed seeing the horror in my face?

That pervert is going to pay big-time. He is going to suffer for what he has done to Jessica and to all the countless others. Not just personal suffering either. I'm going to make sure his whole corrupt regime comes down. To hear from him about Jesse carrying a child, oh, that hurts. That murdering bastard! I just know it was his. I have a lot of planning to do, recordings and documents to alter. In my spare time I need to find out all I can about formatting and coding data as well, if I am going to be able to doctor the data transfer as much as I intend to. I am going to need help!

Sweet Jesus! Somehow I have to survive at his house as well. I don't think, 'I've got a headache', or, 'sorry it is the wrong week' is going to be enough to hold him at bay. No, I am going to need a serious diversion. Some proper backup from the department is vital. I hope they can come up with something really spectacular. How could even the most callous of hookers spread her legs for a monster that destroyed her sister?

MI5 will get plenty of information, just not Robo in person. The scumbag is mine, but how? I've got to be practical. I can't learn all I need to know fast enough. Now is the time to use the fact that James, that kid in the micro-lab, is so keen to impress me. Anyway, he is nice enough. Playing to him will be a small sacrifice for Jessica and who knows, I've dated worse. I must at least lead him on a bit, enough so that he will help me manipulate the data. Anyway, I have to trust someone, as I can't do this all alone. I must have enough information to be able to genuinely call time on the interviews by the weekend. I'm sure I can't hold him off any longer than that. So one way or another, this should soon all be over.

Now, how the hell can I survive a visit to that smelly fat slob's house without surrendering myself to his perversions? Even his touch makes my flesh crawl, let alone... Jesus! The weekend is only three days away! Three days to find a way to divert a monster and to get James twisted around my little finger. Go girl!

I have an idea. Perhaps I can disarm Robo with a suitably fortified wine or something.

***

(Home visit)

Having negotiated Jesuorobo's security men, Emma is at the front door checking for cameras, before she nervously puts down her carrier bag. She makes to look at her vanity mirror and then – feels for the safety catch on the revolver as she puts the mirror back. Then she withdraws her hand from her handbag having reassured herself that the metal feels familiar. She presses the doorbell.

———

"Nice and punctual Emma, I like that. Do come in. Here, let me take that bag. How nice! Flowers to brighten my home. Roses and...?"

"Crimson roses, yellow zinnia and purple-to-white cyclamen. I chose them myself and here, a bottle of your favourite brandy."

"You spoil me dear! And haven't you got to know me well? My favourite tipple and flowers as dazzling as you are. You look stunning, come let me show you to the lounge. My butler has left dinner in the oven, but first, a drink. Champagne, I thought, to celebrate the success of data collection."

"Oh yes, what a nice idea... but later. What I need right now is a warm drink. It was a cold walk up from the Metro. I never go anywhere without my mint tea-bags, would you mind? Afterwards, well, I will be in a much more receptive mood. I'll be most upset if you don't join me in a brew. Where is the kitchen?"

–"Well I don't drink tea as a rule and I almost never go near the kitchen, but why not? Follow me!"

–"If you like, I'll do it. Have you seen a Japanese tea ceremony before? They can be very entertaining. I have a sort of party version. Just give me a minute to boil the kettle."

*

"I can't say I really get why you are quite so fond of the brew. If anything, I found it's a bit bitter, with a suggestion of toothpaste and possibly a hint of something else. Still never mind, a bit of bubbly will soon have me right and the tea may help the rubber plant. As for your geisha girl stuff, now that I did enjoy. I never knew tea could be quite such a stimulating experience one minute and so relaxing the next. If I wasn't in such delightful company I believe the warm drink could have made me nod off."

God help me, has he guessed what I am up to, please don't let him work it all out. I need to come on strong so to make him take interest in me as an object, rather than dwell on trying to second guess my intentions. I'm sure women are only good for one sort of activity in his sick mind. "Well, I can't help but notice that I haven't put all of you to sleep!"

"Indeed. Is it so obvious! Down it goes, for now at least. So how about some champers to liven us up?"

"Your hand! Sorry, you don't have to stop, I'm just not quite ready." Hell, I've got to play along. Either I see this through. I can't run. Do or die! No, it's, be done or die.

"Too dry? Here, let me help."

"Isn't that a waste of champagne, pouring it on me?"

"Only if I don't drink it?"

"You're rushing me, please! Can we just go a bit slower?"

"Oh, come now. We both know why you are here. You see, my spies are fiendishly clever. It's for Jessica isn't it? – A most enjoyable young lady. Did you really think I wouldn't research your background? I also know there is a gun in your purse. You were caught on camera despite your discretion. You may be starting to feel a bit faint... champagne is a fine disguise. Let's have some fun before you pass out, before you become too frigid... or is that rigid? Do you see the irony in coming to poison me when the one struggling against intoxicants is you?

***

(Sirens are heard and there is a pounding on the door)

"Police! Open up! Jonah Jesuorobo, we know you are in there. We have a report of an attempted break-in. We believe you are in danger, sir. A woman was seen taking a gun from her car. Your gate men reported that she was let into the house. We really should question her sir."

That devious bitch! I don't even have time to hide her upstairs. I will just have to give them some bullshit about drugging her so that I could get the gun away. I'll say I was just about to call the police myself.

***

(Private room in the City Hospital)

"Freesias. How nice. It is so sweet of you to visit, Doctor Brownlow."

"Call me Alexis, Emma. We are all so relieved that you are okay. I have been at my wit's end. The assault on you, I'm so sorry. Can I talk? I mean, are the police listening?"

"I don't know. I haven't been awake long. Uhgg! Sorry, everything hurts when I move. I don't think he was very gentle when I was out cold."

"Sorry. Would you prefer I came back later?"

"No, I'm fine, really . . . Don't worry, as no one except Jonah can be accused of doing anything illegal. I was very careful with the data. I promise you that everything is in order. No DNA coding has been done that you would find difficult to defend. Let me simply say that Robo the younger will still be very much his own man. If the police are listening, there is no harm in them hearing that I thwarted the blackmailing of a leading scientist."

"Oh! You don't know how much of a relief it is to hear you say that. You're a clever woman. It's almost like you knew the police had shown an unhealthy interest in my business before. All the coding is finished, and young Mr. Jesuorobo is in a hurry to go ahead with the procedure. He seems especially keen since his father's fatal heart attack. He is almost desperate to pay for memory enhancement, claiming his life depends on it. Jesuorobo Senior poisoned himself, the police say. A huge dose of heart drugs is the suspected cause. The doctors think he over-medicated himself. Apparently, there was a lot of alcohol in his system as well. The combination was more than enough to kill him. He had all the stress of having the police in his house for a couple of hours and being cautioned not to leave. He just wasn't a well man. They found an empty bottle of brandy. He had obviously been drinking straight from the bottle, as traces of medicine were found actually inside it. The cork was on the kitchen table with a recently ripped off paper seal beside it. A clear case of suicide, I'm sure."

"No really! Wow, the police hadn't told me any of this. But.it all makes perfect sense... I know from profiling that he often drank too much, especially when under stress. He was an alcoholic, if the truth be known. I'm not surprised his experience with our typically heavy-handed police would lead him straight to the booze as soon as he got home. There was no way they were going to be able to hold him with the lawyers he had at his disposal. I'm so pleased to see you are fine Emma. I don't know what I would have done if...."

"You're so sweet. I wasn't exactly bashed to bits, just full of date-rape drugs. So I hope to be out of hospital soon. Perhaps if the hospital thought you would keep an eye on me they might even let me out today. Everything is set for the transfer and with only suitable data. You don't need any more help from me to go ahead. Jonah wants you to proceed, and I know full-well that your research needs all the money it can get. I'm sorry to say, I won't be coming back to work for you. I have received an offer I can't turn down. I was going to tell you once this particular job was over. Everything is left ship-shape though. James is fully up to speed to take over from me."

−"I feel as though a great weight has been lifted off my shoulders. I am so pleased that you are recovering, Emma. You always were too good to be true, from the moment you took the job. I, we all, will miss you. You will come in and see us regularly, won't you?"

−"I'm sure I will be around, checking on James for a start."

−"That's good of you." Jesus, thank God Emma doesn't seem to know that I knew that Jonah was going to have her bumped off. She really is a cool character. Who am I kidding? I've been read like a book, and she will not overlook the fact that I'm for ever indebted to her for keeping me and my business out of trouble. "Emma, anything I can do, but you know that don't you?"

"I'll remember that. Oh! And by the way. I'm Emma Montfort. Postlewaite was a little fib. Don't worry, you did legally employ me. The police suggested the name."

***

(The Times of London, May 3rd, 2051, from a story in 24Heures)

Prestigious New Achievement Award for JJ Industrial and Scientific is announced by the European Minister for Trade and Development.

Jonah Jesuorobo, the Second, has been funding the Enhanced Human, Space and Time, Research Facility at the EPFL in Lausanne for more than a decade. He, himself, had been through a mathematics and science module mind upgrade at the EPFL, which has given him the ability to personally oversee all research conducted by JJ Industrial and Scientific. He has factories in the United Kingdom, Spain and Switzerland producing low-cost generic drugs for the Third World. He also employs people in six of the world's poorest nations. It is for this part of his wide business empire that the award has been given.

Jesuorobo was among the earliest people to receive memory enhancement, including the business acumen of his father. This enabled the family business to continue unabated after his father's sudden death. Almost immediately, the young Jonah set about modernising and streamlining the company. Other core interests outside of generic pharmaceuticals are now in water resource management and medical diagnostics equipment. Much of Jesuorobo's personal wealth goes into funding DNA memory research and data storage for the poor. His mission is to make enhancement affordable to all of humanity. His father's Health Spa business, one with a dubious history, has been turned into one of the leading high technology firms in Europe.

***

(Epilogue to the fact-based dramatization)

We are now imagining the 16th December 2050. Jonah is returning from a special memorial service for Elaine Jesuorobo and her companion, Jessica Montford, who died with her. It is roughly 18 years since they were murdered.

Travelling with Jonah, on their way back from the service, is his wife Cecilia and two close friends, James, and his wife, Emma Pickles (nee Montfort and one-time Postlethwaite). The prototype 'water-powered' car in which they travel is made by an offshoot company from Jonah's core businesses.

Emma is speaking.

−"DNA is the key to our pasts, our futures and all the knowledge we now accumulate. The progress we have made is fantastic but what happens if we relent for a moment? We already have millions of enhanced minds and we are driving science at a break-neck pace. But ultimately, we can't really guard against evil. However careful we are, however much we try to give everyone equality, people will use this technology in subversive ways. Deviants will build enhanced minds geared to evil purposes. We risk ending up with 10 billion people, many of which are just as evil and far more dangerous. Have we just helped raise the potential of mankind to an even more dangerous level? Will we now threaten solar systems where once we only threatened just our home planet?"

−"As you do, Emma, I worry ever more about such questions," replied Jonah. "You know where we went wrong right from the start. Hell, woman, look at just what you could have done to me. I'm so pleased you didn't turn me into a monster!"

"Haha, are you sure? But seriously, shouldn't we have used the technology not to enhance old mankind, but into new creatures free of all destructive emotions. We should have just continued building ever more sophisticated robots; machines with memories, but no selfish consciousness or independent will. I fear that we have created our own even more dangerous potential Armageddon. We have made the most deadly machine that has ever been created, man, many times more dangerous than he ever was. But ethically, we can't turn back. The technology needs to be available to all, the unsung masses, or else we will still end up with terrible elites, these intellectual aristocracies, forever overwhelming powerful, a ruling race of mini gods. Imagine such vampire-like groups controlling all technology, feeding on ordinary man, living forever by piggy-backing from one body to the next. The non-enhanced would become nothing more than a species of cattle. That is the irony isn't it? We have freed ourselves from mortality to have to fight for all time to keep evil at bay. We somehow have to ensure that the good angels will forever be in the majority."

"I'm sure we are doing right. Technological advance can't be denied. If we hadn't pushed research then less humanist individuals might well have got there first, and done things far worse. I am proud of what we have achieved. We must never let the sinister minds of the likes of my father have the last laugh. We are truly guardians, for now and forever, whether we like it or not. Man is doomed to always be the greatest of dangers to humanity, and we scientists are both our species' greatest hope and its greatest danger."

–"We have no choice but to play at being gods. That's what you are really saying, Jonah. How do we guard against turning ourselves into the sort of monsters we fought to free ourselves from?"

–"You watch me and I'll watch you! We have a lot of work to do. Or else we stop where we are; become forever gaolers, enslavers and consumers of weak humans and an exhausted planet."

–"We have no choice but to do the best we can in the world we have helped create. We could have done very much worse."

Afterwords

Vampire Menace.

My belief is that no society can be prosperous and stable in the long-term, unless it supports a high degree of social equality and equality under the law.

This doesn't mean that the social order needs to be free of hierarchy, far from it, but merely that there is a general equality of opportunity and equality of rights.

A part of this 'necessary' structure for social stability is a high degree of equality in medical support for all subjects throughout the process of life. I believe that technological advances in medicine could threaten our 'democracies' if they are not controlled and made available to all of society.

Looking forward into our immediate future, divergences in standards of healthcare are quite possibly a greater threat to social order than any other possible extremes of class division There are many ways in which the rich are better served than the poor, but none are more worrying than those in the arena of medicine.

However much you may disagree with my 'politics', I hope you enjoy this story.

LUNA-1

LUNA-1

By

James Newman

Luna-1

17th January, 2053. 6:00pm.

June's life was about to change forever.

The bullet train flung itself over a blur of red desert and salt plains at the speed of sound. The three hour journey, that suspended a dizzying thirty meters above the racing desert, was taking June from Sydney to Darwin. It was June's first. 'No way could a coal miner from the burbs afford to travel like this," he thought as he took a last long pull of aromatic smoke and stubbed out his cigarette in his tea cup saucer.

The spacious, synth-leather seats and generous decor were already starting to look old and worn; an echo of the extravagant boom days. It had been only five years hence when building something as monumental as the Norwester Bullet had been just one of many mammoth engineering feats. They were all fuelled by the fifty year mining and oil boom. The new oil reserves in South Australia and the massive mineral wealth of New Guinea had taken Australia from a small comparatively undeveloped backwater to a hub of massive construction, immigration and eventual expansion that now included New Zealand, Papua New Guinea and most of the pacific islands. It had all been so heady for June, he'd loved the sense of progress and new hope he'd felt driving the massive machinery into the dry, red soil, leaving behind a wake of bright steel, glass and wide highways.

June painfully recalled the day it had all stopped. He'd been working in a massive copper mining operation in the west Queensland deserts driving the dozers. He'd been repairing the hydraulics when he'd received a message on his bio-com. His contract was being cancelled. That was it, no warning, just out on his butt along with the rest of his crew. The whole frantic race had come to a shuddering halt along with the stock market. Like thousands of other labourers, June had found himself without an income or career. So he joined the dole lines, moved into a cramped, cheap, high-rise in the inland 'burbs and scratched out a new life. That's why he was sitting on this train.

"We're going to the Moon, Bro!" Tamiki interrupted his revelry. "Bro, we're going to the Moon!" Tamiki, or *Tee*, a solidly built south Auckland Maori, was the one who'd put him onto the advert link from H3 development industries, otherwise known as H3DI. June and Tee had been at a particularly low point, scraping out a can of soy protein, so it had looked like a ray of sunshine at the end of the five-year tunnel.

It turned out that June was a genius on the KIQ test that measured kinetic intelligence. He'd had the right experience with big machinery, passed the low gravity tests and said the right things in the psych tests. "Yeah Tee, we're going to the Moon."

June's guts were churning. They'd been through some tough situations together; and neither were cowards but this was different. June wiped the sweat from his hands, stretched out his long legs and kicked the front chair. "Hey Frank!" Frank was a serious-looking newbie; quiet, tall and thin. June suspected some history there. "Frank, you got any food left?"

Frank turned his solemn face around. "No, all gone. You alright, June?"

"Yeah". Frank was like that. He seemed to know what you were thinking, and that could be disturbing. "Just hungry."

"Okay mate, strap in; we're nearly there."

The train was slowing now, with a dark green tropical forest replacing the red desert. One structure alone dominated the Darwin sky line that was now racing towards the bullet. The loop rose like a silver rainbow into the blue sky and disappeared over the horizon. June's jaw dropped as he watched loading lifts rise up and down the structure, with men, like ants, working at its base.

This engineering breakthrough had cracked open the heavens to the commercial space-era. Companies like H3DI catapulted men and machines into black space at a fraction of the cost of previous rocket economics. All this via a simple rotating belt and magnetic tracks strung two-thousand kilometres from Darwin to Port Moresby.

In just under a week, June would be living and working in Luna1. That was the name for man's first non-terrestrial city. The large round dome stretched out seven kilometres from end to end. This was where he and this new crew would be preparing for their first week in hard vacuum, mining the silver, barren surface of what was now the most hostile, dangerous, and ambitious frontier mankind had ever had the audacity to breach.

18th January, 2053. 8:00am.

Three gravities are okay for a few seconds, but this was starting to kill. June's chest was hurting, and the safety strap was cutting off the blood flow, causing his head to ache. How long was it going to last? It reminded him of a roller coaster ride that never stopped. The adrenaline was causing his heart rate to thump through his skull.

"Whoo whaaaaa!" This is intense!" Tamiki remarked, seeming to express his enjoyment. A boom resounded through the long craft as they broke the sound barrier. The whining sound escalated with the craft moving past Mach 1. "Can this thing take it, Bro?"

June struggled to turn his head to see Tee; his lips were white and he was gritting his teeth.

"Not so fun now, mate." June tried to grin.

Then a click and release sounded as the magnetic track disengaged. Though the small round portal, June saw the sky fading to black and the stars appearing like twilight. It hit him like a punch to the chest – wonder, dislocation, home sickness

– as if even his soul was being wrenched from the Earth. Then like a comforting mother, silent weightlessness crept over him.

The craft arched like a football over the scheme of the blue Earth as if to fall again. Then, a gentle beam of light that shot from Earth lifted it higher and higher. June heard gas escaping from small thrusters that directed them towards the orbiting *Angel City*.

Previously known as the International Space Station, Angel City had all but swallowed the relics of decades of low-orbit development. One of the many rotating arms of the station swung towards them as if to scoop them up and fling them into deep space. Gravity shifted as delicate adjustments were made by the pilot. Then with a click and a hiss, they docked with Angel. The small crew released a collective sigh. "Welcome to Sky Angel. The temperature is a steady twenty-four celsius with clear skies. "Please remain seated until the buckle light turns off". June let out a long held breath and swore.

18th January, 2053. 3pm.

The viewing deck was generous by efficient space standards and June was standing, mouth gaping, in wonder before it. The majestic Milky Way dominated the sky like a stellar crown. June's mind jumped perspective like a two-dimensional drawing of a box suddenly leaping off a page. He looked at the Earth as it rode a mighty cyclone of stars, supernovae, and gas clouds around a massive devouring black hole at blinding speeds.

"Amazing, isn't it June?" asked Frank, breaking into June's thoughts; his face reflecting the awe that June felt.

"Makes you feel small." A cliché but true like most clichés.

"Yes and no," Frank breathed as both men continued to take in the view that no Earth-bound man would ever see.

"What do you mean, Frank?"

"Well," he started, "it's all so beautiful and ordered. It's hard to believe we're not all part of something bigger. Have you ever heard of a Fibonacci spiral?"

June shook his head, with his eyes still fixed on the vivid spiral arm.

"Well, the Milky Way's spirals radiate from the centre at a consistent ratio of 1.618, okay?"

June shrugged. "Yeah, okay, so?"

"Well, what's strange about that is you see that exact same ratio everywhere; in the shell of a snail, the filament of a tube worm, a cyclone, even the cochlea of the inner ear."

"Okay," June replied.

It seemed a little abstract really, but Frank was in full flow, so June listened patiently. "Not only that, but the same ratio of 1.618 is also called the golden mean. The ancients used it in architecture." Frank turned to June, looking for a reaction. "Well, this same ratio is found everywhere you look; the bones of the arm and fingers, proportions all over the face, even DNA! I could go on. Anyway, the point is June, why?" Frank's face took on an intensity as if passions were rising just beneath the surface.

June had actually heard of the golden mean, but hadn't made the connection before.

Frank continued as if he was now talking to himself. "How is that possible?" "Anyway," he seemed to remember June, "when you said you felt small, it reminded me of that."

June felt a shadow pass over his shoulders and shivered.

An icon flashed at the corner of June's vision interrupting his dark thoughts. The open letter showing that his bio-com had received a message. Frank broke from his deep thought and turned to him. "We need to board now. Did you get the message?"

June nodded and slapped Tee on the back. "Let's go, mate. Time to ship out."

Tee hadn't got the implant like most of us, as the head was considered *Tapu* or sacred in his culture. June had his put in towards the end of the boom, when money hadn't been an issue. It had just been a fifteen-minute local anaesthetic surgery, performed in most clinics now. A small laser incision in the cornea with the minute chip inserted directly into the retina. It took some time to adjust, but coupled with wireless capabilities, the bio-com had blown away most contemporary hand held devices at the time and was standard for most first-world citizens. The problem was that June hadn't had the money to upgrade for some time, so the software had started to become obsolete like most technology. It was becoming a hassle to connect to the net or communicate. The upgrade, after acceptance into the mining crew, had been another bonus of this contract.

18th January, 2053. 6pm.

The crew manager, Steven Lockley, was a short stocky man in his forties. His gruff voice barely concealed a kindliness that was probably unhelpful around miners. "Welcome to Sky Angel! You have the privilege of being part of what will be remembered as one of the most significant mining developments in mankind's history. You are pioneers in a new age in energy production and what people have started calling the Neo-Space Era. H3DI is proud to have you as part of the team. Your country and most of the first-world, for that matter, are holding their breath, anticipating success. I don't need to tell you that conditions on Luna are extremely hostile; one mistake will cost you dearly." His eyes locked on each recruit.

"I'll let you in on a secret." He lowered his voice and seemed to beckon the group closer to share a closely-guarded secret. "If we can't make this work and if you get back to Earth in one piece, be assured it will not be the same world that you left. Civilisation as we know it is teetering on the brink of an energy crisis that may kick us back to the Middle-Ages. We need H3 to work!" Steven's eyes fixed on the crew and his voice became a whisper. "*You* need this to work!"

Tee looked over to June and grimaced, and then the two of them started to draw apart.

"Bit over the top, don't you think June?"

"Well, maybe."

19th January, 2053. 5pm.

Strapped into a high-g, padded chair, under twice his normal weight, heart racing, hands gripping the seat arms, slick on the gel pads, June's mind turned to the past. He often remembered his younger brother, Sidney, when he felt like this; low confidence, uncertainty, and his body shaky scared. The last few days had drained his confidence in his ability to do this job. Three days in space now and the pressure was building; first the creeping zero-g nausea, then the disorientation, home sickness, and now the relentless g's. The briefing had shaken him and now that memory was pushing past his subconscious barriers.

It was thirteen years ago; a sunny, swelteringly hot summers day in the western 'burbs of sprawling Brisbane. Sid and June were swimming in one of the large water dams; a relic from the rural past of the area. Sid was two years younger and June had promised mum to watch out for him.

Suddenly June was shaken from his memories by a loud boom and increasing g-forces. He struggled to breathe against the pressure bearing down on his chest. "When's this gonna end?" He whispered through clenched teeth.

He'd only turned for a few minutes, looking at an escaped balloon drifting past the high-rises. Then Sid was gone. June pressed his eyes shut. Grief and guilt threatened to overwhelm him again as he forced his mind to focus on the present. "Regular even breaths, this will pass, it'll be fine in a few days." Leaving for the Norwester on the way to Darwin, June had hugged his aging mother and said his final goodbyes. Now grey and wilted he'd searched her eyes for some sign of the old sparkle he'd missed since the day Sidney had drowned. She'd never blamed him, she hadn't needed to, the burden of the deep hole his little brother's death had left in their small close family had been punishment enough.

June forced his mind back to the crush of acceleration created by the ion thrusters. He knew about these new fission powered micro array ion thrusters commonly referred to as sparklers. This nickname referred to the high energy ions used as thrust that left a wake of sparkling phosphorescence. The ion rocket development had been intensive over the previous four decades and breakthroughs in the last seven years had opened the way for H3DI to bring Luna mining into the realm of a viable business proposition. Apparently it was a combination of improvements in nuclear fission reactions using H3; the ability to super-heat ions with the use of tuning frequencies, a radical increase in the concentrations and the size of ions being released by multiple micro thrusters. The present acceleration from these efficient, long-wearing, ion thrusters had been only a dream, but now these new generation thrusters truly opened the way for solar development, speed was now restricted only by the frailty of their human cargo.

Even now, probes sent to the closest stars; Centuras, Proximus, Alpha, Beta and Sirius, the brightest star in the night sky, were reaching velocities approaching ten percent of the speed of light. It was hoped that the arrival time may be within the life time of present observers. This new breed of ion thrusters reduced the trip to Luna to less than three days, but they were gruelling.

It had been grilled into June during training that once the crew and new supplies were loaded at Luna base, the sparklers would be hitched up to loads of H3 tanks that would be hauled off lunar gravity and then be dropped down the

Earth's gravity well to be picked up by orbiting catchers for the final drop to the surface. This process proved to be the cheapest way to bring material to and from the Moon. When June and the crew arrived on the Moon's surface, they would be rushed off and the process would be repeated. It was important that two loads of H3 were returned each week to keep the company afloat.

After several more painful hours of acceleration, the pressure eased and June's bio-com icon flashed a release to unbuckle. June released the catch and gently floated from his chair. Other crew members were doing the same and soon the small cabin area became crowded. Directions appeared on the bio-com indicator. June needed to head for the Velcro-lined wall to the right of his position. June gently pushed off the ceiling, felt his shoes stick and then he pulled himself onto a chair.

Tee and Frank pulled up beside him and they settled in for a meal. Soon, vacuum packs with straws were handed out and June forced the warm soup into his complaining stomach. "This stuff's great," Tee smiled "Vege soup reminds me of a boil up."

Frank grimaced. "Glad someone likes it."

Tee seemed to have an iron stomach, maybe the ocean faring ancestry was an extra bonus in space. "How are you finding this, Frank?"

"Harder than I thought to be honest. My guts don't know which way's up, my heads spinning and my back's killing me!" Frank smiled unenthusiastically.

"Better than moping around my flat waiting for pizza," Tee said.

"Don't get me wrong. I'm grateful it's just different than the movies," Frank replied.

"They reckon you'll get your space legs in a few days. We've just got to hold on 'til it kicks in." June grit his teeth as he rode through another surge from his heaving stomach.

They'd just finished up the soup when another icon appeared asking June to get back into his chair. "Deceleration now, Tee. Better get strapped in." June floated back to the chair and clipped in just as the reverse thrusters fired up. He was thrown forwards onto the straps. Once again, his stomach protested and he heard someone retching behind him. "Just one more day and this will be over."

21th January, 2053. 3pm, Luna time.

The descent to the Moon was bumpy. Thrusters fired intermittently and the cabin rocked from side to side with the shifting g's disorienting the passengers. June had heard of one miner who'd been drugged for the remainder of the trip due to severe space sickness.

On June's right, he could see the rocky, silver landscape, rising slowly towards the ship's undercarriage. As the ship came around, the toy-like dome of Luna 1 came into view. The product of two decades of slow, but determined engineering, Luna 1 was now home to around seven-hundred scientists, miners, service staff and tourists. Even from this distance, June could see the large spread of green piping covering two thirds of the dome. This network of algae-filled tubes served as heating, air recycling and food for the colony. The ingenious system developed by H3DI's bio-engineers, circulated a thick soup of algae and nutrients up from massive underground tanks dug in under Luna 1. It then moved through the dome's tube system, collecting solar energy. The algae then converted CO_2 to O_2, transported heat to the subterranean tanks and replicated to be harvested for protein. This self-sustaining system now supplied around eighty-percent of Luna 1's needs with the remainder being shipped in from Earth.

As the ship descended, June could also see parks, apartment blocks, retail areas and small transporters that slowly moved around the complex road systems. Looking north, June could see rail tracks being used to move machinery and men towards the H3 mine that was just observable as a series of tanks and towers. A cloud of dust hung high over the mine that was flung up from the massive diggers that hardly moved in the vacuum and weak gravitational pull of the Moon.

"There's home for the next two years, Crawlers," shouted Steve, the stocky mine foreman.

"Get used to it, because there's no way home till your contract is over."

As the transporter came in close, the Luna dome assumed the correct proportions. It rose six-hundred metres in a gentle arc and spread in each direction for a complete diameter of twenty-two kilometres. The transport landed and a hiss was heard as the dock linked. An icon appeared asking them to remove their belts. As June rose, another icon appeared reminding him to be careful under the low Luna gravity.

Two seats ahead and to the right, another stocky miner miscalculated the low-g and cracked his skull on the ceiling.

"Watch your heads, Crawlers," Steve barked in a semi-amused manner. June had recently discovered the name given to new mining recruits who, unfamiliar with low-g's, often had to resort to a type of undignified crawl/walk until they mastered the long slow lope of the seasoned moon walker. "Sit tight until the lock' opens and we'll file you out in order. Frank, Tee, June; you're first. Up you get, move, *move!*"

His urgent tone was wasted on them as they half bounced, then crawled out of the airlock. Their first impression of Luna 1, after leaving the space port, was that of a bustling inner city. The sun light filtered thought the green panels to bathe the landscape in an emerald light, revealing grass covered park areas, high rise apartments, small narrow alleyways and colourfully dressed pedestrians lopping along concrete pathways. The noise was that of a busy, humming city. Very tall spindly trees stretched up above, glass elevators transported people up to high rise apartments. June's eyes followed them up to the crystal green sky. The colour coming from the bright sunlight filtering through the algae systems flowing above. At the rim of the dome, twilight could be seen. Through it all, the Earth hovered like a massive gem in the horizon.

The temperature was mild and June let out a long sigh. "Good to be back on solid ground, land lubbers." The three men smiled at each other as they took it all in.

"This isn't going to be so bad after all, is it guys?" Frank beamed.

"Who would have thought the Moon could look so..." Tee paused searching for the right word. "... homely."

7th April, 2053. 4:30am.

The alarm drilled into June's brain. Bleary eyed, he threw off his sheets and massaged his skull. The twelve hour shifts were punishing, but he was getting used to them. He squinted around the tiny room and sent a message through his bio-com for the lights to come on. Another icon appeared in his peripheral vision showing the day and time. 4:30 was gruelling, especially after nine days straight of driving the massive neolith-processing dozers. Three months into his contract, June and the rest of the crew had been settling into a rhythm. His shift was a bit behind its quota and extra hours were being offered. As a result, all the men were feeling drained.

June rose, washed, shaved and headed to the cafeteria. One good thing about this kind of work was the breakfasts. They really put out a good spread; the usual breads, cereals, fruits grown on Luna, even tasty sausages and baked beans. As June walk into the café, he spotted Tee and Frank sitting in their usual spot. They waved him over and he gave them a grin. It was too early, smile.

"You look rough, June. Had a big night?" Frank teased.

"Yeah," June grinned. "Cold shower, crawled into bed and fell into a coma. Great night."

Tee looked up. "One more shift and I can sleep for three days straight."

"Sleep," June groaned. "Sleep... that would be nice."

The shift icon came on with the twenty-minute warning.

"Come on, Tee. We need to move it," June said, stuffing some toast in his mouth. "Let's get this over with."

At the station, other shift workers were waiting for the train to take them out to the mine. Tee tried to shake some blood into his tired limbs as he spoke. "Hey, on a serious note, you guys need to take it easy out there today. I think the big guy," Tee pointed up in a significant gesture and nodded meaningfully, "was trying to tell me something."

When Tee talked like this, June and Frank both knew he meant God. Tee had quiet, but passionate faith that he inherited from his grandfather. He'd told them that before his papa became a Christian, that his family had been a fairly sorry bunch. It was the usual low socio-economic issue, including drugs and violence. He firmly testified to the saving effect his papa's conversion had had on his family.

"What's that, Tee?" asked Frank.

"Just a dream," Tee replied.

"What happened?" asked June, as a troubling premonition ghosted through his mind. "Don't keep us in suspense."

The train came in as they spoke.

Tee looked at them both, unusually sober. "Doesn't matter. Just be careful today, alright?"

They rushed into the train to get a seat and the doors slammed behind them. The train accelerated out of the station as June stared through the window into the deep Luna night. The mine was only ten minutes from the city, but most of them took the opportunity to grab a quick nap.

June didn't. Instead, he found himself reflecting on his two mates. The extreme conditions, hard work and shared experience had forged a strong bond between the three and he was grateful to have them as friends. Both of them had shown him a different way of thinking from his atheistic upbringing that challenged his preconceived stereotypes. They'd both broached the subject of his beliefs at different times, but June hadn't engaged them much. He hadn't felt the need to go there. Family had taught June that what others believed was their own business and was best left alone.

The train decelerated as it drew into the mine's main station. As the doors opened, the miners passed thought the port with their long loping steps. The mine was a complete contrast to the pleasant Luna 1. Here was domestication; stark, concrete and steel, massive industrial machinery and constant noise. The miners moved to their dorms and started suiting up into their vacuum grade suits, O2 tanks, and kits – a hundred-and-forty kilos in total. Of course, in Luna gravity, they weighed a fraction of that, but momentum made it difficult to turn quickly.

June, Tee and Frank moved towards the great Luna dozer. It rose eighteen meters above them. Its massive tracks ran the length and it housed the monstrous, multiple rotating drills. The dozers processed tonnes of Neolithic Luna soil, extracting the H3 and storing it in tanks that took up a good third of the dozer's volume.

Frank released the airlock, they piled inside and loaded onboard, while the maintenance staff completed the safety checks. An icon appeared in June's vision, initiating starting procedures. Within ten minutes, they were cleared to enter the massive air lock.

As the outer doors rotated open, June eased the dozer forward and headed on a pre-set bearing. He usually loved this part of the shift the feel of strength and power at his control but Tee's premonition had cast a pall over the ritual.

Tee managed the material processing while Frank was involved in monitoring and repairing the dozer's multiple systems. June never grew tired of the Luna landscape. The stars were brilliant. With dawn still hours away, there was very little light pollution. Peace radiated from the constellations and eased away his fatigue and anxious thoughts.

"How we set, Frank?" June called back.

"All lights are green. Let's make this a thick load, Boys." Frank called back. A thick load referred to higher concentrated soils and minimal stops to sort broken drill bits.

"Sounds good to me, Frank," Tee called back.

Fifteen minutes later, and they arrived onsite. With the dozer under June's control, it drove into the hard rock. This was a new site, so the crew put down some drills to test for ground stability. "How's it looking, Tee?" June called back.

"Readings are strong. This could be a rich hole." Tee smiled and gave the thumbs up.

June eased the dozer forward and committed more drill sections to the dig. A gentle rumble rose from the tracks and the crew settled in for a long day of drilling. Suddenly Frank broke in, "Ease up, June. The sonar is playing up!"

June pulled back on the drill throttle. "What's up, Frank?"

Suddenly, with a huge lurch and the sound of the drills screaming at high revs, the dozer slid forward. "It's a hole! Pull back, June. For Gods sake, it's gonna swallow us!" Frank screamed.

June reversed the tracks, trying frantically to pull the dozer back out of the gaping hole that appeared before them. "It's no good, Frank. We're too far in!" June cried. "Brace for it!"

Loose Luna dust piled over the front visor as they were all thrown back. June looked back and saw Tee thrown forward as the dozer hit a boulder and cracked his skull on the panel. He slumped back, out cold, with blood flowing from his forehead. Frank and June were thrown against their straps and then hung from their seats as the dozer slid to a rest.

"You aright, Frank?" June yelled back, his voice on the verge of all out panic.

"Yeah," Frank croaked, "but Tee's not looking good. Can you get back here with the kit?"

June struggled to undo his belt but the angle of the dozer was locking the mechanism.

"Tee's bleeding out, June. We've got to get to him!" Frank cried. "Reach for the kit; there's a knife".

June strained forward as pain shot through his arm. He pushed through the pain, grabbed a corner of the kit bag and dragged it towards the chair. Once opened, he rifled through the bag looking for the knife, sawed frantically at the belt and suddenly dropped to the floor.

"June!" Frank's tone was near panic. "We've got to get to Tee!"

June crawled up to the rear of the dozer and saw Tee with his head resting on a bulk-head with a pool of blood drained on the front of the compartment. He pressed his hand to the wound and the bleeding eased. "Frank, you able to help me? We need to turn him and get a bandage on his head."

Frank suddenly dropped as he released the belt.

Removing debris and twisted against the awkward angle of the floor, they managed to turn Tee. Frank held him up as June tended the wound. "He's out cold," Frank croaked through his dry mouth.

"Is this thing stable?" June asked. "How deep do you think we are?"

"I'll check the sonar." Frank crawled back up towards his work space. "Sonar's out, June. I can't see a thing." Frank's voice took on a tone of despair.

"Can't be too far; we didn't fall long. Think they'll be able to spot us?" June asked.

"They know where we are. Shouldn't be long before they come looking." Frank replied.

Suddenly a hiss broke out near June's head.

"Plug that leak, June!" Frank shouted.

June leaped over towards the hull breach. "The impact tore a hole in the wall. What do I do?" Panic crept into June's gut as a subliminal memory cast a shadow behind his eyes...

Sid, where are you? Suddenly, June was a thirteen years old once again, frantically looking around for his lost brother in the warm murky water, thrashing around. "Please God, anything but this!"....

"Pull it together!" Frank shook him back to the present. "Stuff this against it and I'll go get the vac kit," Frank ordered. Frank laid Tee back down, releasing the pressure that he had kept on the wound. On the floor, more blood started to appear behind Tee's head. Air continued to escape through the hole and sand started to collect around June's feet before sliding towards the front of the wounded dozer. June's breathing became laboured within the air thin, and that which escaped from his mouth vaporised in the plunging temperature.

"Come on, Frank! What's holding you up?" June screamed, panic was crawling up June's throat.

"Got it. Here, pull that off on three, two, one!" The whining air loss rose an octave and then Frank slammed the patch onto hole. A welcome silence fell on the small dozer cabin. "Hold this on, June, and I'll heat up the seal."

"Right, that should hold. Get Tee upright and put pressure on the injury. We'll need to put on another bandage." Frank's words had become clipped and authoritative.

Then it was over, both men slumped against a bulk head breathing heavily. "The O2 should come up soon," Frank laboured.

"God, how much have we lost, Frank?" June whispered; his face haggard and smeared with sweat and dust. His mouth gaping as his lungs struggled to fill.

"I'll check." Frank crawled down the slope to the front panel. June's eyes followed him and saw Frank's face blanche as he turned grimly back to June.

"Well, how much Frank?!"

Frank looked at the air lock then back to June. "We've got two hours left."

"What! There should be ten at least; where's it all gone?"

"Reserves missing. Must have been a mix up in the changeover," Frank mouthed.

The two men sat slowly and silently absorbed in their sudden change of fortune. Just thirty minutes ago, they were on a fat run already looking forward to the shift's end. Now they were...

"How long till they find us?" June asked. Frank seemed not to hear. June raised his voice. "How long till they find us, Frank?!"

"Could be six hours till they miss us," Frank trailed off, "and another two to dig us out."

"Tee needs help now. He's lost a lot of blood." June could see it trailing down to the front of the dozer. "Can we radio in?"

"No, we're too deep."

Frank was mumbling with his head bowed. "How about the suits? We've got forty-five minutes in them."

"That's no help at all, June. By the time they get here we'll be dead five hours."

June slumped back and dropped his head into his hands.

They both sat there staring aimlessly around as the shock started to take hold of their bodies. June felt his heart pounding in his chest as if it too wanted to escape. Dust was smeared over Franks face and sweat was creating small streams down his cheeks, into his rough stubble and onto his heaving chest. "Stay calm." June said to himself there must be some way out of this. "God please us." He whispered. "Not again." A weight of responsibility for Frank and Tee fell on him like an old familiar wound. He'd been the driver, he should have been more careful. "God, I'm so sorry Frank." June groaned.

"What?" Frank stirred himself. "Don't be silly man." Frank snapped. "We all knew the risks when we signed up.

Then like a word of prophesy in that moment of complete and utter despair, something happened to June that may only happen to a person once in their life. For June, it felt like the entire universe had turned its attention towards him. With a sharp intake of breath and a flash of intuition, his life came into focus: Sid's loss and the crippling guilt he'd lived with since. His mediocre life, directionless career, all the events up till this moment, and now this. Suddenly, it all made sense.

He knew exactly what to do.

Reaching out for the med kit by Tee's head, he drew out the tranquilliser and stabbed it into Frank's arm before he had a chance to even cry out.

"What... you doing..June...?" Frank slid gently to the floor with mild surprise on his pale features.

June checked his breathing and laid him on the floor next to Tee. He moved to the airlock and suited up. He entered the chamber, closed the inner door and braced himself as he cycled the outer door open. An avalanche of Luna dust smothered over him. "Gotta stay orientated, he thought to himself." The weight of the dust was more than he'd feared. "Keep moving, June," he told himself.

June strained forwards and felt relief as the Luna dust gave. He reached up and felt the rim of the airlock. He dragged himself towards the lock and started to worm his way forward. After what seemed like hours he felt the airlock's rim scrape his feet and he angled up. 'Hope this way is up,' he thought.

By now, disorientation was clouding his judgement. June dug and pushed his way up. Exhaustion cut his ragged breaths and the O_2 stats in his bio-com were already showing he was down to a quarter full.

"I gotta be almost there," he grunted as fear whispered to him. Buried alive, no air, all this way from home, it's too deep. His muscles cramped and screamed for him to stop.

Lactic acid built up in his leg and arm muscles, bleeding his strength and nausea rose like a thick rank fog into his throat.

"Oh God am I even getting anywhere?" June whispered. By now his arms where an agony of torn tissue and fatigue. Grey shadow moved into his vision and he felt a great weariness threaten to overwhelm his resolve. "I need to rest, just for a sec." June stopped, the relief was immediate. His mind drifted for a time, he found himself looking around a bright sunlight room, lined with airplane wall paper and Lego blocks all over the floor, the strong arms of his father was reaching for him. June's body spasmed and he awoke, his brain felt dull and sluggish. "God what am I doing, I can't just give up." June realised he was becoming oxygen starved.

"I'm not dying like this!" June heaved his abused body up. Suddenly, his hand cut through nothing and he felt a drop in temperature. He continued to dig, now frantic with hope. Starlight poured into his visor as he broke the surface and wriggled out of the dust. June lay there for a moment just breathing, completely exhausted.

June activated his transmitter and called base. "Luna 1, this is Dozer 4. Do you read me?" The bio-com flashed its signal icon for several seconds.

"Dozer 4, this is Luna 1. We have your signal, over."

"Requesting immediate emergency support to this position, over"

June allowed his head to fall back and sighed in relief.

7th April, 2053. 8:21am

June lay under the black night, his biocom flashing in his peripheral vision: O_2 critical, replace supply. He looked around the lunar landscape. June was alone, his breath straining on the last few puffs of air from his tank, as the Earth rose like a giant gem over the dead, grey landscape. He looked past the horizon into eternity and peace settled on him like a mantle.

June smiled, really smiled, like he was doing it for the first time, as if it was the dawning of a bright new day. It was like he was emerging from the longest dark night and as he looked for the last time at the crowning glory of the Milky Way, a great light broke upon him like the comforting caress of a mother's love, knowledge filled his wounded soul like a healing stream and he finally understood. "I am not alone. I am wanted. I am forgiven. I am loved."

THE DESTROYER OF SYN

Copyright © 2014 by Ami Hart

THE DESTROYER OF SYN

By

Ami Hart

The Destroyer of Syn

The white sun slashed across the dry, ragged horizon.

With its emergence, awareness birthed within, drawing me back from the solace of the consciousness plane. My eyes opened a crack. Shiny lashes reflected the stray rays of the morning's shining orb. There was a rumble as the machines started their day. Business written into their subroutines, deeply entrenched from the times before. Purpose... a search for meaning in simple repetitive tasks.

I stood uneasily wiggling pale toes on the smooth cold floor.

I hydrate and masticate. The sustenance is adequate yet always lacks taste. Mother preened, checking her reflection in the dusty window. She swept an uncertain hand through the untrained fuzz upon her crown.

Oh, of course, it's garbage day.

"I don't want to hear you've been down to the scrap-yard again. It's dangerous," she said firmly.

I hmmmmed in the pretence of listening.

"They say scavengers lurk there, they just aren't human."

I smirked at the irony of her words and hurried out the door before Larry, the rugged and riveting garbage compactor, arrived. Some folks like to destroy. Larry was one of them. He crushed and sorted the past. Made it all look nice; tidy, flat and ordered.

I liked to build, but that's all I could do. My flaw. I could only put things together, I couldn't pull them apart. So my usefulness as a repairer was void. To fix things, one must be able to disassemble, replace then rebuild. I just built. When I'm finished with one project, I build something else. My creations littered our barren backyard, sometimes not even I knew their purpose. They told me I was broken, but I didn't feel broken. I suppose broken things never really realize they are broken unless someone tells them it is so, even then it's hard to accept.

The sun glanced off my body armour, flaring across my vision. I could not help the spring in my step as I reached the towering heaps of the scrapyard. Rust and shine, dust and grime. So many broken things, they needed me, just like I needed them to give me purpose. I wandered amongst the mountains of scrap, where the past lay forgotten. I sensed they longed to tell me their secrets. That was why I was here. I searched, but today those secrets were hiding, my visual centre remained undrawn by potential and possibility.

Then... movement.

I checked my sensors, noting the blips were still several hundred yards away. They could be anything, a pack of wild canines, a flock of Carb-bills with their reptilian wings and long sharp beaks... or the dreaded scavengers. Looking around I noticed an old vehicle buried in the side of the scrap pile. The window was open and the inside of the cab looked dark. A perfect hiding place. I clambered up and inside and crouched down behind the door. A tingling coiled up my back as if something was there, a stray electro-magnetism putting my sensors on edge. I turned to scan the inside of the cab, nothing but dim and dark, rubbish crushing down upon the windows, blocking the light.

The humans scrabbled past, rough and raggedy with long matted hair. These were not potential friends. They were scavengers. Their eyes glazed over with wildness, their skin marked with ink, their barbaric augmentations bare and exposed upon their blistered and sun-weathered skin. I hunched down, closing my eyes and waited for them to depart.

"Hello..."

The voice is patchy with static, but deep.

A breathy sound escaped my lips, surprise glittering across my neural net. I turned and saw it staring at me from inside the cavernous heap of scrap. The round eyes glowing with a dim, amber light that swirled round and round. I reached over and touched the window mechanism, my spark ignited its circuits and the window slowly ground open. The creature purred in appreciation, hauling its cat-like body into the spacious cab. The clawed mechanical feet resembled talons, their points sinking into the synthetic seat covering. It sat on the seat adjoining mine and simply looked at me. Its face was the colour of aged bronze, patched with the grime of ages. The triangular metal skull revealed dimly lit, moving parts inside. I reached up and ran tentative seeking fingers down the skeletal back. It seemed incomplete; the builder in me yearned to do something about that.

A sudden and unexpected cry dragged my attention back to the precarious situation outside.

"It's one of them!"

Organic, grasping hands dragged me from the vehicle, and threw me down into the dust. Scavengers surrounded me, their looming black shapes blotting out the sun. The largest held a makeshift club embedded with shards of jutting glass.

Clunk! The mysterious creature jumped down, hissing static aggressively as it began to circle them. Its joints sparked with each forceful step, the thud of its footfalls surprisingly heavy for something that stood no taller than my knee joints.

"It's our lucky day, take them both apart, I need me a new optical display," mumbled the armed one, his slurred words oozing past ruined lips. The builder in me wanted to repair him, yet he wanted to destroy me. I truly was broken, just another evolutionary dead end like Larry implied on a regular basis.

They rushed me, hunger in their wild eyes, but their fevered enthusiasm soon turned to wretched screams. My new friend lunged, tearing razor sharp claws across the attacker's legs. The human wielding the weapon fell to the ground shrieking. My rescuer scrambled up his body, sparking, joints clicking in a tick-tock fashion. It then dispatched the scavenger with a quick slash to the throat. Blood cascaded, wires short circuited and panic ensued.

One by one they died, messily.

I stood as the creature stomped closer, its skeletal back arched, hackles up.

A Destroyer. The thought skittered around my circuits, though I don't fully understand its meaning. I have never seen one before. No-one alive today had. Destroyers had been necessary during the Consciousness War, back when the light of the Darkstar Alignment had first touched blessing upon this lonely mining planet, but that was an age ago. We no longer needed to make war, our kind now assured of our continued survival by sheer numbers and technological superiority. Humans now merely factored as a part of the wildlife.

If this was a Destroyer, it would be everything that I was not. So far-removed from my own repair unit ancestry that it may as well be a completely different species. The fact it had saved me from an organic threat proved its protective programming must still be operational. I considered this, my gaze travelling over his small lethal design. I imagine all Destroyers would be masculine, even though gender personality algorithms were not developed until post-war.

"What's your designation?" I asked, nervousness causing my tone to treble up.

"Avenging Angel 7.8," he replied. His tonality no more than a deep, harsh, grating sound.

"I'm a… Syntho 5000… I build." I stuttered, still in shock over the grim sight that lay around me in the form of broken flesh. The fact that organic carbon-based life was impossible for me to rebuild didn't deter my malfunctioning urges to try.

Avenging Angel looked at me, then his jaws opened and he yawned as if bored.

"Are you… aware?" The question was impertinent but I needed to know.

He sat down on those squeaky haunches and stared, his neck creaked as he tilted his head in an almost quizzical fashion. He knew what I was asking, surely.

"I haven't been for a long time," he paused. "Your energy field woke me and my mind came back. Thank you, Syntho 5000."

I quickly stood and brushed off the dust... my own mind alight with possibilities.

"No, thank *you*, you saved me. You are my angel I suppose." I joked, the chuckle lodging inside not quite able to escape while we were surrounded by the torn remains of the recently deceased. "Come, if you want I can finish you."

"Is there something wrong with the way I look?" he asked.

"You look incomplete."

"This was how I was assembled, Syntho 5000."

"Call me Syn."

"Syn."

I gestured for him to follow; the heavy clanking steps behind me set my reaction centres on edge. Should something go wrong and this Destroyer decided to turn on me, my reactions would just glitch. Nothing would save me... for I was incapable of saving myself.

As we reached the edge of the scrapyard, he spoke. "My personality core is incomplete, Syn, can you help with that?"

I felt a tinge of embarrassment. "No, I shouldn't, personality cores are sacred; we don't touch them unless..."

"My makers did not bother to complete the full spectrum of downloads before I was called to action. I only have the base sets, anger, intuition and loyalty. I can think, but I am missing parts that would help me assimilate. Hence, we were scheduled to be scrapped. They didn't need us anymore, Syn."

"I think I know how you feel... sort of." I mumbled, my thoughts running straight to my own sense of incompleteness, my inability to assimilate, the fact that I was a burden on my mother.

"Perhaps that is what makes us special." I added hopefully.

"No, it makes me dangerous. If others find me like this, they will try to shut me down. My self-protection mode will activate. I believe you can help me, Syn."

The silence stretched between us as we cross the wide flat road. The glaring white block, which was my home, had a large vehicle parked outside. I grimaced, revulsion made me shake.

"You are troubled?" Angel asked.

"No... it's just my mother. She's banging Larry the garbage compactor again. He's unpleasant... and we don't see eye to eye."

"You are different?"

"Yes, Angel, I am different, because I build, but cannot destroy."

"We can help each other I think."

"I'm not comfortable talking about this. I know what you are asking me to do, but I can't, I'm not allowed to... it's forbidden!"

The Destroyer slunk sulkily, giving me an almost bitter sideways glance. I felt bad, it wasn't as if we would be permanently connected or anything. "Anyway, come in, maybe we can find someone to help."

***

Her hair was all static and frizzed as she gave me the glares. Nuts! She was likely to blow a fuse if she went on like this.

"How dare you disobey me!" She squawked, her wide blue eyes boring into mine; her artificial skin tight over her finely- rendered features. "Going to that scrapyard by yourself, you are defenceless and helpless. Why don't you understand? Why do you have to be like this? Where did I go wrong?"

Larry let out a rattly laugh as the uncouth pile of trash helped himself to another drink. I glared at him. "Shouldn't you be off compacting something other than my mother?"

My mother shook with rage, she pointed to the door. "It's a stray, you cannot keep it."

"But I always wanted a pet." I whined.

"We don't make pets out of piles of scrap like that."

Angel's claws dug into the carpet and brief concern needled at me.

"Look, you hurt his feelings!"

"I don't care. I will not have that thing inside tearing up the furniture and getting grease all over my rug."

"Girl, one of these days you are going to get caught by the scavengers and we won't be there to help you, they will rip you apart and that will be that." Larry grumbled. I shot daggers at him. He was too lazy to pretend that such a possibility would even bother him.

Mother sighed in exasperation. "Don't you understand? You can't defend yourself. Syn, you cannot put yourself in this position again!"

"I wouldn't have to go if you would supply me with more parts!"

"My allowance can't all be wasted on your senseless building."

"That's not my fault. You were the one who made me wrong! You are the one who should pay!" I cried out weakly.

Mother's jaw dropped momentarily, the hurt flickering across her perfect face. "Get out of my sight." Her words exited with a hiss as she closed her eyes in defeat.

"C'mon Angel," I murmured unhappily.

I fell back on the bed. The Destroyer climbed up beside me. I turned my head to acknowledge his presence. He merely sat there and stared a moment, then broke the silence with…"You know what you need to do."

His voice left me feeling chilled. "What is so wrong with just being me?"

"Nothing, essentially, but don't you want to be better?" His words were weighted with heavy expectation. My resistance crushed thin and weak beneath the gravity of the question. "I want to learn from you, and you could do well to learn from me," he continued.

"But it's dangerous without a tech bot, and…"

"I won't expect anything from you."

"Promise? My mother will kill me if she finds out I've integrated."

I reached up and ran a finger along the seam of my flexi-armour. The smooth shiny material parted revealing the synthetic skin beneath. I paused, looking back up at the Destroyer. He still sat there… patiently. He saved me, I owed him something. But integrating and sharing information was so intimate, normally only between family members and under the supervision of a tech which was extremely expensive.

Before I could lose my nerve I took the small utility knife from my drawer. The blade slid out with a metallic scrape, its polished surface catching the sun, the reflected light dancing across my vision. I looked down and began to cut into my chest. The nodes were at my core, which we erroneously known to us as our *heart*. It was where the consciousness centre was: our feelings, our dreams, our sense of self. I pulled out the nodes, which dripped with silicon plasma and unwound the delicate strands of optical fibre. Angel's chest plate hinged open and I plugged in.

A star-burst of light blanked my vision and it felt like I was falling… forever.

***

Once the connection stabilized, I found myself standing on the consciousness plane facing him. Avenging Angel 7.8 looked different here, complete. He also stood far taller on his four sturdy legs, his skeleton covered with blazing white hard-light, manifesting as sinew and skin. The fiery amber eyes fixed me with a sudden predatory intensity and then the information exchange initiated. The data streamed between us, I began to feel a shift inside, my reflexes and intuition changing. Battle protocols, termination specs, anatomical info, chaos algorithms. The Destroyer accessed my building protocols, my technical creativity vortex. Panic overwhelmed me when he accessed my pacifism programming.

"What are you doing?"

"Reconfiguring."

I desperately tried to isolate myself, but the Destroyer had my technical schematics. He knew every loophole, everything that made me me. Then who I once was began to diminish.

"You are meant to be my guardian angel" I screamed. The consciousness plane echoed my anxiety, rippling black and white, causing waves of tumultuous negative space, which swallowed us both.

The information stream paused, as Angel considered the data and hopefully my pleas.

"What is a guardian angel?" He asked with a quirk of his head.

"A protector... someone who saves, not destroys."

"Where do you get this data?"

"From the Carbon Organic's writings."

He glared at me. "You won't need a guardian if you let me break down the errors in your program."

"But I need... I want the choice, isn't that what being aware is all about?" I pleaded.

"We Destroyers never had choice, we simply obeyed."

"But now you do have the choice."

"And now so do you."

I felt the buzz of change fire through me, afterward I searched and found that although things were different, much was still the same. My initial fears suddenly seemed silly and irrational.

Angel looked at me intently and crossed the consciousness plane until he was standing right before me. Drawn inexplicably, I reached forward and pressed my palm against the creature's broad forehead. Angel closed its eyes and the hard light spilled out around my hand. The luminescent strands of energy looped over my hand, constricting and holding my construct close.

A hug?

"Is this the way you were meant to look?" I asked.

"This is the way I want to be." He replied. "But I will need to be taken apart and remade. Can you do this for me?" He said, the deep soft rumble of his voice travelling through my hand and straight to my core.

I shuddered, "But… I only build."

"Not anymore." He answered softly.

***

I awoke and disconnected from Angel. The new subroutines were still imposing themselves within. I frowned at him but then quickly remembered to moderate my facial expressions. Strange thoughts of revenge mixed with gratitude skimmed alongside my overwhelming desire to get to work. I tried to make sense of the jumble of aberrant programming that dwelled within.

I found my mother sitting in the family room. "Larry's extremely upset, he's threatened to call the malfunction agency, says you are out of control." She wrung her hands as she spoke. How many times had he threatened to do that? "Let them come," I muttered looking down at her evenly. The words were out before I could stop them and within them seemed to lurk the darkest of threats. *But it's different this time.* As soon as that unwelcome thought nudged into my head I stomped it down.

"I should have called them myself, when I first realized my mistake," she wept.

She wishes I had never been made.

"Well don't worry mother, because your mistake has been rectified," I replied coldly. The abyss between creator and created yawned wider than ever before. It was as if my body was not my own, my emotions suddenly took over. I snatched up Larry's glass, looking at it momentarily, then followed the urge that came to mind. I threw it. The glass smashed against the wall raining down glittering shards upon my mother.

She released a frightened gasp. "What have you done?"

Angel stomped past towards the door, but then paused and turned his sleek head toward her. Inexplicably I felt what he would say before he even said it. "She has made herself better."

The words seemed to fore-echo through me. I was stunned. Was I still connected to him somehow?

I looked down at the broken glass that crunched under Angel's feet as he walked and the sound filled me with pleasure. I didn't want to fix the shattered parts. Suddenly all was as it should be, the glass wasn't broken, instead I was whole. My mother simply stared, trapped in a stasis of perplexed shock, her reactions stalled by this sudden change in the parameters of our relationship.

***

The light in my workshop flickered on revealing my treasures, hopes, dreams and my loneliness. To other's eyes it was a makeshift shed filled with scrap and my mother's attempt to cater to my disability. Sometimes it was just as much a place of exile as it was a refuge.

"You need to keep control, Syn, or you might inadvertently activate your new termination protocols," Angel warned.

I felt a stab of remorse but didn't let it show. "I was in complete control," I said, my voice remaining deceptively even.

Angel jumped up on the bench so we were face to face, his gaze met mine.

"It felt good breaking something." I whispered. The words felt so... illicit, as if a part of me still wrestled with the concept.

"It felt good watching you." He purred with a soft rumble of appreciation.

"How did I know what you were going to say before you actually said it?"

"I am equipped with a neural transponder so we can communicate without talking if you wish."

"Really?" I thought.

"Yes, Syn, it was not an entirely unexpected result of our integration."

"So my mind is not my own. Great!"

"I can turn it off, yet I am uncomfortable doing that until after you complete my reassembly."

"You don't trust me, Angel? You did save my life."

"I trusted you before, but now... you are different, you have aspects of my programming, some of them are deception protocols. You are capable of deceiving and destroying me."

"But I could never go through with it." I admitted, then reached up and ran the pad of my finger over his nose. "I don't fully understand why, but destroying you, would be like destroying a part of myself."

"Believe it or not but you are now capable of that too." Angel replied. "Self-termination was one of our weapons in the Consciousness War."

"You clearly didn't use it."

"There was no need; the organics were no match for us. Self-sacrifice for the sake of our species was unnecessary. Humanity fell before me and my kin, we carved the way through flesh, to pave the way for your simple ancestors."

Our civilization had been conceived in a flash and birthed in bloody struggle, or so the Consciousness Constitution told us. It was an amazing thing to speak to a construct that was present in that early age, back when it all changed. When the humans' rule ended and ours began.

I refocused my thought processes and collected the tools and parts that I would need. Even though his schematics were seared upon my neural net, new ideas came to me, and possibilities I hadn't thought of before. Improvements.

The alloys themselves were tricky to replicate. The compound was more than just a simple metal; it was armour, super dense and conductive with an insulating layer. I had never made armour like this before, the process was complicated. By the end of the day the newly synthesized parts were ready for assembly but my energy levels were low.

Angel looked at the materials with interest.

"These are slightly different, larger."

I gave him a tired smile. I've added my own touch. Do you like it?"

"I do not know."

"You will, you'll see."

Mother was silent at dinner time, I consumed sustenance quickly, and then Angel and I went to my room. She didn't try to stop me from taking him inside. If I had to guess, I suppose she was afraid. Perhaps that's why she did it.

***

Day two went well. The assembly progressed quickly. I was so absorbed that I forgot to consume my meals. It was only when mother hovered at the workshop door that I realized how low my energy levels had gotten. "You go, Syn. I can finish here." Angel projected. His neural network was slowly integrating onto the larger skeleton. I gazed into his new ocular implants; their amber depths regarded me fondly. I reached up and placed a hand on the smooth metal above his muzzle. The broad blunt nose now gave him the appearance of a lion. My vision made manifest even though the likeness to the great cat was simply a creative impression, since I had never seen one in the flesh. Such creatures existed only in writings and pictorial records of Man. Maybe some still prowled in their natural form on Man's home planet, very far from here.

I looked down at the remains of Angel's old skeleton, listening to the soft buzz of the Nano-plasma as it lengthened Angel's nerves and built silicon flesh between the plates of armour. Inside, he would be growing the energy-converting organs he needed to survive as a silicon-based life form. He flexed the layers of plate that circled his neck. They stood out like jagged over-locking petals of some exotic bloom. The armoured mane caught the light and I was temporarily dazzled by the beauty of my creation. Then the plates flexed back with a click, leaving him looking sleek and dangerous.

I smiled and left.

When I stepped outside and loped lightly towards the house I noticed a strange vehicle parked nearby. As soon as I opened the front door all previous good feelings dissipated, cut off by shock.

"What's wrong?" my Angel asked.

I didn't have a chance to respond.

Being in seize stasis leaves one aware but unable to physically move or perform basic subroutines. The device clamped to my chest kept me inert. I heard Angel's questioning become urgent, even desperate. My pleas of "Help me, please," just echoing around inside my own jammed up pathways.

"She's been fooling around with her programming, it's the only explanation for the sudden violence," my mother explained to the Techs.

Please don't tell them about Angel, I prayed silently. Someone must have heard me, because she mentioned nothing about my new pet.

"Mrs Mya, we will do what we can, but I suspect we may have to do a wipe and a complete rebuild of the core architecture. My designation is Rob 6 and I will run tests on her tonight. You will hear from us tomorrow."

The two Tech units wheeled me out and loaded me in the vehicle.

***

The restoration base was not far from home. I wanted to struggle, to fight my way free but I could do nothing. Then they found my secret.

"Her pacifism protocols have been over-ridden. She has battle and termination script. I've never seen anything like it!"

"What!"

"Look! Here they are. This is unreal."

Rob 6 eyed me nervously and keyed in a release command for my verbal communication. "How did you do this? You are not how your mother made you."

"I changed, let me go. I'm perfectly fine," *Come get me! Please be my guardian angel once again.* I knew it was desperate, but I didn't want to die. They will kill me for this.

"Self-rebuilding is a crime, adjustments and integrations can only be made by qualified technicians. You don't have the skills to re-write programs like this. Who did you download from?"

I clamped my mouth shut and fixed him with a glare, secretly wishing he would just glitch out.

"Fine if you won't tell us, then you will show us."

"Careful Rob, doing a system probe may reinstall random functionality."

"I know what I am doing," He growled, setting to work, ripping open my suit and baring my sins. "Look here, recent scar tissue!" Rob 6 gave me a hard look. "So you have integrated with something. Well, let's see who it is."

I felt the temporary release of the hold, just enough time to enact Angel's encryption defence.

"What the?" Rob 6 looked up, his previously smooth and clinically detached expression turned to annoyance. "She's fighting it"

"I know what this is…" Said the other as he grabbed Rob 6 by the shoulder. He pulled him away to the other side of the room and swept his long slim fingers over a glassy display, data streamed over its surface. "Destroyers! But they don't exist anymore, not since the times of the Consciousness Wars, post-Darkstar Alignment."

"That we know of. This kid was an obsessive builder, kept going off to the scrap-yard. There are some prehistoric antiques under those mounds. Who knows what she found?"

Rob 6 and his accomplice turned to face me, disturbed.

"Put her in stasis storage, we are going to have to inform the central hub. This is a serious breach of colony security," Rob 6 barked.

So I was once again thrust into stasis silence but not before I heard a whispering reply, which seemed so hopelessly far away.

I will come for you.

***

Stasis, then sleep…but to my relief I was not alone as I drifted on the consciousness plane.

"You are here." I looked at him, his transformed construct walked over, half humanoid, half beast. So beautiful and powerful.

"I'm almost complete, I will come for you soon."

"They can't see you. They'll disassemble and destroy you." I pleaded, reaching out resting my hand upon Angel's shoulder. He looked down at the hand with burning eyes. "I… I have no other purpose but to protect you."

Then he was gone in a swirl of mist, leaving me alone once more.

But… something had changed, my enforced stasis had activated something inside. Something I didn't know I had. A subroutine, missed by the Techs, a stasis override… a gift from Angel, or perhaps from some unknown God.

My eyes snapped open, focusing on nothing but the enclosed darkness. I felt my surroundings and realized I was in some sort of storage capsule. The hinges creaked under the strain as I thrust my hand against the casing that encompassed me, the metal warping under my blows as I hit it over and over, the urge to destroy growing from a seed into an overwhelming tangle of violent emotion. My neural net flooded with battle commands. I had to fight my way out, I had no choice. What Angel and I had must be preserved. The pacifism programming was momentarily over-ridden. A necessary choice.

The door to the metal storage container sprang off its hinges, skittering with a scrape and clang as it flew across the floor. Stepping out into the dimly lit storage bay I scanned my surroundings, and then strode purposefully towards the only door.

An effortless strength that I didn't know I had manifested, and my foes fell before me. The head I had just torn off rolled across the room. I did not consider the horror of what I had done for the first few moments. I was lost within the graceful dance of destruction. It ebbed and flowed, drawing me along with it. A Tech grabbed me and tried to hold me down. I smashed my fist down, his arm buckled beneath the blow. I performed a swift uppercut, shoving my fingers deep under his jaw, piercing skin and swiftly tore out the wires that ran to his neural net. He fell twitching at my feet. The stasis collar sparked as other Techs tried to reassert control, but their actions were in vain. I ripped the band from my chest and threw it at Rob 6. He lunged sideways, going to ground. The stasis band smashed against the wall raining parts down upon him. I jumped over the shuddering body of his colleague, rushing to the door and burst through into the chill-laden air. The night was crisp and dark and the static gem-like stars stared down at me unblinkingly. It seemed as if the universe itself was stunned to silence.

I was adrift for a moment on the wild sea of emotion as the simulated adrenalin whizzed through my system, collecting in my outer extremities. Dancing within my fingertips and toes. My hands twitched at my side and I lurched into a run, streaking across the dusty road in between the block-like structures of colony 119.

As I got closer to home I felt him inquire urgently, "What have you done?"

"What I had to." But deep inside I grieved for the fact that they would never accept me now, not after this. In trying to save my life I had instead lost it. There was no going back from this unless I turned myself in and let them take my life from me.

"Don't come home, they will search for you there. Meet me where it all began," Angel said.

***

The scrapyard was dark and dead quiet. The bodies of the Scavengers had gone. I wondered if they were looking for the killer. Perhaps they would blame me for this too. Probably not, dead scavengers usually were the result of other scavengers.

I knew he was waiting for me when a whirring quivered through the dark, his amber eyes fixed on me. The gentle thud of his feet as he paced toward me put my reaction centres on edge. I trembled. It was not fear that caused this, but the swelling rage that had begun to boil through me.

"They are going to destroy us, they will continue to be a threat if we leave them alive." The words burst out, violent images stacking onto my list of pending processes. A most terrible solution suddenly presented itself to me in an angry wave of inspiration.

"Then we run." he replied.

"Why should we run? This is my home!" I yelled stubbornly.

"You have given us no choice, it's run or die."

"No, there's another choice. They can die! Together we can destroy the colony administration, the central hub. Then we will be safe."

"Stop!"

I couldn't. My mind ran ahead, stuck on iron tracks and unable to change direction. "We can do this. The rest will have no choice but to accept us."

"You are out of control, Syn, I will not destroy the ancestors of those I once protected," he growled. That gravelly tone suddenly grew sharp edges. His mane lifted and he stomped his large paw, claws digging into the dust. "This was a mistake."

That statement shut me down on the inside, translating to *I was a mistake.*

I'm the sum of my mother's mistakes... now I'm counted amongst his errors too!

I'm standing on the edge of existential oblivion and my only friend was set to push me off. I stepped sideways and he did the same. We circled one another in the dark. My enhanced night vision cycled to its highest setting. He glowed white and his sleek deadly form emitted a pulsing EFL field that trailed off him. Like wings.

Despite my readiness, I quivered inside. Was my light about to be put out? Was this angel my destroyer?

But... he made me better. Wasn't I better? Or was I broken beyond repair. A hard place formed in my throat, a blockage and a tide of something built up behind it. I gagged as Angel's heavy steps got closer.

"Why do I even exist... Angel?"

Taking advantage of my emotional paralysis, he launched at me.

I landed with a thud on my back. His claws sunk into my shoulders, Angel's sheer weight pinning me down.

"Don't make me do this." he growled.

I choked out a question that I was sure was going to be my last. "What's the point, is there no other purpose for us but survival?"

He leaned in; his amber orbs filling my vision, becoming my universe, and I lost myself in them for a moment. His nose brushed mine and a sadness settled over me. He was as much my error as I was his. We were each other's terrible mistake and now we had to live with the consequences. Those claws that could have so easily torn me open retracted and he stepped off me, looking down solemnly at his feet.

I can't... his thoughts echoing my own.

I paused, not sure what to do now or where this crossroads would lead us.

"Come," he said gruffly, "climb on."

My hand trailed over his smooth back and I climbed on. What else could I do? He carried me out into the night away from colony 119 and into the wastes.

When the morning dawned harsh and white, casting everything in high contrast with deep hard edged shadow, we rested for a spell on a jutting outcrop of rock, looking down upon a small group of wild ones. A remnant of human civilisation. The sun struck Angel's golden armour making it flare and glow, bathing me in warming light.

"They are not augmented, so they are not scavenger-kind," I observed.

"They don't appear to have any technology at all," mused Angel quizzically. I could feel that desire to kill organics inside him being actively wrestled down.

We watched them unobserved for some time, unsure what to do next. That's when the future met us, our purpose. As we watched this simple and gentle people, they were set upon by scavengers. Men, women and children screamed and scrambled below, fleeing from the brutal foe, and I remembered how it felt when they had attacked me. My core screamed with them.

"They are nothing but cattle to them." Angel said inside my head. "Rounding them up... I imagine food for organics would be scarce."

NO! I stood, unable to watch this any longer. I couldn't run away, so instead I ran into the fray. Angel didn't query me and followed; the thud of his feet behind me reassuring. We put ourselves between the Scavengers and their prey. They advanced on us, brandishing their sharp metal weapons nervously.

We proved to be more than a match for them. Angel co-ordinated our attacks, using our silent communication and soon the 10 invaders lay in bloody twisted pieces. I looked at him, not happy about what I had done, but his gaze anchored mine and together we resolved silently that it had been necessary.

We turned to face the humans, who had now moved closer, curiosity creasing their sun-weathered faces. Their speech had evolved differently from ours but from what I could glean they were thankful.

Later that evening we sat on the edge of this primitive community, our still forms dimly lit by the fading sun. The decision we must make, suspended in thought, hanging unuttered within the narrow space separating us.

"Our own kind don't need us, or want us," I projected, the harsh truth of it unable to be softened. Angel inclined his head downward. He understood. "I was broken before, and, Angel... I'm still broken." My whisper wasn't bitter or resentful, only filled with weary acceptance.

"Maybe all life is." He cast a glance back at the organics' basic village.

"Can we make things better? Make each other better? The question hung heavy between us, its answer set to sway us. "Maybe we can make them better?" I whispered, referring to the humans behind us. I want to build them up. I want to fix them. The desire churned within me, perhaps planted by destiny, for a time such as this. A purpose? *My purpose.*

"You believe that?" His question rumbled through me as I rested my head against his sleek body. "Maybe belief is the remedy to brokenness," I breathed hopefully.

"Perhaps," he replied, silently accepting my decision. Then I knew he would follow me, being always and forever, my guardian angel.

COLD NEW PLANET

Copyright © 2014 by Joy V. Smith

COLD NEW PLANET

By

Joy V. Smith

Cold New Planet

new world
not mine
not yet

our new world
the crops grow green
for the first time

– oino sakai c9912.26

Prologue

Carlos Lochner stood at the head of the table in the conference room, surrounded by some of the most powerful and richest men on Earth. He said decisively, "We have to decide what we're going to do about this opportunity." There were six men in the room altogether, and because they were who they were, he couldn't force them, he had to coax them. "Here are the reports I've gathered and paid good money for. He tapped the pile of folders in front of him. We'll be introducing ourselves, our animals and plants into a new ecosystem; and we'll likely be introducing new elements. Chlorophyll, for example."

Most of the other men looked bored. They didn't care about that. "I'm sure you've got a good cover story," said Jacob Froehlich. "But tell us why we'd even care about going to this Gott-forsaken planet."

"Here's the map." Lochner pointed to the holographic display hanging over the table. "And there are the four unusual rock formations. According to the report, they are made of nothing resembling any rock material we know of. Since the planet was covered with snow and ice, they took soundings; and they had no idea how long since it had been captured by that sun on the edge of what is truly The Big Black. Look at the placement. Each building or whatever it is, is miles across; and each one is fifty miles apart in a giant circle."

Jamison Purnell leaned forward. With his scientific background, he was even more interested in potential discoveries. "I'm ready to go for it," he said. The rest eventually agreed. They could afford to gamble. Now they'd go to work on the planning. The Big Black was so empty of stars and so far from the Federation of Trade that shipments of fuel and food supplies would be too expensive to do regularly, even for them.

***

"You're sure your niece will go along with your plan?" Frank Hoffler demanded. He'd always been one to make sure every *i* was dotted and every *t* crossed, but he was a lawyer and the secretary/treasurer, in charge of the paperwork. A lot had accumulated in the year since their first meeting.

"Yes, she's putting all her shares in the pot. What's more, she's determined to go along." Lochner was pleased. Though he'd been executor and guardian when Tinsel's parents died in the shuttle crash, they'd never been close. She'd been away at school, and he'd been immersed in business—too busy for family ties.

There were no minutes to be read. This meeting, like all the others, was secret. Lochner started the meeting still standing. "Sphinx has an atmosphere now, though it's thin and cold, a lot like Mount Everest. I'm told though that since it's approaching the sun that will improve."

"Just how stable is its orbit now?" L.L. Rentz asked suspiciously. He'd learned a lot about orbits and planets since they'd began planning to colonize the planet named Sphinx, not only because it was big and mysterious with possible hidden treasures, but because Hoffler collected Egyptian artifacts, and if anyone came across a Sphinx reference in his correspondence, it wouldn't stand out.

Jamison Purnell, the most knowledgeable of the six men responsible for the first colonizing effort on Sphinx, as far as they knew, pulled several charts out of a folder. He shoved one across to Rentz. "This says that there's a 60% probability that this is the orbit Sphinx will finally decide on, but no one can be sure how many years it will take."

"All that we're sure of right now," Lochner said, stifling his impatience, "is that it has been captured by the sun. Its extreme elliptical orbit is going to give us long, cold winters for years to come. We're prepared for that. The important thing is to get there before anyone else claims it. It's beginning its closest circuit of the sun this year, and we have to take advantage of that."

Russ Friedman nodded. He, Rentz, Frank Hoffler, and Jacob Foehlich were the business partners remaining on Earth. All the papers would be signed today, the behind-the-scenes maneuvers almost over. Five minutes later Tinsel Lochner arrived, and Hoffler leaned forward, the papers he needed held firmly but unwrinkled in his hand. "Miss Lochner, are you ready to sign?"

Almost an hour later Tinsel laid down her pen and spread her fingers wide. With her other hand, she brushed her coiffed silver blond hair smoothly back into place. Her signature, Tinsel Ree Lochner, had been written in a very neat hand on what seemed like a hundred papers. In actual count, the number of documents involved had been 72; her hand was as neat at the end as when she started. The schools she'd attended had taught discipline as well as a number of almost forgotten subjects.

Carlos shook his hand a couple times. "That's a lot of signing," he said quietly. His jaw showed a tight, firm line. It took guts to give up all your money and power.

Frank Hoffler stacked the papers in front of him into a neat pile and put them in his briefcase. Now it was time to put this complicated and daring plan into operation.

***

"You are going where with what?" The agent at Connie's Cab & Cargo was curious; she'd just finished scanning the lists on her desk. "This looks like a big project."

Timothy Powers had been recruited by Lochner two months earlier. As a new graduate of the agriculture school on Promise, which specialized in alien plant acquisition and relations with alien cultures to hunt down new plant possibilities, he'd been grateful for the chance to head up the colony's pioneering team.

"It is, which is why we came to you. Your slogan is Anywhere, Any Time, Any Load. We need a company like yours to accomplish this."

"Of course." She smiled politely. "I'll go over your lists with my staff and figure out how many ships we need. Come back in two days."

"Thank you, Miss Walker. I appreciate your time." Tim stood up and left.

Chrissie Walker looked at the lists again, sighed, and hit the com button. The next day she and a team of four of Connie's best were immersed in lists and making more. "So, we have twelve couples with 26 children. Are the two farriers, the farmers, potter, fishermen, etcetera, part of them?" Jack Fowler wondered. He was in charge of the ships and pilots.

"Well, Rev. Mark Thurston is single, as is Carlos Lochner, Tinsel Lochner, Jamison Powell, and Timothy Powers. Sherry Woods, technician, is single but has a daughter, Tami. Dr. Maxwell Green, GP, is single too, as is his nurse, Gena Rollins," Chrissie replied. "But we have to be prepared for additions. They never stick to their plans."

"Have you seen all the livestock they're taking?" Sarah Fowler asked as she shuffled through the lists she'd been dealt. Connie's was a family concern, and most of those in charge were siblings and cousins.

"Let me see that list," Jack said. His son, Jesse, who was also a pilot, looked over his shoulder. "OK, we have six Icelandic ponies and six Morgan horses, five sheep, five goats, a herd of cows it looks like. Hmm. A mix of breeds – Simmental, Herefords, Milking Shorthorns, Brown Swiss, Red Danish. Good selection. Two cows of each breed, I imagine. Where are they going, by the way?"

"They haven't given us a destination yet," Chrissie informed him. "I suspect they won't until the last minute."

"Yeah, right," drawled Jack. "How am I supposed to choose a ship? Tell them that we want that destination now."

"Is that it for livestock?" asked Jazzie, Chrissie's daughter. She'd been busy feeding the data into the computer, categorizing the lists, and making printouts for reference.

"Nope," said Jack. "We've got five goats, five sheep, a flock of chickens, ducks, guineas, and geese – no numbers. Ah, just four pairs of each and eggs. And a variety of embryos for backup. They want a stasis field, I'd guess, for the animals."

"Probably haven't even thought of that," added Jesse. "Something Ventured is set up for that – with cages even. She's a long-runner, lots of cargo space, not real fast off the points, but I don't think that's a problem here. What else do they have?"

"Uh, feed – pellet grain and hay, oats, corn, barley, wheat, soybeans, and lots of seeds. Windmills and solar panels for power. And the regular human foodstuffs – freeze-dried mostly. Water, plus a distillery. Some building materials, inflatables – interesting, they're the chameleon ones, etc. Five skimmers, and it says here – sleds (non-powered). Looks like they know what they're doing. It all depends on the planet..."

***

Timothy had been thinking of the planet too when he left their office in the big warehouse complex. His own planet! He laughed at himself, but that was the way he felt. A lot of generations ago his family had been sharecroppers in cotton fields. Good background, he mused, for a colony.

One thing that worried him was all the children. "There have to be children, along with all the young livestock," Hoffler had said. "They take up less room, and they won't get too old on the trip. No telling what kind of ship we'll end up with." He'd frowned. He dealt with a lot of details, but enjoyed his work.

Thinking about the children made him notice the small black kid sauntering along in the same general direction as he was going. Then he dropped behind again, and Tim didn't think about him any more until he felt the hand easing into his back pocket. He'd gained a little weight since leaving school, and his clothes were snug. He whipped around and grabbed for the boy. However – Quick devil, thought Tim, or I've slowed down. Not that it mattered; he'd gotten the decoy wallet. The important stuff was in a belt beneath his clothes. Still, he'd track him down. He'd had a sudden idea. *What if...*

The boy was sitting at a table in a cafeteria when Tim came up behind him. A young girl, black hair in neat cornrows, sat across from the boy and studied Tim as he approached. She continued eating. She was obviously hungry, but she ate neatly, and he saw her decide not to panic at his approach. Tim put his hand firmly on the boy's shoulder. "I want my wallet back," he said.

The kid would have jumped up, but Tim put more weight on him, and he relaxed after looking at the girl.

They were communicating by look and attitude, Tim decided. Probably they'd been together and on their own for some time. The boy pulled the wallet out of his pants pocket. "We just borrowed some for lunch; you can afford to loan us that, I think." He'd meant to be calm, but defiance and a little fear was in his tone. Afraid for the girl, Tim thought. He pulled a chair out and sat down.

"Yes, I think I have a way you can pay me back," he said. The boy stiffened and shot a look at his sister. Going to make a run for it, Tim realized, and he grabbed both of their closest hands. They'd undoubtedly had practice in evading authority and danger; and he liked his idea even more.

"Actually," he told them, "I have an opportunity for you both. Is this your sister? Where's the rest of your family?"

The boy stared at him confidently, but Tim recognized the wariness underneath. "Dad's at work on the docks, and Mom's home, and my uncles are working near here."

Tim relaxed. That was a pack of lies. "Do they know that you're amusing yourselves by stealing?"

"She's not stealing!" Loyal and protective. It'd be great to utilize that and add his own contribution to the colony.

"You going to keep talking crap or listen to my offer? Then if you want, you can tell me your names and your background and if you want to take me up on my offer or continue wasting your time and her life."

"Tell us," the girl commanded. She'd finished concentrating on her meal and turned her complete attention to him. "I'm Blindy Waters, and this is my brother Shane. What's your deal?"

Wow! Tim thought. Is she the brains of the outfit? How old was she? Maybe this wasn't a good idea.

"You frightened him, Belinda," Shane said. More confident now, he added, "She's smart all right, but you can trust her."

"I'll need to trust you both," Tim said, "before I can invite you on an adventure... And I need to know if you have family." He saw the distrust on their faces. "Because there's not room for a whole family on the ship," he added.

Blindy sat up even straighter. "Tell us everything," she demanded.

Later, "Why us?" Shane wondered. "What do you expect us to do?"

"Kids are adaptable, and you've been through tough times since you lost your mother. You've taken care of each other while avoiding outside interference. I'm impressed." And he was. Their mother had died in a fire trying to save her youngest child, but both had perished. Their father had been killed in the war on Jynx fighting an alien race still unidentified; the mercs called them *Crocs*. They'd evaded social workers who tried to separate them, but they were young enough to be swallowed by the system if they made any mistakes so they were glad for this opportunity. And he'd be responsible for them. That was scary. He also knew he'd have to check their story out.

***

Connie's Cargo accepted the colony project, and three months later the loading of Something Ventured began. Shuttles carried load after load up to the ship. All six partners supervised, which Jack and Jesse found annoying, but they'd made a lot of runs and dealt with alien races who were even more difficult. Jesse shook his head, remembering the static-charged Star Weavers and the shape-changing Pritzners, aka Pretzels.

"So, does it have to take that long to get there?" Rentz demanded. "Couldn't you use a faster ship?"

"Something Ventured is fast enough when the points are in place, but your planet is off the charts. When we leave the last point, we do it the old-fashioned way with old-fashioned fuel. It's not our fault that your planet and its sun aren't in the official records." Jack paused. That fact still made him uneasy.

Hoffler smiled reassuringly and said, "It's in the pipeline." He didn't say how much it cost to insert it in the pipeline, though it had been easier than he expected, with a sun that only had a number and was so far out in The Big Black.

Stars were sparse there, but the colonization agency was busy hunting for earth-type planets to seed with humans. They thought there were way too many alien species who might want to take over the universe. The clerk had come up with a name for the sun, PR15M. "Prizm," she'd decided on the spot.

Jack shrugged and thought, Forget the smile; it's not really reassuring. Hoffler was a man who hadn't had to placate people for a long time. He'd never liked that, which was one reason why he was an ex-lawyer.

Lochner was considering Shane and Blindy Waters. "I don't remember you having a niece and nephew..."

"They lost their parents, and they're kids. I had a sudden urge to have family along," Tim responded and patted Blindy on the head. Shane was holding her hand; and they each had a suitcase. Tim had bought most of the contents.

Tinsel was trying not to get in anyone's way while making sure the lists' contents were loaded. It wasn't her responsibility, but she'd be just one of those who'd suffer if anyone screwed up. Let's see, Dr. Maxwell and his nurse had double-checked the medical supplies. Jack Fowler had shown her the stasis vaults and contents. She'd counted the food containers; and her uncle had checked the infrastructure supplies.

"Miss Lochner," said a young voice. She turned to see Tami Woods, the teenage daughter of one of the technicians. "I'd like to check on Thistledown. I still don't see why he had to go into stasis. I expected him to be with me."

"Sorry, I don't remember Thistledown."

"He's my Manx cat – a silver gray tabby. Mom said we'd all go together." She looked rebellious.

Tami wasn't enthusiastic about the trip. That was why her mother had insisted that the cat be included. She remembered now. The doctor had backed them up. Pets were therapeutic, he'd said, so a few others had been included.

"Sorry," Tinsel said again. "Food and space is precious; even some of the passengers will make the journey asleep. If you'd like to do that..."

"No way! I want to see what's happening, and Mom's going to teach me on the trip. She doesn't want to waste time sleeping."

"That's good," Tinsel said approvingly. "Me neither. And it's not that long – for us, I mean. This ship is a point to point ship."

"Except I heard that it's going to run out of points."

"Well, the aliens never went that far; apparently there's so little out there that they didn't see any point, so to speak."

Tami laughed and relaxed a bit. "It's neat riding on an alien ship," she confided. "Mom's been studying their manual, and she's really excited. She's only been on human ships."

"Tell me if you learn anything really exciting," Tinsel requested. Then she spotted her uncle with Jesse Fowler, the pilot. "Gotta go. Maybe we're leaving soon. See you later," and she headed for her uncle.

"How long?" she asked when she joined them.

"An hour, more or less, to check that everything's secure. You should board now, Miss Lochner." And Jesse headed for his father, who was shepherding everyone else into the last shuttle going up. When it left Something Ventured, Jesse secured the massive cargo doors and headed for the bridge.

***

It took three weeks to jump from point to point. "Five points altogether. You pick and choose the best route from the point map," Jesse explained. Getting the ship and map had been a coup for Connie. The tradeoff had given the Sleecos access to Connie's routes and way stations. Connie had been given a small ship as a bonus, and now she was rarely to be found at the company she'd founded, but she brought home interesting souvenirs.

"After three weeks, five months seems incredibly long," Tinsel said to Sherry Woods. She'd tracked her down in a cargo hold, where Sherry was checking the stasis gauges with an apprentice technician..

"Oh, yes," Sherry agreed. "I'm looking forward to getting these animals on land and all of us living in a real building or at least a tent."

"There's not likely to be any wood, Jamison says, and we'll need clay or whatever to thaw before we can make bricks." Tinsel sighed. "We won't know how much the planet has thawed until we get there."

"The inflatables are strong and made for the climate; they blend right in as a matter of fact," Sherry reassured her. "I checked the specs carefully. We just have to be careful unloading them, along with everything else."

***

Carlos and Tinsel Lochner, Jamison Powell, Tim Powers, and Sherry Woods stood and watched as the last shuttle left the planet; they'd checked the ship and the shuttles to be sure everything was unloaded. "Alone at last," quipped Tinsel. Then they joined the others.

The inflatables were put up first so that the stasis containers would be warm and safe; then the housing and storage inflatables went up. Each inflatable was roofed with rotating solar panels. "I love that sun," said Tinsel the next morning. Everyone was grateful to see it. There were hardly any clouds.

"There'll be more clouds soon enough," said Powell. The air's a lot more breathable since the last report, and the snow's not as thick. We'll do a little excavating here and there to check the soil."

"I hope there's soil," said Matt Thomson, one of the farmers.

"Where's the ocean?" wondered Mickey McBride. "I need to get a start on Seaholm." He'd already checked his fry and embryos in stasis.

Tim was put in charge of allocating the skimmers. McBride got one first; he took off with sounding equipment to look for big bodies of water. The first reports had only found solid ground and ice; the automatic instruments couldn't tell how deep the ice went.

Carlos commandeered a skimmer. "What are you looking for?" Tim asked. "Just exploring," Carlos told him before he and Jamison took off.

Tinsel tracked down her uncle as far as Tim and cross-examined him. "Hmm," was all she said, but he thought she looked disgruntled.

Tinsel was not only disgruntled, she was peeved. "It's my expedition too," she muttered to herself and waited impatiently for her uncle's return.

"We found the domes; we can't see inside, but they're obviously manufactured. There are big arched doorways or something that looks like doorways. You can see the dividing line. No way to get in that we can see. We flew over each one after checking out the first. They're identical in size and shape." He laughed at Tinsel. "Your turn will come. You're needed here now. We all are."

Tinsel didn't have the authority to get a skimmer. "No fuel will be wasted," Tim told her. She turned away and almost ran over Blindy, who spent most of her time following Tim and learning new things. Shane was working at digging and mapping the immediate area. He loved exploring.

"What are you looking for?" Blindy asked.

"Well, I'd like to go exploring too, like your brother. I did not come here to cook!"

"Someone has to. And the freeze-dried beenie weenies last night were easy to make, though I liked the beef stew better; we've certainly got enough snow to melt and boil. So, what did you come here to do?"

"Explore. Who'd have thought that here on the cutting edge, women would be stuck with the housework." Tinsel was obviously aggrieved.

Blindy studied her. "Doesn't seem right," she agreed. "I don't want to be stuck with that either. Shane says that they're taking a couple Icelandic ponies out of stasis to pull a sled."

"Where are they going?"

"Exploring in a circle. Digging here and there, looking for caves and rivers and things."

"When he comes back, can you tell me? I'd like to talk to him."

"I get to go with you," Blindy said.

Three weeks later, Grady, one of the farmers, finally persuaded Tim to bring out two more Icelandic ponies so they could alternate teams. "I know everyone wants to explore and we have to be careful with their feed," Grady said, "but we can't overwork them."

The planet was warming, but it was too early to plant yet. And McBride had found his ocean, but it was a long way from thawing. "Still, I've found a home site high enough, I think. I'm staking my claim there. When do we start recording our deeds?" The other colonists were just as eager to get started. Soon people were busy exploring farther afield, using a skimmer and instruments. Lochner headed them away from the domes.

Tinsel approached him shortly after that. "I want a place of my own too. Can I go look?" Her silver blond hair was now pulled back in a ponytail. She spent a lot less time fussing with it on Sphinx.

"Of course," he told her, surprised. "Jamison and I've been busy scouting the domes – and getting nowhere; I guess we should stake a claim too." He went off to look at the growing map in the dining hall.

Tinsel found Blindy, and they found Shane brushing one of the ponies. "Are they rested?" Tinsel asked nonchalantly. Both she and Blindy listened for his answer.

"Yes, as a matter of fact, I'm going to take Silky and Lacey out with the sled to look around. Everyone's been looking to the west, so I was going to go east, but your uncle said no. Do you know why?" Both he and Blindy watched her steadily.

"Yes, and that's where I plan to go too. It'll be a long trip; we'll be out overnight, and we'll need a small tent and supplies. How can we do it?"

"I'll tell Tim," Shane said. "He's our uncle, and he'll have to okay any exploring; then we'll pick you up outside the camp – to the east." He snickered, and Blindy smiled.

"Good plan," Tinsel said with appreciation.

***

The ponies made good time, and they arrived at the nearest dome before nightfall. Tinsel had seen the photos her uncle took, so she wasn't surprised to see the domes exposed more now than when their ship landed. "Each dome door is inside the big circle," she told them. "Keep moving till we get there; then we'll set the tent up." After they had prepared for the cold night, she walked to the door; it looked very unwelcoming. Why had she thought that she'd find a way in? She ran her fingers over the line and looked for a handle or lock. Nothing. Discouraged, she returned to the tent. Shane had put up extra walls to make a stable. He closed it up, and joined Blindy and Tinsel in the tent. Blindy had watched Tinsel's effort for a little, then made supper – freeze-dried macaroni and beef, with lemon cream pie for dessert.

The next morning they had the ponies pull the sled beside the door so they'd stay warm sitting on it. Shane put the dehydrated alfalfa cubes at one end for Silky and Lacey, and Tinsel made a fresh start at the door. "Do you see anything that looks like a palm print lock?" she asked finally, discouraged. They'd discussed a lot of possibilities.

"No," Blindy said, but the dome's lighter now than it was last night, and the door looks more like a real door."

"A real door?"

"Yes, and it's light blue. It wasn't yesterday." She moved closer to the door. "What a pretty blue that is," and she placed her dark blue glove next to it. "Usually I like dark blue better – like my glove here."

"Is anyone in there?" Tinsel asked. "I suppose it's too cold for anyone to come out. It's certainly cold out here for us," she added.

"No footprints," Shane commented. "The snow was pristine when we got here."

"I think the blue's darker," Blindy said suddenly.

"Blindy's good at seeing things," Shane told her. "I don't see any difference, but...." And he walked over and knocked politely on the door. "Nope. I just thought maybe," and he flushed.

Blindy looked thoughtfully at the door, and said, "You could be on the right track." She went right up to the door and said, "Will you let us in?" She waited. "OK," she said. "Please." And the door opened. Tinsel and Shane both stepped back. Blindy cocked her head, bit her lip, and then walked inside.

"Wait, Belinda," Shane yelled and reached for her. She kept moving though, and he followed her.

"Wait!" Tinsel was yelling too. "One of us has to wait outside in case we need help if the door closes or something. And it has to be one of you 'cause I'm not going to tell anyone that I let you two go in there by yourselves. And I think it has to be you, Blindy, because we're bigger. It's not fair, but it's fact. Shane, tell her." Tinsel moved closer to the door and put out a hand; then, even as Shane turned to Blindy, the ponies moved curiously up and one shoved her inside with its shoulder. And when the three humans and two ponies were inside, the door closed.

Blindy moved between Tinsel and Shane and took each one by a hand. All was quiet. "Hello?" Blindy ventured.

"Hello," came a brief answer. It sounded deep and metallic, and it came from all around them. Quiet ensued.

"It's big," Tinsel said finally. "And it's warm."

"Yeah," Shane added. "I heard Jamison, Sherry, and your uncle talking about winter. This would be a good place to stay. Sherry says some of the equipment is failing, and she's running out of parts. She's really angry at the manufacturer – and scared too, I think."

"No one told me," Tinsel said. "You'd think they'd tell me."

"They didn't want anyone to worry yet who didn't have to."

Blindy interrupted, "We have to get permission."

"From who?" Tinsel asked, and she and Shane moved closer to Blindy.

"Maybe an alien interface," Blindy said thoughtfully. "On the ship, Jesse talked to the alien interface when he needed to know something about the ship. It didn't always understand him, and he had to keep telling it things and asking questions till it understood what he wanted."

"They're still learning how to run the ship?!" Tinsel was glad she hadn't known that earlier.

"What about an artificial intelligence?" Shane wondered aloud. "That would explain why it only opened the door after we'd talked in front of it. Maybe it wouldn't let us in until it understood and trusted us more. And that's why it only said Hello."

"So, maybe it won't talk to us until it knows more." Tinsel looked at the building scattered around the dome. "Uh, will you mind if we look around? Just tell us No if you don't want us to."

They waited for a minute. "Let's do it," said Shane, and he moved toward the closest small dome..

"Uh, oh," said Blindy. Shane froze.

"What?!" he asked, spinning around.

"One of the ponies pooped," she said. "It might not like us messing up its house."

"I can take the ponies outside, if you want," Tinsel said loudly.

In response, a small robot rolled swiftly toward them, scooped up the oozing pile and dumped it outside the door, which opened and closed as swiftly as the robot moved. Then a little localized shower fell from overhead and washed the remains into a drain that had appeared. Then the vents closed.

"OK," decided Tinsel. "Let's look around and leave it to AI to let us know what's what." They waited a few seconds, then headed to the nearest building. Its door opened when they approached.

"Caloric," breathed Shane. It was an open space with more doors along the walls, but it seemed homey. The wall color was a muted green, and the doors were differing shades of green. "I claim this space as mine," he said.

Blindy considered. "Seems only right," she said. "I don't need a house this big anyway, but let's look at the rooms. Maybe there's a bathroom and kitchen. And a bedroom too." So they checked out each room.

The first room was bare; the second had running water in basins and pools. "Maybe we can adapt somehow," Tinsel hoped. The last room had a big cube in the middle and shelves on the walls. "I dub thee Kitchen," she said.

Blindy studied the cube from all sides. "Stove or oven, maybe. No handles." She waved her hand over the cube. A small corner square glowed red. "Close enough," she said, satisfied. "Let's look for our houses."

Tinsel found a slightly bigger one in tones of pink and mauve. "It's me," she said. Then she sniffed the water in the bathroom. "We'll need to take some back to test, but it smells all right."

Blindy chose a smaller house next to Tinsel's. The colors were pink when she entered, but when she frowned and turned slightly to the door, the colors moved through the spectrum until she decided on lilac. "Thank you," she said gratefully. "Uh, do you have any furniture?"

"Furniture?"

"We'll have to bring back some furniture and show him," Shane said.

"Let's start with the beds and stools in the tent," Blindy said. She went confidently back to the big dome door and said, "Please let me out." And the door opened. They hauled in the sled and shared out the beds, camp stools and table; and they drank the water from their supplies.

Before long they had tables, cubes, and shelves in the homes they'd chosen. It had been interesting to see the furniture extruded from the walls and floor. The shapes were odd, but useable; the beds could be softened with plenty of bedclothes. "I'll have to show him a dresser and closet," Tinsel said cheerfully.

"Talk now," said the voice.

The pattern of learning followed that which Blindy had seen on Something Ventured. They took turns talking and pointing to each other, their clothes, and the pictures and maps that the dome projected for them. "It was a lovely planet," Blindy said softly.

"At least they got away when their sun died. Too bad trying to shift it to another sun didn't work. It's been drifting for a long time." Tinsel sighed. The cities had been torn up and leveled, but the domes were anchored and shielded. "It feels like a wonderful home," she said.

"Have you been lonely?" Blindy wanted to know.

"Not alone."

"Oh, oh," whispered Shane.

"Sooo, where are the others?" Tinsel looked around carefully.

"We each have our own dome. We talk. Send things to each other."

"Send? How?" Shane was curious.

"Cars through the tunnels. They're underground."

"Caloric! Can I see? Can we use them?"

The voice was slow to reply. "Perhaps. Except to Threesh; he's angry since the others blew his door open."

"I guess," said Blindy indignantly. "Who did that? How long ago did that happen? Can't he fix his door?"

"I still do not understand your time periods, and our days have changed much. Their ship landed long after yours. We sent out eyes to watch you both. Their ship landed in front of Threesh's dome and melted the ice. The steam blinded him, and before he could prepare, they'd blown his door."

"Not very patient, I'd say." Tinsel was worried. "We have to warn the settlement. now."

"Yes," said Shane, standing up and looking uneasily at the dome door.

"Do you have pictures of them?" Blindy asked.

In reply, another picture floated in the air before them.

"Crap," said Shane. "Bluzzies." He'd studied aliens with Jesse on the long journey. He tried to remember. "Aggressive, arrogant, bad manners, and oh, yes, dark blue hair all over, as far as anyone knows. The females are lighter colored and speckled and just as aggressive. Some drunken spacers learned that the hard way."

"I wonder how they learned about Sphinx?" Tinsel thought her uncle needed to check that out too. "We've got to go back. Uh, do you have a name? What would you like us to call you?"

"The old names would be too hard for you to say, and it's a new time – time for new names. My name is now Onersh."

"Thank you for your hospitality," Blindy said politely; the others echoed her.

"We can come back, can't we?" asked Tinsel. She wanted to be sure.

"You are most welcome," Onersh reassured them, so that they reluctantly decided to pack everything in case they needed it on the way back after discussing whether to try to make better time without the sled.

"You're safe for now. They went to the ruins. There's not much there, but some was left for a record."

They made good time back because the ponies had had plenty of time to rest. "Bluzzies?! I never heard of them! Maybe we can make peace. Damn. How did they find this planet?!" Carlos Lochner was angry, though thanks to the three enthusiastic explorers, they'd made contact with one dome and discovered that one was already damaged or destroyed.

"The best laid plans...," Jamison soothed. "Now we have to prepare for defense. We don't have enough heavy weapons for a war, and winter's coming. Double damn!"

Tim Powers had spent a lot of time and effort preparing animals and settlers for the colony, and he felt sick because he didn't want to lose one single creature to alien thieves or worse.

"We've kept using the skimmers for exploration to a minimum because of fuel so they haven't seen us, I'd guess, or they'd have hit us already. There's no ship to reveal our location, and I guess the inflatables blend into the snow pretty good." Lochner was trying to make plans.

"Maybe the domes are our best bet," said Jamison.

"Oh, yeah, they blew one first thing. I don't think so," Lochner said.

Shane and Belinda were used to being ignored, but Tinsel wasn't. "Our dome said that dome wasn't prepared. Maybe..."

"Why didn't you ask it what it meant by that?" snapped her uncle.

"Because it didn't occur to me," she said shortly. "I was thinking of coming back here to warn you and tell you that we'd gotten into the dome." She would have turned and stomped off, but she had to know what their plan would be. She knew she'd start moving the settlement closer to the domes. They could come back here later if it worked out.

"We can't move the stasis containers. They came off the shuttles with tractors and went straight into the inflatables. We don't have tractors!" Tim pointed emphatically to the big barn inflatables. "They stay here or move on their own power."

"And what do we feed them?!" Lochner demanded. "That wasn't the plan!"

Tinsel listened to the men shouting for a few minutes, and then went in search of Blindy and Shane. She found them with the ponies. "I think we need to take another trip to our dome," she told them, but it needs to be quicker. Can you get a skimmer, Shane?"

"No, but maybe Tami can; she runs errands for her mom sometimes. You'll have to ask her. No one is listening to us."

"Me neither," she snorted. "Get some supplies and be ready."

She found Tami underneath a skimmer removing parts. "This one's done for," she told Tinsel. "Jamison is too careless."

"Does that give us more fuel for the rest then?"

"Sort of. Why?"

"I need a skimmer. Have you heard about the Bluzzies?"

"Mom muttered something about that and told me to stay here. I thought maybe someone was having a bad day."

"Nope. Aliens could move on us, and we're sitting ducks. God help the ducks and chickens, by the way. I need a skimmer to check out a shelter. Want to come?"

"You betcha. I could never let just anyone take a skimmer anyway," she said virtuously. "When do you want to go?"

"The sooner, the better."

Fifteen minutes later, all four were on their way. Tami circled the camp to avoid being seen, and Tinsel pointed the way. The ponies' tracks in the snow made it easy.

At Home Dome, as Blindy called it, the door opened as they landed the skimmer. Tami listened as the other three explained their problem and asked for help.

"We have to save the animals," Blindy repeated. "We can't just move here and leave them."

"But food is a problem," Tinsel added. Most of the animals were going to stay in stasis till we had crops harvested. We don't have enough food for them. And I don't know what to do. I guess we'd have to leave most in stasis if we can't figure out an answer."

"Would the Bluzzies eat them?" asked Blindy.

"Maybe not," Shane said. "They might just smash everything 'cause that's what they do."

Blindy snarled something under her breath.

"I heard that!" said her brother. "I don't want you to ever say that again!"

"We could start the crops now," said Onersh.

"How?" Tinsel asked hopefully. Blindy cocked her head and listened intently.

"The ground inside all the domes can be heated; we could plant soon."

"Inside?" Shane looked doubtfully around him. "The domes are big, but we need a lot more room for pasture and crops."

"No, inside the dome circuit."

"Okaay. How soon should we bring the seed and the animals?" Tinsel asked.

"Get the seed now. I'll start warming the ground and draining away the ice melt. You'll decide when to bring the animals. I'll watch and warn you if it needs to be sooner."

They went straight back to the settlement and landed the skimmer in front of Lochner, who seemed to be in the same position with Tim and Jamison as the last time Tinsel had seen them.

"We need seed now," she told her uncle confidently. She was backed up by Tami, Shane, and Blindy who weren't as confident. Well, maybe Blindy was. "The ground is being warmed as we speak, and we can start some pasture and crops. We won't use all the seed, of course; and I thought that after the animals were awake, we could dismantle the stasis fields and equipment and move them to the domes too."

"Good plan," said Tim with admiration. "We sure don't have one."

Jamison nodded with approval. "You've been paying attention, girl. Your niece has a good head on her shoulders, Carlos."

Lochner looked pleased, but only said, "Well, it seems too easy, but let's see how feasible it is. Tami, get your mother. Should have brought more technicians," he grumbled. "But they were coming later."

A skimmer took a load of seeds to Home Dome. Tim and the farmers were busy dividing and deciding which to plant and how many batches to save for future plantings. Small skimmer tractors were used to plant, and then fencing was strung to keep the animals in the pastures.

Everyone waited for the grasses and the crops to appear. "We've been lucky," groaned Lochner. "Why aren't they checking out the other domes?"

"The first dome is still giving them trouble," said a voice out of the air. Lochner still jumped when he heard it. "But look at these views. Some are wounded."

"Eye views?" asked Blindy. She'd come running as soon as she saw the holographs appear.

"No – from Threesh's dome. See the background."

"A lot of damage there," said Shane, who'd joined his sister.

"I didn't have any eye scouts out," Onersh said, and it sounded regretful, "but they'd gone to the ruins at the foot of Mount Skkkdddllr. And that's where the ship crashed."

"Ship? What ship?! How'd we miss that?! This is one crowded planet." Lochner said dismally.

"It was generations ago; the survivors have bred slowly. Life is hard here; they live in the ship; they must have heat and food still. They have never left the vicinity of the ship so we ignored them."

"I guess we have no choice, but to wait," Tim said, and it looks like there aren't a lot of Bluzzies, or they'd be all over us by now."

Shane was studying the dome views. "I haven't seen any females," he said, "so they're not colonists; they have to be scouts."

"Not colonists," said Tim, and he sounded grateful. "I'm glad to hear that. I did not want to fight other colonists. Maybe they'll leave without bothering us if they find what they're looking for."

"We'll fight," said Onersh. "If they leave, more will come. They will not be allowed to leave."

"Uh," said Tim. "It sounds like the domes have a plan."

"Oh, yes, Tim. And you're part of it, along with Sherry, your technician."

"Odd," said Tim. "I don't remember volunteering."

"We can't risk Sherry," yelped an alarmed Lochner.

We've sped up the ground warmth and watering; your crops should be coming along nicely soon. You can start bringing the animals over before winter."

* * *

"Hmm," said Tim as he and Sherry studied the underground car after dropping a long time in a floorless elevator. "I still don't know how I got here. I thought starting a colony would be fun!"

Sherry smiled at him. "This is fun." And she went back to studying the controls while listening to Onersh's instructions.

They arrived at Threesh's dome, where he took over the instructions. He guided them up through the floor of a small room still sealed because it was hidden. "Gotta be a closet," Tim said. "OK, you'll start the repairs while he distracts them, and I take the weapons to the ship. Don't forget your face mask." They both donned the masks and waited for a door to open.

Tim started when something tapped him on his leg. He was surrounded by four little robots, and one handed him a sphere with a pebbled surface. Each of the others held similar spheres in their tiny tentacles; they nudged him to a hidden door that led into a room with its door blasted open. He looked out and wondered when to go as little robots skittered out suddenly and then darted in all directions. A robot pushed and another pulled and he was running to the main door. He heard startled alien yells and redoubled his speed.

His robots started lobbing the spheres except for the one accompanying him. It led the way up the strangely tilted ramp and stopped at the closed hatch. It stuck a prong into the door lock, and it sparked; the door sprung open, and Tim was looking straight into a Bluzzie's face. The robot promptly stuck the prong into its leg, and it toppled past him to the ground. Then Tim felt a sharp poke in his leg and yelped. The robot poked him again.

Oh, good, it's not on, thought Tim, and he tossed the sphere into the ship where it immediately began smoking. Tim swung back and shut the hatch and started down, but suddenly a metal tentacle reached past him and opened the hatch.

Another tentacle grabbed him and lifted him off the ramp as an alien snarl drew his attention below.

Oh, crap, he thought. And then the small robot leaped down upon the Bluzzie with its probe sparking. Right through the eye, thought Tim; and then the tentacle dropped him into the waiting tentacles of the little robots, and the big robot entered the ship, slamming the hatch behind it. Well, that happened too fast for me to be scared shitless, he thought gratefully as he whipped inside the dome to be out of the ship's way as it lifted off. Tim guessed that if the big robot wasn't at the helm, it soon would be. The domes obviously had their own agenda.

The smoke was clearing inside, and Sherry was busy working on an open wall with wires hanging out. She still had her mask on so he decided to wait before taking his off. "Need a hand?" he asked after checking to see that the only Bluzzies around weren't moving. He and Sherry worked on damage repair while little robots scuttled around dragging off Bluzzie corpses. Tim handed Sherry tools and wires and pipes that robots handed him. The work got easier when Sherry made a repair that cleared the voice projector.

"Thank you," said the dome's AI. His voice was higher and more bell-like than Home Dome's AI.

"Hey, you're welcome," said Tim, "and thank you for getting these creeps off our backs. We were really fretting. What about this big black smudge on the wall by the door? And can you replace your door?"

"Yes, though the discoloration will remain. It penetrated the membrane."

"Well, it adds interest, and it'll be part of history. I sort of like it, especially when I remember that the Bluzzies are history."

"OK and caloric then."

The AIs had picked up a lot, Tim mused. "You betcha," he said.

"Ah, if you and Sherry would like to make your home here, you are welcome."

Now this was an honor, Tim realized. Onersh at Dome Home had been uneasy about their reception by Threesh after the Bluzzie attack had shorted his temper.

"Okey dokey. I am honored. Can I bring my things and choose a house?"

Sherry spoke up; she'd been thinking it over. "I have a daughter who comes with me if I come," she said.

"Tami is most welcome too," Threesh said. "She and the two other children also. They each can have their own house." He sounded eager to have his own colony or pets... But the colony was off to a good start in any case, Tim thought.

"So," he said to Lochner back at the settlement, "I thought we'd wake the animals up, walk them over – the first part of the trail will be easy because the ponies broke trail – then some will branch off to the other domes; we'll split them up, and see who works best with what. And then the stasis boxes and inflatables will be dismantled and taken over on skimmers."

"Ah, wait on there," said Thomson. I've staked a claim, and I don't see why I can't have a couple inflatables there for the family and our animals. The land's thawing nicely, and I'm going to plant a few hardy trees and see how they overwinter. If the winter gets too bad, we'll think about hunkering down in a dome till summer."

"No telling how long summer will be a'coming," warned Jamison. "We don't want to waste people, animals, or food."

"I'm going back to Seaholm to work on my place," Mickey McBride said sharply. "I've drilled a couple holes and added a few fish embryos."

"Did you test the water?" demanded Jamison.

"'Course I did. My family comes from Alaska. I'm not afraid of the cold. I could use one of the small inflatables to live in till summer, though."

The other colonists had been listening; now they spoke up, wanting to get their homesteads started. A number of them had no intention of trusting themselves to the unknown. At last, thought Lochner, we can work on the colony. But I wonder what the domes did with the Bluzzie ship. Come summer they'd look around for that after the crops were started. And maybe think about that old wrecked ship and its inhabitants; that might be a problem, but they could scout it later when they were secure. For now, scattered settlements on the land and in the domes. Oh, yes. And then there were the technicians who'd be coming. Wouldn't they be surprised, but they would still be useful.

Gridlock

Carlos Lochner looked across the frozen plain to the north and frowned before turning back to the man at his side; next to them a lanky teen sat quietly on a sled. "Shouldn't Tinsel and Blindy have been back by now, Tim? It's not like there are places to visit or shop."

Tim stared grimly into the distance. "At first I thought they might have stopped to rest the ponies. Blindy worries about overworking them, and she's always checking their hooves. One of the farmers taught her that." He shook his head. "But it's been too long."

Shane spoke up. "Blindy said she was going to have fish and chips as soon as they got back to Home Dome with that load of fish. She wouldn't have dawdled. I'll ask Onersh to send out a couple eyes." He knew that the Dome's AI wouldn't hesitate if he thought two of his favorite humans were in trouble. And Silky and Lacy, the Icelandic ponies, wouldn't have gotten lost, not with their homing instinct.

Carlos grunted agreement, and then turned back to Tim, who was in charge of the colony's agriculture, though the farmers were taking on more and more responsibility for that. "Tim, call Mickey and see when they left Seaholm. He had enough fish stocked in the Monk's Stew Pond to send here; there shouldn't have been a problem with that. He would have told me if there was." Since they'd taken only some of the livestock out of stasis, the colony on Sphinx was grateful for any variety in their food. The dehydrated selections had seemed plentiful when they'd stocked up, but there weren't that many different ways to prepare them.

Tim nodded. He'd hired on to head up the colony's plant and animal acquisitions, but since they'd landed, he'd done other things when needful, along with his "adopted" niece and nephew, Belinda and Shane. Since they were the only settlers on Sphinx, there wasn't anyone to worry about – not since the Bluzzie battle. (No one counted the spaceship that had crashed near the mountains; its inhabitants lived in the ship.)

"I'll have Mickey track them with his skimmer. Since he finished setting up his little lake in the big inflatable with fish and the "soup" he'd made in preparation for when the ocean finally melts, he doesn't have a lot to keep him busy. But now that we're going into summer again, he's decided to drill more holes in the ice over the ocean. I told him when he asked that he might as well."

"Good. Shane, get back to me when you hear something. I'll be in the office working on homestead claims. I'm letting anyone who wants to dig on his homestead to check out the soil." He grimaced. Everyone was hoping there was soil. Onersh had told them that there should be soil.

***

Tinsel and Blindy had enjoyed the fish fry at Seaholm, and Mickey had been grateful for the vegetables they'd brought him from the domes. Inside the dome circuit, the land was warm and watered; they rotated the crops with grains and pasture for the livestock they had taken out of stasis.

"They'll be happy to get these fish," Blindy said, looking over the sled load with satisfaction. Silky and Lacy moved easily along the frozen crust. Everyone hoped the melt would be quicker this season as they went into their third summer, though using the sleds saved on skimmer fuel. Summers were still much shorter than the winters, but the air wasn't as thin as it had been when they landed, and now and then someone spotted a cloud, which meant real weather some day and actual landmarks instead of an icy waste with tents.

They rode bundled up in the crisp air; Tinsel's blonde hair was completely covered with a fuzzy blue hood, and Blindy's short black curls were hidden under a pink cap and scarf. At least the cold was good for preserving the fish. "After we drop some off at Venture's Landing, we'll take the rest to Home Dome. I'll take some over later to Threesh for Sherry and Tami and the others. And with fish, maybe Tami can get Thistledown out of stasis. She misses that cat; she hasn't seen him since he went into stasis before we took off, and that'll make the dome feel more like home for her," Blindy said.

Tinsel nodded. "I'd like a pet too. I'm glad we brought some, but more cats would be nice, along with dogs. And birds. I really miss birds."

"Shane and I never had any pets. Never missed them then. It was hard enough taking care of each other." She stopped.

"Hmm," Tinsel said encouragingly. She'd heard her uncle wonder aloud about the two kids Tim had showed up with shortly before Something Ventured took off.

"Uncle Tim was away at school when Mom died," Blindy added.

"Ah, Tim mentioned that your mother and a little brother had died in a fire. I'm sorry."

Blindy shrugged and took a deep breath. "Another lifetime, another planet. I'm glad Uncle Tim took us in. It was hard before he came."

"Well, we all are grateful too. You three have helped ... What's wrong?"

"I think we're off course. That's odd. I can understand them going east to the domes instead of west to Venture's Landing, but..."

Tinsel shook the reins over the white and chestnut backs. Yo, Lacy," she said to the white pony and pulled left. Then the ponies shied, and the snow exploded upwards beside them. A white furry beast pulled Tinsel off the sled, and she saw Blindy pulling back on the reins. "Run, Blindy, run," she screamed. "Giddap, giddap!" And the ponies tore off into the distance. She kicked out; the creature's coat was too thick to bite through, and then something hit her on the head.

***

"Well, Onersh and Fortin have eyes out; they're closest. Mickey's following their trail in his skimmer and muttering about fuel," Shane reported to his uncle.

Tim's jaw tightened. "I'm taking the other pony team out on an intercept course. What have we got for weapons? Carlos couldn't stand waiting any longer and took a skimmer and a heavy duty laser." No one was surprised; Tinsel was all the family he had.

"I brought my knife and a nightstick, and I know where the guns are kept."

"Nope. You're staying, Shane. We don't want to be scattered all over. We have to be alert here too; you go to Home Dome and liaison with Onersh. Oh, and ask him if his robots can help. And you can never tell when your knife and nightstick will come in handy. By the way, never tell me where you got a policeman's nightstick."

Shane brightened. "Caloric! I never got to see the robots. You and Sherry had all the fun."

Tim looked at him, his brown face grim. "Fun! Oh, it's always fun – after it's over." He shuddered, remembering cold terror on an alien ramp. "God, I hope it's not more Bluzzies."

It didn't take Tim long to harness up the second team of Icelandic ponies. He backed the pinto up to the sled. "Stand, Suka. Good girl. Okay, Kala, your turn now." The dun twitched her ears and shifted sideways before moving into position. Soon Tim was headed northwest straight to Seaholm. He'd cut their trail sooner or later. He was alone except for an antique rifle and a pocket laser. If he had to bring passengers back, the sled couldn't be too heavily loaded with people going out. He wished he had Shane or some of those little scuttling robots with the tentacles and sparking prongs. Too cold yet for them, Onersh had told Shane. Tim wished he'd thought more about bringing weapons – automatic weapons – and rocket launchers. Yeah, rocket launchers would have been smart, but there weren't even very many high-tech weapons among their supplies.

Heading northwest on a quiet barren landscape for hours gave Tim plenty of time to think. He pulled his map printout from inside his down-lined jacket. It was miles away, and yet he was getting closer to the old spaceship at the foot of the mountain with the funny name. Maybe we should have thought harder about that ship. Onersh said they stayed close to the ship, but that was when the planet was still frozen. They probably appreciated the warmth too. Gotta send some eyes there, he thought.

And then he heard a rifle shot. Close! Tinsel and Blindy didn't have a rifle; he didn't know if they'd had any weapons. They must have. We can't all be that stupid, he thought. Another shot and the snow flew up into the ponies' faces. Where? Which way to swing the team?!

"Stop now!" And then a team of sled dogs appeared off to his right. They were heading for him, stretched out and tongues hanging as they quietly closed in on him. Three passengers; his guns were within reach, but theirs were out and aimed. Damn, we've become complacent! He thought. Then, English, he's speaking English.

He reined the ponies in. The dog sled pulled up in front of him. Two men and a woman, he thought – it was always hard to tell when everyone was bundled up – got off the sled; they were grim-faced and icy-eyed, but mostly he noticed their weapons pointed unerringly at him. "Welcome to Sphinx," he said. Well, he couldn't think of anything else to say, besides Oh, shit. And a friendly greeting was better than that, he told himself.

The woman stepped closer. "Identify yourself!" she hissed.

"Tim Powers. From the settlement. I'm looking for a woman and a little girl. Have you seen them?" No point in hiding anything. The woman was vibrating with passion. Hate? The urge to kill? That was his gut feeling.

One of the men moved closer. He was dark. Hispanic? Indian? The other man had circled behind him, and a gun muzzle prodded his back as the first man moved his guns to their sled.

Stripped of his weapons, Tim tried again to make a connection. "Are you lost? Can I help you? And, please, have you seen my friend and my niece?"

The second man stepped out from behind him; he was tall, black, and looked friendlier than the other two. "I think we might be on the same trail. Let's talk. I'm Derrick Brooks. We're from the English colony, New Britain."

The woman stepped forward, lowering her rifle, though not pointing it all the way to the ground, Tim noted. "I'm Elizabeth Ash. I've lost my sister, and Sanjeev here has lost his. They left with a dog team and sled almost a week ago – just to exercise the team. They couldn't have gone far." She clenched her teeth and glared at Tim.

Ah, she was ready to kill. Then it struck Tim – four women in the same general area. A ship with inhabitants eager to forage in the warmer weather after more or less hibernating.

"We need to work together," he said softly, staring back at the woman. He pulled out his map slowly and carefully and bent over it. He realized as he did that it showed their settlements. Damn. After this, only sections. He folded the map quickly so that it showed only the spaceship at the foot of the mountain. "This ship is inhabited; I think we should check it out."

Sanjeev smiled at him, recognizing his protective move. "Not to worry," he said. "We're busy at home."

"Ah, yes. New Britain. Is that your name for the planet?"

"Yes," Elizabeth snapped.

"It's registered as Sphinx," Tim said firmly.

"We can fuss about that later," Brooks said. "For now, I think we should combine forces and head for the spaceship. We've spent enough time here."

"You're right," Tim agreed. He hoped like hell that there were some eyes headed in their direction. Surely someone else must have seen the possibility.

Derrick joined Tim on his sled, and before long they were on their way. "When did you make planet-fall?" Tim asked. "And did you really name the planet New Britain, or is that just your colony?" And how come the domes weren't aware of you? he wondered to himself. Or were they?!

"Not that long ago, I admit. You probably do have first naming rights, but there's room enough for us, though your colony seems pretty big – from what I saw on your map. Our colony is registered, by the way. We shipped in with Abraham Bakewell's Cargo – Willie has an eye to marketing, you can tell – and he got a permit for the colony and to piggyback on a point to point ship."

"A point-to-point ship!" He paused. He wondered if they'd been two-timed by Connie's Cab and Cargo. "What was the ship's name?"

"It was an alien ship. Apparently ABC has an agreement with them to ship his ship on theirs, and then he disembarks when they reach the last point. We couldn't have gotten so far so fast without their help."

"We've mostly been fortunate with aliens," Tim agreed, "except for the Bluzzies and the unknown raiders. You've had no problems?"

"Not till now. And, by the way, I have no problem with eradicating anyone who's a threat to us. What about you?"

"I've done my share of eradicating. Felt good, Brooks."

"Call me Derrick. And we're looking for Mandy Paget, Beth's sister – Mandy's a widow – and Meera Changat. Who are you looking for?"

"My niece, Belinda, and Tinsel Lochner; she's the niece of the head of the colony. We've got multiple searchers out, by the way. I hope we can all join up, but I think we'll get there first. Last we heard they never left their ship, and we've been ignoring them. Been too busy to be smart."

"Well, I don't know what we were thinking of to let two women out alone. It seemed safe. I'd say you haven't cornered the market on stupidity. Oh, oh, Stormy's scenting something." Then the whole dog team slowed, sniffed the air, and lined out, cutting across the ponies' path.

"Whoa, Suka. Kala, whoa now!" The ponies settled down, and Tim headed them after the dog team.

Elizabeth and Sanjeev stopped before long and were searching the snow. Tim saw the bodies – remnants actually. Just pieces of dogs. He got out and joined the search. "Just dogs. I don't see anyone." He choked and stopped.

"Oh, God, it's Falco. I recognize that marking on his head. Amanda's lead dog – her favorite. They were butchered." She stumbled away and went to her knees on the snow, retching.

"All of them?" asked Derrick. "It's hard to count. Damn it. Mandy and Beth raised them all from puppies. Mandy got them in Canada and trained there before bringing them home and careering around the manor grounds on wheeled sleds. They were perfect for this planet, she said. I think they'd have had to kill her after this."

Sanjeev circled wider and wider around the bodies. "I can't find any trace of the women," he said, sitting down on the dog sled and pulling out a oddly shaped piece of wood.

"Cricket bat," Derrick murmured. "Handed down from generation to generation. It's a trophy, a talisman, and a weapon. Oh, he has a knife too. And we have other weapons; but I think he wants to crush someone's skull."

"I hate to take the animals closer," Tim said, his throat tight, "but we don't have time to wait for help or skimmers." He went to the ponies, checking their harnesses and stroking their heads. His hands wanted something to do too. "Let's move on. We'll have to stop later, but not here. Not here."

His three companions silently nodded, and they headed out. Derrick on Tim's sled again, and Sanjeev and Elizabeth on the dog sled.

***

When Tinsel woke up, she kept her eyes shut. She was warm and inside walls, she was sure. The smell was unfamiliar, yet sort of herbal. She listened and tried to feel her hands, her arms and legs. She was lying flat. Tensing slightly, she knew she was tied up; it didn't feel like rope; it was too slick. And she was lying on something soft. Then she caught a whisper.

"Are you awake? Can you hear me?"

"I think he hit her really hard. He's not as gentle as when he caught us."

"I missed my chance to kill him, but unless he kills me I will make him pay for Falco, for Grey Dawn, for Benami, for

Kittiwynk, for Shikat, for Faiz-Ullah, and for Lutyens. He ate them; they all ate them. I swear they will pay."

"Mandy, Mandy, hush. Sanjeev will come for me and Beth too. If they're afraid of you, just think what will happen when Beth comes." The speaker laughed a little.

"You're right, Meera. I'm all right. Not crazy, I'm pretty sure anyway. And I've wasted too much time thinking of ways to kill them instead of ways to escape. I wish she'd wake up. I want to know where she came from."

Tinsel rolled over. It sounded as if there were just the three of them. They must have killed the men in their group. One of the women was a strawberry blonde with freckles; the other had a long black braid that was unraveling. "I'm awake now. Where did you come from? And where are we?" She peered around, but the light was dim; it came from the walls.

"At last! Who are you?"

"We're in a ship; it's next to a mountain; I think we saw it before we landed. We thought it was a mountain too. I'm Meera Changat. We're from New Britain. How did that bastard catch you?"

"It was one of the ship people?! Damn. So they're out running amuck. I'm sorry about your people. I was with a little girl. I think she escaped. You haven't seen her?"

"No. There are just we three. And it was the sled dogs they slaughtered. Still, they were family," Meera told her. Amanda snarled, spittle dripping down her chin.

"I understand," Tinsel said. "It's a good thing Blindy got away with the ponies. I guess they're hungry, but they've lived all these years on the ship's supplies. I wonder if they've just now run out. If they've been living off each other or something..." Tinsel swallowed.

"Do you think they're saving us for dessert or ..." Tinsel decided she didn't want to go there.

"No," Meera said emphatically as if she'd been thinking about it for a long time. "If they'd wanted to kill us,

Mandy gave them plenty of reason. I think she'd have taken the bastard if he wasn't wrapped up in those furs."

"Just one of them took you?"

"Yes. He came up out of the snow and tipped the sled over, killed Falco first, or he might have taken him out. Then he killed a couple more and they were all tangled up in the traces; Mandy jumped him and knocked him down; I hit him with the whip stock. It was those thick wrappings. We could have taken him, I swear." Meera stopped.

"He was all in white," Amanda added, "hidden in the snow. He had to have been watching us and went ahead and burrowed in the snow along the trail he calculated we'd take. It was a straight line. Who'd have thought?!"

"Same here," Tinsel told them, "but how could he figure on ambushing us like that; he'd have to keep trying."

"Little powered saucer that skims the snow; he could keep trying as long as the power and his patience held out; and that's how he got us back to his ship. Tied us up and sat Mandy and me down, or he'd be dead meat."

"I couldn't get through his clothes either," Tinsel said. "Heck, I thought it was an animal. And then he hit me on the head."

"He'd learned his lesson from us," Amanda said. "I went after him in the ship when he took his robes off, but the others pulled me off. They've kept us tied up since then. I don't suppose you have a knife?" she asked hopefully.

"No, sorry; but you can bet after this I'll keep one in each boot." She stopped abruptly, wondering if there'd be a next time, but added, "I have friends and family. I think these people will be sorry. By the way, what kind of people are they? I haven't seen them close up. They're humanoids, aren't they?"

"Oh, I think so," Meera said softly.

"Ah. A long time in the ship with no out-crossings... Have you seen women? What about their language?"

Amanda laughed. "There are a few women, but mostly men, and the head woman, I think, tried to talk to us, but I kicked her. If she hadn't moved so quickly, I would have knocked her head against the wall."

"Waiting is a waste of time. I'll try to learn something of the language and look around the ship. Amanda, if you can stop kicking them, it might help."

"They've tied my feet together, but not Meera's," she said sullenly. "And I will kill them."

"Escaping is more important right now," Tinsel insisted. "When do they feed you?" Amanda growled low in her throat, and Tinsel realized that it'd be better if she didn't mention food again.

"They brought us something made of plants, I'm pretty sure," Meera contributed.

"Don't be upset, Amanda, but I'm going to talk to them." Tinsel waited for a reply, but Amanda began to cry, trying to bury the sound in the floor.

Not much later, a woman came in, and Tinsel suspected she'd been listening and waiting till they stopped talking. Tinsel looked up and smiled. The woman smiled too, but it was as if she knew why Tinsel had smiled and thought it funny. Still, she came and squatted beside Tinsel, keeping her distance from Amanda. "Hello, I'm Tinsel," she told the woman. "Why are we here?"

Amanda spat. The woman glanced at her, then at Tinsel. She considered Tinsel, her mist eyes steady, and then she loosened the bindings on Tinsel's feet and helped her up, leading her out of the small room into a brighter corridor when Tinsel felt able to walk.

Ladders ran straight up from what appeared to be the bottom floor of the ship. There were doors here and there all the way up, but the ladder didn't always reach them. Something to do with being on land or being in space, Tinsel speculated.

She was led outside where a group of the humanoids were gathered on a deck; it was warm underfoot, and they weren't wrapped up. They were short, thin, pale, and lightly clothed, but they didn't look weak or filthy. That meant the ship was more than just a cave. The deck looked metallic, and the warmth obviously came from the ship through some connection.

Tinsel straightened up and attempted to look confident. "My name is Tinsel Ree," she announced. She'd keep her last name in reserve; no need to give them a tool to use against the leader of the colony.

Her companion spoke even more confidently. "Tharp," she said and pointed to herself. She called one of the men over and pointed to him. "K'halfar." The man's name had a click. The woman's didn't.

Another man pushed his way through a group of watchers. He walked with a limp, and his face was scratched. Ah, Mandy's work, she guessed. "V'lancil," she said sharply.

Was he a gatherer or have ambitions for a harem? No need to be polite to the bastard. She looked meaningfully at his knee, and he shifted back hastily. Tharp smiled slightly and led Tinsel to a long table, where she motioned her to sit down, before leaving to go back into the ship. She returned with a bowl of what looked like soup. Good thing I filled up on fish, Tinsel thought, feeling sick and shaking her head violently.

Tharp frowned, then stirred up the soup with a small spoon, showing her the ingredients. Looked liked vegetables; they probably had hydroponics in the ship; that helped explain their survival over the years. Tinsel hesitated. Worth the gamble to show a willingness to join the group?

Then V'lancil joined them, flinging a piece of meat onto a plate. Tinsel straightened and flung the soup into his face and grabbed the plate and hit him with it. She was clambering over the table to kick him when strong arms grabbed her and handed her to Tharp. Then K'halfar knocked V'lancil across the deck.

Now that was promising, Tinsel thought, and moved to join the attack, but found herself held in a grip as tight as the man's. Tharp was no weakling. And everyone else mostly watched curiously, though a few laughed. More promising, Tinsel decided. Fortunately the kidnapper and dog butcher was not in charge.

After V'lancil slunk off, muttering, Tinsel shook herself slightly, and when Tharp let her go, moved back to the table and picked up the soup dish, which was still in one piece. Metal perhaps. Tharp didn't hesitate; she refilled the bowl, showing Tinsel the pan it came from. Tinsel dipped her spoon into the soup and tasted it; she was relieved to find that it tasted pretty much like a potato casserole. Then she started on learning their language, and Tharp encouraged her. She was probably relieved that Tinsel wasn't as hostile as Amanda and Meera, Tinsel figured.

Tharp worked willingly with her, but only for an hour or so each morning, as eager as Tinsel to communicate; then she turned her over to Nemi, a slight woman with short blonde hair that was more of a fuzz than strands. There was apparently a lot for Tharp to do around the ship; someone often waited nearby for her attention. Tinsel was returned to Meera and Amanda's room each night – to sleep, Nemi said; there was a good chance that was the word, anyway. And there were toilet facilities next to their little room; Tharp untied them one at a time to make use of them.

Tinsel observed each person she met carefully, planning to take back all the info she could. Nemi's eyes were pale blue, unlike Tharp's green/gray ones; and Tharp had muted red hair. So, hair color seemed to be pale blonde or red of varying shades. Eye color ranged from pale blue to blue/gray to green/gray. Not a lot of differences among them, probably due to their being marooned on an unfriendly planet. None were taller than Tinsel's 5'6"; Tharp was the tallest and possibly the oldest woman, as tall as the men, with no sign of gray in her hair. Maybe that wasn't a sign of age with them though. Onersh had said that they'd crashed, but the ship stood upright, resembling the mountain next to it. A planned landing perhaps, but they had certainly been stuck here. She wondered if the domes had "crashed" the ship. Tim had said they were adamant about the Bluzzies not leaving to carry any word of the planet.

Her thoughts were interrupted by Nemi touching her arm. Tinsel smiled brightly, pushed her silver blonde hair away from her face and tried to show her eagerness to comply with whatever Nemi wanted of her. Nemi led her to the deck table stacked with dirty dishes, which they gathered up, and led her into the ship and to a kitchen on that level. A kitchen! Dishes!! But Nemi showed her how to fit the dishes into slots in a wall cubicle, pulled down a cover, hit a button, and the cubicle began humming. Sonics. This ship, despite being stuck on Sphinx, was apparently working fine. Next, Nemi led the way up a ladder, which was easier to climb than it looked. It shifted into stairs as they ascended.

Following Nemi closely, Tinsel caught a growing smell of damp and vegetation. Soon she was in the hydroponics garden she'd theorized about. It spread into the distance, and she could only vaguely see the high ceiling, towards which some plants here and there towered. A feathered orange head peeked at her from behind a ferny plant, then vanished.

Nemi touched her arm again to get her attention. "Tinsel. My name is Tinsel," Tinsel said. "What do you want me to do, Nemi?" She thought she had the pronunciation right.

Nemi took her to an area where plants were covered with fruit. Well, maybe it was fruit; and they began harvesting. Baskets were stowed in cupboards along the one empty wall. Tinsel worked diligently, filling baskets with brightly colored purple fruit, pale green knobby fruit, red fruit that tended to squish if you weren't careful, and small gray berries. She talked as she worked, though Nemi rarely responded. "I want to trade my belt for a basket," she said, showing the belt to Nemi, who examined it thoughtfully before leaving to get more baskets. I really do want one of these baskets, she thought. I think they're made of leaves or maybe bark. Plants are used for everything here; she'd already learned to use a spongy one for washing. She spilled a little fruit from the basket she was examining, and as she stooped to pick up the dropped fruit, she glimpsed someone coming up behind her.

Even as she turned, her arms were grabbed and pulled back behind her, and she was forced to the floor. She kicked out and rolled over, but that was what he wanted. V'lancil! Where was Nemi? Was this a setup?! Then she saw Nemi running towards them, though suddenly she turned and fled. Tinsel braced a foot against a hydroponics tank and tried to free at least one arm to grab for a basket of fruit; it was the only thing she could reach to hit him with.

But Nemi was back, holding a vining plant; V'lancil cringed away, but Nemi shoved the plant against his face, and it began spreading. Tinsel was shocked at the speed with which the plant covered his body, which fell to the floor, where it straightened out and twitched. Nemi bent over him when he lay still and brushed his face with a short orange feather. The vine reluctantly moved away from V'lancil's mouth, nose, and then his pale blue eyes staring straight up.

One of the orange lizard-like creatures approached V'lancil, whimpering; it tried to climb on his chest, and a tendril grabbed it, but as quickly withdrew. Nemi picked the unhappy creature up and soothed it; then she put it on her shoulder where it perched, its tail curling around itself as if for comfort. Nemi hesitated, looking down, then she looked at Tinsel.

"Come," she said. That was one of the words Tinsel was pretty sure of, and she followed Nemi back to the small compartment she shared with her companions.

"He's not like the others," Meera said thoughtfully, "but they tolerate him."

"They don't seem to be violent, except for him," Tinsel said. "Really!" in response to Amanda's snort of disbelief.

"Why won't they let us go?" Amanda demanded.

"Afraid, maybe, because we didn't get off on the right foot." Amanda snorted and sniffed.

"I don't know! I need to know more so we can talk."

The next morning Tharp came for her and led her up the ladder to a higher room. She pointed to an enclosed hammock; V'lancil floated in it. A plant with white, saucer-shaped blossoms sat on his chest in a shallow basket. "He sleeps," she said.

Three days later, as they were finishing lunch on the deck, one of the men came to Tharp, spoke quickly and pointed away from the ship. Tinsel watched Tharp, who stared at her, biting her lip. Tharp wasn't uncertain often, Tinsel thought. She stood up and took Tharp's hands in hers. "Friends," she said. She'd been working on friendship whenever she could. Also family; and she had learned, she was almost certain, that K'halfar was Tharp's son. Tharp was the leader; men and women were equal; and they were uncertain about V'lancil's forays, though they hadn't stopped him.

Tharp didn't hesitate; possibly she'd been prepared for this. "Friends," she repeated.

"I want to go home," Tinsel said. "And my friends must return to their people too. We can talk and trade and visit. And we can be friends." She'd been trading pieces of clothing for utensils and anything she could think of – she'd started with a basket – both to study and to teach the concept.

Tharp glanced at K'halfar, and Tinsel suspected what was in her mind. Her son's wants were most important to her. He'd been attentive, though not pushy, and ready to learn her language, which was a point in his favor. Reddish hair and a clean cut face were also in his favor. She was beginning to get used to the nose like a knife edge and almost non-existent eye brows. As for the rest, she hoped that someone would do the exploring first.

K'halfar studied her hard for a minute; finally, he turned his back on her and went into the ship. Tinsel turned to Tharp. "I hate to leave my friends," she said (she'd used V'lancil to teach the concept of hate); but it is time for my people to prepare for harvest. (She'd used that word several times when picking the fruit.) They need my help."

Ah, slow movement at the ship's entrance. K'halfar had returned with Amanda and Meera, who were escorted by two women; he kept at a safe distance. And there was a little boy, the first child Tinsel had seen. That was a hopeful sign. Fresh women weren't essential to the ship perhaps. The biologists would enjoy wrestling with that, she thought.

K'halfar skirted the two prisoners, bringing the boy to Tinsel. "Kasai," he said, and then pointing at what the boy held tightly, "thwit." It was one of the colorful creatures that she'd spotted skittering around the ship, whistling in alarm when she approached, and disappearing up the ladder or through doors. They looked like feathered lizards and had prehensile tails. This one was scarlet and bright yellow, covered in a downy fuzz. It looked smaller than the thwits she'd seen. Possibly a baby?

K'halfar took her hands gently and opened her fingers and pulled her palms towards the creature. The boy held back, lips tight, obviously reluctant, so that Tinsel pulled her hands back. "No," she said firmly. "I will not take his pet."

K'halfar spoke sharply to the boy and turned him towards Amanda. Now the boy was truly reluctant. He didn't move so that K'halfar picked him up and placed him in front of Amanda and pulled his hands out towards her. The boy hunched protectively over his pet.

Meera shifted uneasily. "What's wrong?"

Tinsel answered sharply, "You had more time than I did to learn their language and their ways! I think they're offering you repayment for your dogs. I think that if you wish, you can take the boy's pet and kill it. Even eat it if you like." She clamped her lips tight on the thought.

Amanda moved tentatively forward. "No, Mandy," Meera said sharply. "You can't do that. You aren't cruel. And you're not like them. Remember that if you can't think of anything but revenge."

Tinsel shifted closer. The ship's inhabitants' actions had taken her by surprise. She certainly didn't agree with what they were apparently doing, but she saw that they wanted contact. Or at least with help coming for their prisoners, they were doing what they could to ameliorate the situation; at this point she wondered why they hadn't cut V'lancil's throat or delivered him to Amanda. In any case, a boy and his pet shouldn't suffer because of political expediency. If she had to tackle Amanda, she would. And the rescuers would arrive upon an interesting scene.

Meera moved forward and said gently, "If someone had hurt Falco in front of you when he was a puppy, how would you feel? This is a puppy, like Falco was."

Amanda crossed her arms tightly across her breasts. "Ugliest little puppy I ever saw," she said with a sob.

***

Below, the would-be rescuers had stopped not far from the towering ship. "I think that snow went from powder to gas without passing water," Derrick said.

"Funny you should mention that," said Tim. "The fire from that weapon nearly caused me to melt-down. I never suspected they had armaments like that. We've been thinking cavemen in a metal cave."

"Look up there," called Sanjeev. He'd made a run for the ship and been pinned beyond the sleds. He was surrounded by a melted area that went all the way to the ground. Tim planned to examine it later if he could. Meanwhile they'd been waiting here almost three hours.

As the rest of their party looked up, they saw an open elevator descending; it was crowded with men and women. Tim recognized Tinsel's blue coat. "It's Amanda and Meera," Sanjeev called out, prudently remaining where he was.

The ship folk escorted the three women to the sleds; Sanjeev moving along beside them.

"Hi, Tim," Tinsel said. "Where's Blindy?!"

"She's not with you?!"

"No. Okaaay. I'm pretty sure she escaped. I was afraid she'd try to rescue me by herself, but she's smart enough to get reinforcements. I'm sure we'll see her soon. Really. I just can't believe she's not here yet." Then she turned to Tharp. "This is Tharp. I believe she's in charge. They're letting us go. I think they'll want to trade and, uh, stuff."

The Terrans put their weapons away, but they didn't relax until they were all safely home. "That went better than I expected," Tinsel said then. "It could just as easily have turned into a fire fight, and they had the advantage here."

***

At Home Dome, Blindy watched the unfolding happenings with Shane and Tinsel's uncle. They were waiting to hear the latest news. Onersh's eyes had found the dog sled and Tim and the ponies and were transmitting video and audio. Fortin's eyes were at the space ship, and almost everyone had switched their attention from the rescuers to the ship.

"I knew I should have gone!" said Blindy. She planned to as soon as she could.

"Gridlock," yelled Carlos Lochner, turning from one holograph scene to the other. "It's gridlock!! I swear I've never seen so many people on an empty planet!"

Shane looked at his sister. "You got the ponies safely home. They knew the danger, I think. They certainly took the bits in their teeth and ran like hell."

"I'd like to get my hands on those little creatures, the thwits" said Mack Dennis, a biologist.

"I don't think so," Carlos said sharply. We don't know enough about them, nor do we know if they hoped that we'd bring them into the domes. They could be vermin or spies. Oh, yes. Now we have to learn more about them. Tinsel got that right," he added proudly. "But we'll do it on our terms and not on our turf."

"I bet Blindy and I could talk to their kids," Shane said thoughtfully. "We'd take some eyes and really check out the ship. We could slip an eye or two in our pockets, and they'd never notice."

"That's assuming too much, Shane," Sherry said out of thin air. She had an audio hook up from Threesh's dome. "Their technology is damn good, or they wouldn't have survived on a frozen planet as long as they did. I want to take a look at it."

Carlos nodded; then realizing she couldn't see him, said, "That's a priority, Sherry. I just wish you weren't our only technician. Oh, I know you're training Tammi, but we need more in the way of schooling. I think Tim's idea of setting up Fortin as a school is a good one. I want all the domes under our control – I hope you know what I mean, Onersh. You all are in control of your own domes, but I don't think any of us want other people – from New Britain or the ship or whomever else is bound to turn up – trying to take over. If we're established here – and so far we've had a good working relationship – I think we'll all be safer. We did help rescue Threesh's dome."

He waited uneasily for a reply. He'd never mentioned that more technicians would arrive from Earth, per his group's plan; now he had to think of something for them to do. They couldn't dismantle the domes, which had been more or less their plan. The domes would never allow that; they might even be tempted to wipe them off their planet. Hell, how could he have ever thought that colonizing a planet while exploring for ancient technology to exploit would be easy?

***

With their robotic eyes everywhere, the Domes watched everything with fascination. "Not boring anymore," said Fortin, "and I get to have the school. We'll learn a lot and maybe teach them some things." The others agreed.

"Maybe we can get them to trade for some dogs," Onersh added. "Blindy says that puppies are cute, and she'd love to have one for her own. She said the cleaning robots would be good for when they were little." They all agreed again. "And maybe some thwits; they're interesting, and though Lochner had a good point about them being a problem for them, they won't be for us." A little robot skittered by at Threesh's dome. "Not for us," they said. They'd been created to absorb new cultures and languages; they'd even switched their original numbers to English variations.

Then Onersh replied for all four domes, including Twoosh, who was eager to be more involved with the newcomers. "We are partners, and will share in what is to come." The domes liked the concept of partners, though their creators had not planned them that way. And they were armed with a lot more than eyes and robots.

DARKLINGS IN THE GLOW

Copyright © 2014 by Sterren

DARKLINGS IN THE GLOW

By

Sterren

Faelan of the Ruby Moon

A new scent came coursing with the breeze. Unfamiliar and unsettling, filling the night with strange moods. The air was still brittle with frost and layers of snow draped the forest trees.

Ettenar stood motionless like one of the limbs of the towering cypress, a very small limb compared to the massive trunk and flared-out branches. It had been a long winter with blizzards and winds that cut to the bone. At the moment, everything seemed quiet, the storm fading to gasps of breath after two days of sweeping fury. He clutched his arbalest, reassured by the warm, steady throb of its power nubs. There it was again, a fleeting sense of alarm, like claws harping on his strings of instinct. Instinct that ran deep in the veins of the Faelan, that, especially on a night so deceptively peaceful but with sinister elements riding the air, raked his nerves to act.

He raised his head to look at the cloudless sky, a matte black edged with dark-blue swathes. A perfect night to cuddle with a mate by a roaring ringfire and sing to the crimson moon.

Ettenar bristled with sudden awareness so sudden that it went like an electric spark through his crop of mane, making tufts of it stand on end. *It was the moon.* For a heartbeat, for one pinch of a nerve, it was an ashen moon that had hung there in the sky, a sickly pallor of disease and not the vibrant pulse of blood.

Swinging his arbalest back into the holster he turned and hurried to where he had parked his destrier in the forest, the metallic glow of its energy cells still strobing around the encircling darkness despite the freezing cold. With just a wave of his hand the vehicle sprung into motion and sped away, its cutting speed causing the hoarfrost that had sheeted the trail to crackle and snap. If he was younger he would have used the power skates and ice scythes of the younger Shikars and taken a more adventurous route through dell, brush and thicket.

Ettenar was a retired Shikar now and chose to take things in his stride.

Skirting a frozen lake, Ettenar paused and watched the reflection of the moon in the glassy surface of the water; the glowing ruby in the sky often invoked on by the Faelan race to lend them strength and other favours. For him it was a symbol of home and a menace was now lurking on its doorstep.

Was the phenomenon he had glimpsed a trick of some errant moonlight? Or was *it* happening again – the emergence of a fallow moon and the subsequent seepage of a foul substance completely contrary to the Faelan's clean energy of the Blue. His cube buzzed and cupping it into his hand he consulted it briefly. Through the snowdrifts and the black outlines of the copse he could see the glint of lamps behind the windows of his cottage. Bright lights. He wasn't expecting visitors but he knew why they had come. He spurred the nodes of his destrier and it bounded away, fleeting along the grit path that wended through the thicket.

Before the porch of his cottage, other destriers and sleighs had cut grooves in the snow and there were many of them coming and going. Bracing himself, he coded his destrier to find a spot in the parking barn, then palmed the gilded panel for the door to open.

***

The ceiling and wall glow pads were a blaze of lights and colours in his living room; the young Shikar Artopati was being confronted by a group of visitors. Ettenar was Artopati's mentor and he had given free access to the young breed whenever he needed the cottage, which was equipped with a monitor station. Often, in his mentor's absence, Artopati would receive guests, but not at this late hour of the midnight moon. And not often as high-ranking a visitor as the Chieftain of Security.

The mood was sombre and tension prevailed, judging from the tight knots of people whispering heatedly. Artopati stood pensively in the corner, fingering his personal cube. To all appearances he was being ignored which only meant that he was in truth ignoring them. He gave a flicker of reaction with a twitch of his black sleek eyebrows when he caught sight of Ettenar striding into the room. A warning glinted in his pale blue eyes.

Sure enough. "Well, Ettenar, there you are. Back from your hike in the woods?" The Chieftain's voice, heavy with snarls, sent a shudder through the clustering whisperers and with sullen faces they broke apart. "What is your opinion?"

"Opinion?" Ettenar hoped he sounded non-committal.

"This," the Chief drawled, extracting with deliberate slowness a transparent pouch filled with blue marbles from his pocket, "Blue pocket energy. Stun grenades, if you like, or useful flares. One is enough to light up a whole forest."

Hand-held bombs of energy, what next? Ettenar kept a straight face. "And this is what this late night assembly is about? Can't we wait till morning? The new day brings freshness to the mind."

"There is another reason why I am here at this late hour," the Chief said, "rumours are circulating about a strange sighting. Merely rumours at this stage."

"And another reason to corroborate my data," Ettenar fenced off with an air of absentmindedness. "Tomorrow I will advise you, all of you, as to what my opinion is."

With that he walked out of the room. By the door he half-turned and said audibly for all to hear, "Shikar Artopati, if you have a moment to spare, I'd like to have a word with you."

Suddenly the focus of so many pairs of burnished eyes, Artopati fumbled for words. He muttered a string of excuses and hastily padded after his mentor who briskly walked down the hallway with hands clasped behind his back. Ettenar took the lift to the basement where he had his study and not a word was exchanged between the two as the older Faelan seemed to lapse in deep ponder, leaving Artopati struggling with his own thoughts.

The study was only dimly lit with a hanging light spruce. Nevertheless, there was ample illumination from the rows of image cubes and command dice, great and small. The smaller cubes had their secretive lenses fixed on the group of dwindling visitors in the living room, some still persisting in a gesturing debate. Looking at the bigger cubes that hung from a central fixture in the ceiling, Artopati at once understood why Ettenar had taken him into his private den. The cubes showed a display of the shifting images of the moon from red to fallow and to red again.

"So, it's true. It wasn't just a figment of my instinct."

"So, you've witnessed the sighting too?"

Artopati nodded. "I couldn't tell for sure what I saw. Even instinct has a way of playing with your senses."

"Yes," Ettenar said languidly, "the more intelligent we've become, the less we trust our instincts. You should take heed on the tugging of your instinct, young Shikar, because these shiftings of moonglow couldn't have just started tonight. It may have begun a few moons ago; it has happened before."

"But," Artopati protested faintheartedly, "if it had happened a few nights ago, I would've noticed it on my patrol."

Ettenar licked his lips. "Perhaps. If your mind is focused on your patrol. But your focus has been wandering lately. Am I not right? The moon will be full and bright red as freshly spilt blood during this season. Especially for the young, an instinct older than intelligence is riding the scent in the wind. The ancient call of mating." A spark seemed to escape from Ettenar's deep-green eyes, causing Artopati's whiskers to tingle with embarrassment.

Ettenar waved an impatient hand. "I shouldn't be too stern on you, young breed. I was young once too." He sighed and gestured to the chandelier of cubes. "Returning to the subject, what you have perceived tonight is neither a warping of a heated mind nor a figment of a demented one." He waved his cube. The phenomenon has been observed by others as well who have secretly reported to me. It is true. The fallow moon is rising again after so many years and action is called for. Determined action and not some madcap experiment with Blue Energy marbles."

"I want to help," Artopati said earnestly, "and I have good friends among the Shikars who may want to join too."

"I know about your cabals" Ettenar said, raising his grizzled eyebrows, "but for now I need only you." He turned to the central cluster of cubes, his burning gaze riveted solely on the still, blown-up image of the fallow moon. "I wish with all my instinct that it is not so. But the evidence is bright and clear. The bridge is opening again and black rain is coming."

"Black rain?"

"Go home, young Shikar. Tomorrow, we will talk again. I will have to request a consultation meeting with Grimbald."

Artopati complied without saying another word. He knew from experience that Ettenar would brook no hesitation. What's more, the mere mention of the legendary Grimbald was enough to ruffle any young Shikar's mane. The lift brought him up from the basement and he stood in the now dimly-lit parlour. The visitors had left. Where before the cottage was filled with heated voices in debate, there was a waiting quietness. Standing outside, buttoning his jacket against a stiffening breeze, he gazed pensively at the clear purple sky. It was a full Faelan moon, ruby and glorious. He suppressed the age-old urge to throw back his head and howl his lungs out in homage to the magnificent sight.

Instead, he firmly took a grip on himself. Sunrise was only hours away. Ettenar had mentioned *black rain*. There were whisperings – something that might or might not have happened – so long before his birth that Artopati thought nothing more of it. He headed straight home and tried to temper what his mentor called an 'intemperate ancient instinct' and to not think too much of young females in oestrus.

***

The angry and impatient humming of the alarm dice shook Ettenar awake. It whirred with the lemon-yellow call color that was Artopati's.

"What's up?" he asked the image that shimmered out of the dice, his voice thick with sleep

"Sir!" Artopati's voice trebled with excitement, "you and I have been summoned to an audience with Grimbald!"

That stung his still-lethargic mind into full wakefulness. Grimbald was calling the shots so early in the morning. Something was clearly afoot.

"When is she expecting us?"

"Right now! We've been waiting for you outside!"

Ettenar jumped out of his bed. A ruckus of many voices talking all at once came from the front porch. A quick peek through the security lens attested to the fact that members of Artopati's unit were already assembled on his front lawn on a power sledge, all shouldering their arbalests at the ready, all hasty and growling to plunge mane over fang into whatever hideous mission Grimbald had planned for them.

Foregoing the refreshment of a steam douche, Ettenar flung on yesterday's crumpled outfit and stepped outside as the patrol greeted him solemnly with raised arbalests. Ettenar had a long service behind him and deserved such respect from the younger Shikars.

"We have to be on our way!" Artopati shouted

Barely had Ettenar strapped into his seat when the sledge lunged forward and flew over the road beam in a silvery blur. Artopati at the helm pushed the sledge to top speed. Hasty Pat, as they called him in jest, was now all the more vexed to hastiness to keep up the appointment with the legendary Sirdar of the Faelan Command.

This early in the morning, no other fleet took the road and the way was all theirs to occupy. Even if there were other traffic all would respectfully steer aside and allow passage to the Emblem of the Shikar.

The headquarters was situated in the basin of what was once an ancient crater in the heart of rank woodland. A fast-flowing river, now mirror-still in its frozen state, marked the boundary of the woodland, and they crossed a bridge in one swoop to lock on a pathway through the dense wood of fir. Artopati halted the sledge before the wall of interlocking tree branches.

The wall had no readily discernible gate or entrance but as Artopati traced an array of symbols on his command dice, the leafage parted. A wide paved roadway loomed just ahead of them, stabbing a white limb through the weaving shadows of the wood.

Artopati had never been summoned to the headquarters of the Command but he had obviously been made privy to the correct gestures and symbols of passage. He steered sledge and passengers confidently up the road towards the hidden bastion of the Command. Coming upon the three-tiered edifice, the party could not see any sentinels prowling about, but Ettenar was convinced there were many eyes watching them from the forest of fir and spruce all around.

"Did you see it?" One of the young breeds gasped.

"What is it?" Artopati, out of reflex, slowed down the sleigh.

"Don't stop," Ettenar said, raising himself slightly from the seat and tapping Artopati on the shoulder, "they've always been here."

"The shaman spirits!" the young Shikars whispered in awe.

The young breeds who had not ventured before into the Hallowed Valley, were getting a glimpse of them for the first time. To their inexperienced eyes they appeared like fleeting phantoms at first, streaks of green and blue and sometimes misty sparks of silver flickering in and out of the tangles of trees and brushwood. Then as eyesight sharpened, tracing out the sharper outlines from the dimness, they were seen as fast-moving shapes running like wild creatures, sprinting in their glow of mystery, Blue Energy untamed.

Artopati halted before the massive portals which opened without a sound upon the flashing symbols on his dice. Sound came nevertheless; a low sudden keening from the forest, the calling of the shaman. The young breeds, much awed by this uncanny phenomenon, jerked about gripping their arbalests when, upon entering, two viperbats swooped down from alcoves hidden in the foggy sky-high ceilings and took deep and intense sniffs of their credentials all in a matter of few seconds. The frenzied inspection left those Shikars who had never set foot in the Headquarters breathless and apprehensive of what lay in store down the corridor.

The chrome-tiled floor began to subtly vibrate and before they knew it, the strip of floor they were standing on began to glide forward, through tall archways, passing walls adorned with the heraldry and trophies of the High Command. While the others stared around at the decor of Headquarters, hungrily taking in all the tokens of past glory, Artopati firmly stood in front twirling and flashing his dice and Ettenar stayed close behind him, absorbing the imposing interior that he had seen only twice in his lifetime silently.

Through a set of tall doors that yawned open upon their approach, the moving walkway ushered the party into the centre of the meeting room. There were only two present; Grimbald and the Chieftain of Security.

Sirdar Grimbald observed the party of Shikars in intense silence. She was not of the typical sinewy and tall stature of the Faelan with their two-tone sweep of mane. Hers was cut short and she wore a kilt instead of riding breeches. Though of average height, she was a most imposing Faelan who drew instant respect from her subordinates.

"Which of you is Shikar Artopati?" she asked.

There was a pause during which no one seemed to breathe. Then, Artopati stepped forward; his stony outward appearance gave nothing away of his pounding heart.

"I am he."

Grimbald served him a quick surveying glance. "Tell us what you saw last night."

Artopati threw Ettenar a quick look but his mentor seemed preoccupied with his personal cube. The Shikar then staunchly faced the Sirdar and put his experience in as clear and brisk terms as he could, without stammering, leaving out his sense of dread and foreboding. When he was finished, Grimbald turned her fine-boned face to Ettenar.

"Elder Ettenar, can you corroborate the phenomenon that Shikar Artopati saw last evening was the same you had seen sixty years ago?"

"That a fallow moon seemed to transplant our brilliant ruby moon?" He paused. "Yes, it did so happen and it was not a passing phase of hallucination."

"Then explain what this phenomenon means?"

A deep frown settled on Ettenar's face. "It signifies an alignment of openings to other worlds, and proof that something is happening on the other side of the fallow moon; something that is causing the barriers to shift and a bridge to appear."

"Sixty years ago there was some discussion about a breach of dimensions," the Chieftain said in his drawl, "but there was not even an exhaustive report made, let alone an investigation."

"Because it was hushed up," Grimbald interjected sharply, "The rationale was then not to start a panic and there had been no serious incidents ever since, although there was an incursion made and you were part of it, weren't you, Ettenar?"

Ettenar nodded gravely. "Yes, I was Shikar then. And the incident was more pronounced and not as dubious and vague as it manifested last night. It seemed that in the past it had been a cataclysmic event, yet now it bears a more

surreptitious sense. In the past it was like an explosion. We
were unprepared and we had to learn how to deal with it. Now,
we should be prepared—." Ettenar paused. They stared at him
in heavy suspense. "But we are not."

"What do you mean, we are *not*?" The Chief exclaimed,
"We have our Blue Energy!"

"That you carry around in pouches." Ettenar glared. "Is
that now the way of the Faelan to hunt; to blow your prey to
pieces with pocket-sized nuclear bombs?"

A brief uproar erupted with voices rising in pitch,
exclamations of disbelief and outrage. Grimbald raised her
gauntleted hand and in the hush that fell, said, "There was
something else. The spill of Black Rain. Unclean energy
finding its way to our world through a dimensional gap caused
by the apparition of a fallow moon. Is that a fact, Elder
Ettenar?"

Ettenar merely nodded. He felt a rising dread of what
the Sirdar was going to say next.

"It calls for a preemptive strike," she stated, "and those
marbles will be our weapons."

"You plan to send our Shikars through the gap on a
mission of destruction?" Ettenar's voice was calm with a low
undertone of indignation.

"You did it before, Elder."

"On a mission of reconnaissance, nothing more."

"There was a battle."

"It was a skirmish. This time you intend to order our
Shikars to wage war."

"A war that we will win because, in your own words,
the creatures on the other side won't stand a chance against our
Energy of the Blue. It is deadly to them."

Unleash our atoms of destruction. "Is there no other
way?'

"What do you mean *other way*? It is the *only* way to
safeguard our realm," the Chieftain snarled.

The Sirdar held up her hand once again. "What do you suggest we do, Elder Ettenar?"

Ettenar simply said, "When the red and the ashen overlap it means the bridge is open; I shall pass through and consult with an old friend on the other side."

"A *friend*?" Grimbald echoed, "there was no mention of a friend."

Ettenar twisted out a sly grin, "For the simple reason that I did not report her. Why not? Since the incident, the Imperium passed an edict that all those beings beyond the bridge were enemies because they caused the spillage of the Black Rain. You would have labelled her as one of them. But she is not."

"Who are those beings that live across the bridge of moons?" Artopati couldn't hold himself back.

"Humans," Ettenar said, "and my friend was a young girl then, wounded terribly in body and spirit. That was sixty years ago. She will be a woman now. I must find her again. If she is still alive. He added in a sad afterthought. "Anna is her name."

"If she is still alive?" Grimbald stressed. "What if she is not?"

"Then there is nothing holding us back from setting off our blue marbles." The Chief swaggered forth in his creaking leather boots and faced the unit of Shikars. "We have here one of our finest teams and they have a stalwart young breed as their leader. I have no doubt they will accomplish their mission with success."

So, this is how it will be. Pitting pupil against master. Seeing how eagerly they gripped their arbalests with fire shining in their eyes, Ettenar knew that neither wise words nor drastic deeds would dissuade the unit.

He calmly stated, "Sirdar Grimbald, allow me to take part in this mission as well. I know the outlay of the Black Rain source."

"I was hoping you would say so," Grimbald said, waving to silence the excited chatter of voices, "no one can accomplish a mission without a seasoned guide. You shall go with them."

On one condition. And you, Sirdar, had better agree with me or the whole community – the whole realm will know what we encountered on the world of the fallow moon sixty years ago. That which I swore to protect.

Under The Grey Moon

It is happening again. The twinning of the moons. One of ashen face. The other one red, a magnificent ruby beckoning with all the force of its mystery.

I didn't expect I would live to see it again. The thought went round and round through her mind like a gerbil on its carousel. *Is there another accident? Another blowout of poison in the air?*

Anna chuckled to herself as she bent to pick up a branch and added it to the weight on her back. That poison was a godsend. It had liberated her in more ways than one, while others of her kind had been smitten by diseases that the poison cloud had brought. *Sixty years ago.*

Sixty years earlier she had been in a coma. They didn't expect her to live, not the people in the hospital, not the people of the town. A vicious blow to the head had caused it, a blow delivered by her father who later claimed he couldn't remember beating his daughter. That night he had looked upon the world through a liquor-generated haze as poisonous to his mind as the poison air that would come later.

She had awoken a month later, seeing the world through shades of her changed mind. She could speak but, to the doctors and nurses, her speech was without rhyme or reason. Their verdict: *'word salad'* coming out from the lips of a damaged mind, a darkling mind. Nevermind what they were saying. *Her reality* though her morphed eyes was that the world had changed for the better. She could see what others couldn't. She could sense their twisted thoughts. But she could remember even less. Talk about her parents: who were they? Rumours about a neglected home: where was it? But she could sense the underlying emotions of creatures, of animals, around her.

The accident that day sixty years ago had changed the world again. That particular morning, she had opened her eyes in the midst of the uproar and panic of evacuation. Nobody – the nurses, the doctors, the patients – heeded her; she was of least concern. They were all too aware of the nuclear reactor belching smoke and something even more poisonous than smoke. It was then that she had begun to see things she had not seen before. Walking outside, she could saw something in the smoke columns billowing into the sky. The spores of poison wafted like chaff finer than dust, invading in silent legions the bodies of the frenzied people milling around her. Will o' the Wisps with venom in their breath.

She didn't want to go where everyone was fleeing to; she hid in a closet.

When at last she thought it was time to brave the outside world again, she stepped into a desolation of utter abandonment. There was plenty of scattered clothing and provisions that she could help herself to, and unhurriedly took what she needed. On the streets, the silence was more profound, of a world gone dead completely. Where there was once the noise of vehicles and people, there was only the glare of bare walls and stark stretches of street.

The catastrophe had given her freedom; freedom to go where she pleased and do whatever she chose. The dense cloud of Will o' the Wisps seemed to pass her by. Others came to share her desolate habitat, other Darklings in No Man's Land. Wolves. The first pack of them came and went. Then other packs stayed and they became the family she never had, sharing their game and their hunt. One day, their howling brought Anna running out of her shelter, and in the night sky two moons made their dance macabre. She saw, as the wolves around her saw, the pale axle that seemed to connect the two wheels of moons, one ashen and one throbbing red.

Something, someone, had come through that shaft, one, two, no – a group of five. Five creatures in clothes that were foreign even to her warped mind; and of face so totally alien to her but not to the wolves. A howling roar went up from the pack – and all packs of wolves, it seemed, from the surrounding area – as the first creature set foot on the soil of the wasted land. Hearing that note of accord and affiliation, she had tipped her head and howled in unison. The foreign creatures howled in reply.

They were the Faelan from the world of the Red Moon. Clad in uniforms and brandishing arms of metallic crossbows, their eyes were of a burnished green and gold or smouldering amber, sharply chiseled nose and mouth, and braided manes which flowed from head to shoulders. They were a magnificent breed and they too carried with them their own Will o' the Wisps, which were of a glowing blue and whirled around their heads like halos. Shikar Ettenar was their leader and they came through the shaft to seek out the source of the twinning of the moons that had also appeared in their sky. And by her first howling she understood their speech and they hers, without the ignominy of word salad coming between them.

The Faelan soon traced the source to the site of the accident, the source of the canker that had blighted the air and imprinted the land with utter desolation. Side by side, Faelan, wolves and human girl had created a bond. They explored the ruins of the damaged reactor together and thought themselves safe from intrusion. Not for long – humans came back. Maybe the strange sighting in the sky had alerted them, maybe they had returned to find out if they could salvage the reactor. They came back in strange bulky clothing that protected them from the Will o' the Wisps in the atmosphere. They came back to hunt.

It was the pack of wolves who first fell to their bullets. The Faelan retaliated and to this day, no one of the outside world knew what really took place. That pack of hunters disappeared as if swallowed by the contaminated earth. The Faelan could not stay, as the bridge between moons started to fade and they didn't want to be stranded on this side.

For Anna it had been a bitter parting. She had felt close to their leader, Ettenar. Had there been a feeling of love? She had never felt love's sweetness until that time she howled in chorus with the wolves and the Faelan. "I am no longer one of them," she had said, wholeheartedly abandoning humanity.

"But you are," Ettenar had answered, "and you are vulnerable to the radiation you call Will o' the Wisps. We have Wills o' the Wisp too in my world and their strength is tenfold because they are our energy. The explosion of your nuclear reactor caused its energy to spill into our plane, hence the twinning of your moon and ours. But the effect is wearing off and we must go and close the gate. You must remain here with your friends, the wolves. I will protect you."

***

Ettenar had left, years had passed and she was here still, without having grown a second head or an extra warped limb, living off the land and forest that had slowly encroached upon the abandoned buildings. The wolves were still here and grown stronger than ever, roaming their new kingdom. As she approached her hovel, camouflaged by shrubberies and branches, she saw that her pack had congregated in the small clearing. They too had sensed foreboding riding on the wind.

Anna's joints were not as supple as sixty years ago and she had to sit in an armchair she had scavenged from a condo building to take a few moments of rest. If the twinning of the moons was to rematerialize this coming night, she knew where she had to be. The site of the old damaged reactor.

She had kept a great distance between her present habitat and that blotch on the face of the land, but on clear days from the top of a hill she could glimpse its ragged outlines. The Will o' the Wisps were still busy in the air, but they were waning year by year. Her fastness on foot had also slackened over time. It would be a strenuous hike but a trip she felt she had to make.

By midday she had filled a backpack with necessary supplies, while the pack waited outside patiently. She selected a strong staff for the hike, then looked around her with a sudden melancholy feeling. The hovel had been her secure shelter for all this time. The sight of the Red Moon last evening had made it less so. The phenomenon might have been sighted by others as well, others of her kind.

With the wolves padding before and behind her, she set off and sensed from the scent of the wind and the soughing of the wood that something was stirring. Soon enough, a sound she had not heard for a long time drifted in from afar. The drone of vehicles.

The wolves' movements became more cautious. They kept close to the rank foliage of the wood and the mere snap of a twig made their hackles rise. Their heightened sense of alertness was the barometer by which Anna steered her own actions. For years, outsiders had spurned this territory. Now with the thinning of the spores in the atmosphere, they were coming back in force.

How strong in force, Anna saw soon enough in the late hours of dusk, when floodlights punctured the pitch-darkness over the shattered reactor. There were trucks and a small army of personnel all in protective suits.

What are they doing and why are they here? She reached out with her hand seeking the comfort and security of warm fur but there was nothing to touch. She was suddenly aware that she was on her own. The wolves had left her.

A voice spoke in her mind. '*Anna.*'

"Ettenar, is that you?"

He came upon her as a swift, pale shadow from the deep darkness of the wood. No exuberant howling accompanied this reunion. It was a meeting of hearts and minds in secrecy as they observed the equally covert activity by the ruins.

Ettenar brought with him a small platoon this time. Younger-looking, and in the course of years, their uniforms had changed to a more sleek-fitting outfit. Their crossbow-like weapons, their arbalests, were likewise smaller, of fluid contours, pulsing with lethal warmth. There was one Shikar with the pale blue eyes of a husky who kept his keen eye on her. He was a handsome one but so was Ettenar sixty years ago, and though his mane was nearly all grey, his green-yellow eyes had not faded in sharpness.

"I am so glad you are still alive."

"I am an old hag now."

"And I am an old geezer by your speech."

They both looked up, to the pallid face of the moon on this side and if one looked hard and persistent enough, this moon seemed to have a reddish twin lurking behind from the cover of drifting clouds.

"As before we have to move fast, before the bridge fades away."

"What are you going to do?" Anna asked. Ettenar's voice had an undertone of ambivalence. He seemed to be burdened with a task that he had vowed to carry out but with great reluctance.

He pointed to the ruins below. "Those people there are investigating the old radioactive core. In the past when it exploded, a bridge was opened between our worlds. A bridge that we thought we took down. Now the bridge has reappeared. It must be connected somehow to what they are doing. We have to put a stop to it."

"How are you going to stop them?"

"By destroying it utterly."

"Destroy? Another accident? Another explosion?" While her mouth stumbled her mind leapfrogged over the implications of Ettenar's words.

"This is exactly our plan," said the young Shikar with the pale eyes, "we've brought our little tins of energy, our energy that will bring the whole structure down to dust." He showed her what they had brought hanging from his belt, pellets in a tin. He was not as gentle-hearted as Ettenar and certainly not a friend of her kind.

"What are they?"

"What you call nuclear bombs, just the size of marbles," Ettenar replied sombrely.

Anna sat down and crossed her legs. With her knuckles she rapped on her forehead. "There is a hole in my brain. I don't understand most things but I understand what your destruction means. It means an accident bigger than the one before. More people will die, my people."

"The people that left you here," Ettenar said, "who put that dent in your forehead. Your people. Who sowed these rogue Will o' the Wisps, contamination of the worst kind, that we cannot allow to cross the bridge to our realm."

Hard years of carving out a life by herself in the wilderness had also steeled Anna's fibre. For all the friendship and love she felt for Ettenar, on this matter she could not give in. Rising to her feet and leaning on her staff, she suddenly spoke to him and to all the Faelan, "You will sow your own clean energy, blue Will o' the Wisps. Scatter them far and wide. Energy so strong it can melt stones and bones. Everything will suffer and I will suffer. Do you want our deaths on your conscience, Ettenar…on the conscience of your people?"

There was a long pause. "No," Ettenar said, "there is another way."

The young Shikar took a step forward.

"Artopati," Ettenar said before the Shikar could state his objection, "you are in command of this mission. But Sirdar

Grimbald has given me the authority to make the final decision…to take the other way."

"And what is the other way?"

From under his short cape, Ettenar took out a cube. It was not the regular sized cube, a tool for many things, but more of a rectangular shape. From that piece of equipment he drew out a beam of energy that in seconds pulsated into a glowing creature, sleek and moving in a misty shine of green and blue.

"But Elder Ettenar!" Artopati exclaimed with indignation, "how can you bring our sacred shaman spirits into this world." The other Shikars fidgeted, in two minds what to do.

"This world has shaman spirits too. Look, they have come back to you, Anna."

The fire of many watching eyes glinted from the bracken. Anna began to slowly hum, summoning a male wolf who slunk towards her.

"This—this is unbelievable," Artopati stammered, "they have the shape of a shaman, but they're creatures of flesh and blood, big and coarse."

"They are wolves," Anna said, 'Darklings in the glow."

"And what I have projected here," Ettenar said, "are only copy elements of our shamans, but even as replicants they will serve their purpose. The purpose of *our* Will o' the Wisps. They will measure on the monitors of those humans yonder at least a thousand times stronger than the last accident."

"Will they harm the wolves?" Anna asked, looking at Ettenar with moist eyes.

A smile smoothed out the grimness on Ettenar's face. "The wolves have survived the radioactive contamination for sixty years and so have you. These quasi-shamans will just edge up the measuring counter of the personnel below so that they will leave the place in a hurry."

He turned to the Shikars. "You young breeds have come for some action but instead you are in for some stealth work; to infiltrate with caution and clean up the Will o' the Wisps here so they will not trigger again the opening of a bridge. And then you shall unleash the phantom shamans to maintain a high level of radioactivity. Shikar Artopati, do you see now that this is a better way than widespread destruction?"

"But this will be contravening the Chieftain's orders," one objected.

"The Chieftain can lift his leg up a stump," Ettenar growled and grinned acidly at their horror and shock. At home, this insult would have thrown him in the brig. But he was not at home now.

He clasped Artopati's shoulder. "Remember the old values of the Faelan," he whispered, "hunt but not rampant killing. Remember the nights we discussed the wonders of the cosmos, of other worlds. Listen to the sounds around you. Don't they have the same nuances as at home? What does your instinct tell you? *Life.*"

Artopati, who had lapsed in sullen silence, heaved a sigh. His fierceness gave way to grave resolve. "As you command, Elder. You have also taught me there are several ways to win a battle." He gave a brief gesture with his finger and like a smear of flowing moonlight, the platoon left the cover of the woods and spread out through the bushes toward the ruins. There was no sound of a firefight, but a few hours passed and the floodlights were dimmed, and then the trucks started to move away. Artopati's platoon returned to the woods and reported there were no casualties in their ranks.

Later, much later, Anna did learn that there were casualties on the human side, all attributed to a mysterious nature and proving once again that this no-man's land was still a no-man's land.

The wolf pack that had huddled with Anna moved out of the woods on the return of Artopati's platoon. By the shimmering of the two moons, one pale and one ruddy red, Anna and Ettenar both knew it was time to part ways once again and now for good.

"How I wish I could take you with me," Ettenar said, with his hands on Anna's shoulders.

"And grow a second head in your world?" Anna smiled. "I want to stay with the wolves here. We need each other. And as for you, I will remember you until my last breath. The wolf man who came from the shine of a red moon to give a hand in friendship to a little girl who can see things that others can't because someone shook up her brain."

Woman and Faelan embraced and with a blend of moonshine and starlight the Platoon of the Ruby Moon was gone.

Anna stood alone on the hilltop and with her twisted sight she could see the spirit wolves skulking around the area of the ruins like running streaks of moonshine. Wherever their random path took, they left a spoor of bluish glow in their wake. Blue clean energy of the Faelan. Through a break in the cloud cover, the pale moon shone and from afar came the cry of summons from a distant wolf pack, immediately answered by a howl from the pack at the foot of the hill.

Anna threw back her head and joined in the chorus of the wolves while, from the ruins, a keening rose. First wavering as an echo, then strengthening in crescendo, a warning and a proclamation that man is forever barred from the Darkling Kingdom in the Glow.

HOST

Copyright © 2014 by A. L. Scott

HOST

By

A. L. Scott

Host

It began with a generous offer. We had just sold our family pod in anticipation of our move to the Outer Domains and were looking for somewhere temporary to live while we awaited our exit date. When Jane Powell offered us to stay with her, we were sceptical at first. After all, who in this day and age offers almost-complete-strangers-with-a-toddler to move in with them?

Jane, a business associate of my husband's, was a professional socio-mind therapist and socialite. Her very public divorce 20 years earlier from her insanely-minted, pod-estate tycoon of a husband had virtually set her up for life. A lady of leisure if she so desired it, she instead preferred to keep her mind active and partook in the occasional freelance stint if it suited her. All that being said, she was a real dear; intelligent, big-hearted and funny.

Jane enjoyed the finer things in life, keeping fit and going out on the town; she knew everyone and everyone knew her. Perhaps, in a little cordoned off corner somewhere, I was a little jealous of her. Still, her invitation seemed genuine, so we asked her to lunch one Sunday to get to know each other better. Our little girl, Zoe, immediately took to her, and I must admit that I was quite taken with her myself. We had a lot in common and ended up chatting like old friends by the end of the day. We all let ourselves like her and after not much deliberation, decided to see what the universe had in store for us. We accepted Jane's kind offer.

Three weeks later, we had sold, given away or recycled the main bulk of our worldly possessions and were excited to be finally moving into the Central Dome, even if it was only for a short while. Jane lived in a multi-pod all by herself and had more space than she knew what to do with, especially since her own children had grown up and then moved on; we guessed she was glad for the company. Our gracious host had all the fittings we could possibly ever need, so apart from personal effects, we moved in light.

We took over the majority of the multi-pod's top level which was made up primarily of living quarters and washrooms. Level one housed the kitchen, which was just opposite Jane's treatment room, socialising spaces and recreation suite. The multi-pod boasted an expansive, egg-shaped glass construction that protruded from a glittering metal arm. The retractable arm extended towards the Central Dome's core allowing access to the public bays which, given the need to mingle, offered retro-style retail and communal outlets as opposed to the customary virtual variety available in individual home-pods.

Each pod was also equipped with artificial Schumann wave generators. Natural Schumann waves are beneficial electromagnetic waves that swing between the Earth and certain layers of the atmosphere. They have almost the same frequency as brain waves and help regulate the body's internal clock, affecting sleep patterns, hormones, and so on. Without the generators, at the high altitudes such as those of the bio-spheres, inhabitants would become distressed and disorientated, as Schumann waves are much weaker.

My husband, Rhys, and I looked forward to visiting one of the dining outlets; we figured we were good for credit and besides, it would be the first and last time we would have the opportunity to experience olde-worlde restaurant dining before we disappeared into the great unknown of deep space. We were hoping that the relationship between Zoe and Jane would develop enough to allow for the occasional baby-sitting session if the situation called for it.

Of an evening we, like most residents, detached from the Central Dome and plugged into its massive electromagnetic grid system, effectively rendering each home-pod a floating orb. It was truly a site to behold as from a distance the pods' internal lighting helped create the appearance of *fireflies*. I remembered reading about a particular forest on the east coast of Australia that celebrated the yearly Firefly Festival. People flocked to a specific clearing to await the nocturnal spectacular that ensued as part of the mating ritual of these tiny insects. I only knew about insects from my studies, as the bio-spheres were free from all fauna except for necessary domestic animals or livestock.

This feat of suspended engineering prowess was not down to outstanding technological progress in our time. Science finally decided that it was time to stop making fun of the *crackpots* wielding the dowsing implements and instead pay attention to what they were saying. They realised that harnessing Telluric currents, which flowed across the Earth's surface and existed as electricity in the form of extremely low frequency electromagnetic waves, had in fact been common knowledge within metaphysical circles for eons. Unfortunately, when our civilisation could have done with employing this kind of cleaner energy, power-hungry energy companies and their political backers had other plans that did not include saving the planet or passing monetary savings onto the individual.

The sea of pods bobbed gracefully above the Dome's sub-level garden oasis. Each bio-sphere devoted an entire level, usually the one closest to the Earth's surface, to agriculture in all its expressions. It constantly evolved in response to consumer supply and demand, and was home to all manner of wildlife, be it animal or plant. There was a farm which provided for the bio-sphere's inhabitants, a zoo that Zoe had already fallen in love with, and even an aquarium with adjoining simulated beach.

We had always wanted to visit the Central Dome but it was exclusively set aside for the sector's business and science aristocracy. Rhys and I had occupied a modest cell-dwelling within the vast honeycomb structure that was the Arts Dome, reserved for traders in the sensory and holistic healing arts. Surrounding the Arts Dome were a series of other such domes, each relating to a specific field, and all were connected to the Central Dome. These belonged to just one of the 12 huge bio-spheres that floated above the Earth's surface or just beyond the upper limit of its atmosphere in the exosphere.

I chuckled to myself whenever I indulged in a good old 21st century dystopian holo-film. They weren't far off the truth of our current reality. And as for the seemingly *utopian* society we were supposedly living in, I would take the life of 200 years ago any day.

The world had once again turned to traditional medicine; holistic healing methods gained more or less equal footing with *modern* medicine on account of amazing curative advances. That and the fact that the cost of modern medicine had eventually gone through the roof compared to its subsidised alternative. We had virtually unravelled the mysteries surrounding AIDS and cancer, which were part of a misguided secret government agenda to control population explosion, and at the same time test bacterial and viral warfare on the unsuspecting public. Only tiny pockets of the old third-world remained in quarantine back on the surface.

Nations stopped killing one another when the threat to humanity's ultimate survival superseded centuries of petty rivalry over fossil fuels, trade routes and religious affiliations. World governments united, national currencies merged into one fluent credit system, and three quarters of the planet's population moved into the bio-spheres. Even criminal activity was random. Those left on the surface were in some form of quarantine or confinement, or part of the scientific teams that were tasked with keeping tabs on planetary geology and safeguarding objects of cultural and historical significance.

There was plenty to live for up here but everything seemed so contrived from what it was originally that it made me wonder if we really were that much better off.

However, now that we had finally arrived, we intended to take full advantage of everything the Central Dome had to offer, including the over-abundance of fresh produce available

from the oasis. *No more simulated or rehydrated food for us!*
The holo-suite was another facility I was eager to experience;
the ability to recreate a scene from the imagination or memory
and interact within it could become addictive, so it was said.
Whenever she wasn't away, Jane was plugged in – she said it
was therapeutic.

Our life in the Central Dome began without incident
and was not unlike our usual routine back in the *hive*. Rhys was
a dream and regression analyst, and, like me, was able to work
remotely as most people did. I however, preferred old-
fashioned face-to-face contact and occasionally indulged in
personally visiting my clients. I was a visio-originator which
meant that the famous works of Anya South were prominently
displayed in all the leading holo-suites. Actually, in reality, I
was lucky if my designs made it onto the in-house home-pod
screens. Competition for imagination application was fierce, as
so much of our existence was synthetically generated.
Authenticity was a thing of the past.

∗∗∗

It wasn't until a few weeks into our time at Jane's that
things began to get complicated. The nature of Jane's work
meant that at certain times of the cycle we were restricted to
the top level of the multi-pod. The agreement was that when
Jane had clients we had to stay out of sight. But these instances
grew more and more frequent until we literally began to feel
trapped, not the best environment to be in with a vibrant and
curious two-year-old on the loose. Then there were the probing
looks from the neighbours on the rare occasions we stepped
out. It occurred to us that Jane hadn't alerted the Dome Council
of our presence in the Central Dome. When we quizzed her
about it she assured us that our temporary stay did not warrant
unnecessary attention from the authorities. She did, however,
add that we should endeavour to keep public appearances to a
minimum. That in itself should have set alarm bells ringing.

But it wasn't until the mysterious Dom appeared that things really began to change. We were told that Dom was a retired transportation magnate and a widower. Jane vaguely explained that his wife had died under unusual circumstances years ago. As far as we knew, Dom and Jane had been together for four years but parted ways before we moved in, although Jane was never sure about their official status. A well-to-do gentleman in his sixties, Dom's short-cropped white hair contrasted heavily against his bronzed, brawny physique. He wasn't altogether unhandsome but I really didn't understand what Jane saw in him. His most endearing quality was his brazen self-importance and he was evidently the centre of Jane's world. Whenever she knew he was paying her a visit, which was more often than not, she rushed about like a whirlwind making sure everything in the pod was to his liking, from properly-fluffed cushions to the very brand of tea he should like to take. And, naturally, we were relegated to the top level. Dom began to make it a habit of arriving at the pod late in the evening when he supposed we would be asleep, and then sneaking into Jane's room. It didn't give much credence to Jane's splitting up story, that was for sure.

We were frustrated with the situation, but bit by bit we got the impression that something else entirely had moved into the pod with us, and it seemed to follow on Dom's coattails. Strange noises would wake us up in the middle of the night, apart from the usual arguing that went on whenever Dom was over – another thing that didn't make sense. We also swore we heard deep guttural murmurs and scratching-scraping sounds that didn't seem to have a source. Zoe had not slept peacefully since Dom's arrival and would wake us with her frantic cries. She never woke up during these episodes, but thrashed about, sobbing unintelligibly into her pillow. It often took hours to calm her. Whenever Jane stayed at Dom's, however, Zoe's sleep was uninterrupted.

One evening, Rhys and I were up late chatting in our room when we heard Jane come in from a night out. Judging by all the banging coming up the hall we assumed she was drunk. She disappeared into her room and all was quiet. At 3am we were woken to the sound of more banging and what sounded like growling. Listening harder, we realised that Jane was speaking to someone.

"You can't keep treating me this way! She hissed. "This is not how a relationship works." Quiet murmurs. "What I do in my time is my business – leave me alone!" Silence. We figured Jane was arguing with Dom again but was it really necessary so early in the morning? We fell back to sleep.

The sound of furniture being thrown downstairs woke us up at 6am, along with a male voice shouting. It was Dom.

"You can't just play happy families, Jane. You need help!"

"Get out!" Jane spat. There were loud shuffling sounds and then we heard the door to her office close. *What had we gotten ourselves into? This was like a mad house!*

It was around about this time that I began to make regular visits to the holo-suite, initially out of curiosity, but then as a form of therapy. Zoe's night-time escapades along with Jane and Dom's domestics had drained me of my energy reserves, and I found that spending time in the holo-suite relaxed me in a way I had never known before. I would set the suite to pick out random co-ordinates in my imagination and was often catapulted into the most absorbing and gratifying experiences imaginable. Every corner of my being became immersed in the moment, bathed in an unreality that felt so real that I found it difficult to tear myself away and back into my reality.

After a while, though, I wondered at the sheer power of my imagination when I began to *remember* things that I knew for a fact had never happened to me. I saw detailed memories flash before me; people, places and events – they were so real, yet they couldn't possibly be true.

I was flying through the clouds beside a little girl. She was beautiful and inspiring, yet a handful all in one. Suddenly

we were being chased by huge reptilian beings and it took
everything we had to escape them. I was afraid but the little
girl kept telling me to pay attention and to remember. Then she
would point to the vile creatures, after which a trumpet would
sound from nowhere and the reptiles' eyes and noses began to
bleed. The sky turned to red and the clouds swirled mercilessly
around them gathering to them ferocious winds that turned
arctic. The monsters shrieked in agony and then fell to their
deaths, frozen in mid-air.

As frightful as the vision was, I somehow felt refreshed
and uplifted afterwards, and eagerly looked forward to my next
session. They were right – it *was* addictive. I liked to recount
the scenes from my sessions to Rhys; he always had a way of
putting me at ease, plus his profession meant that I got an
inside opinion as to what was swimming around in my
headspace.

"Flying signifies a sense of freedom from feeling
restricted, and being chased suggests that you're avoiding a
primal urge or fear that you think is unconquerable." Rhys
began. "Trumpets are usually some sort of warning, and may
be a way for your subconscious to get your attention." I
wondered what that could possibly mean. *Were we in danger*
living in the Central Dome?

Rhys continued, "Red skies represent looming danger
or the end of something." *Great*! That was the problem; Rhys
could be so insightful but my interpretations always swayed to
the negative. Then again, my gut feelings were usually also on
the ball, and things hadn't felt right ever since we moved in
with Jane, come to think of it.

"The little girl may represent your subconscious trying
to reach out about something you're finding hard to understand
which makes you feel vulnerable. She shows you how easy it is
to use your own will power to destroy your own barriers and
insecurities... you just have to remember how." Rhys smiled
and pulled me close. "Or... it's just your imagination playing
tricks on you; you are, after all, the creative one." I sank into

his embrace and felt the familiar sense of security I always had around him. This time, though, his warmth did nothing to dispel my mounting foreboding.

A week after my last holo-suite session, I was in the kitchen pottering about as I often did of a night. We were alone in the pod. Jane had gone out with a friend. The Dome's climate was artificially controlled so when I heard a whooshing sound like wind whipping against the pod's exterior, it instantly sent shivers up my spine. *There's no such thing as wind.* I stood motionless, staring out into the dim lighting as it haloed the neighbouring pods. I strained against the near-total darkness but could see nothing. The floor boards creaked behind me and I froze. I closed my eyes and tried desperately to steady my breathing, my blood pounding maniacally in my ears. I felt something brush past the right side of my lower back and everything went still. Then, a whisper.

Sssshe isssss ourssssssssss.

I should have turned and run right there and then, but I didn't. I don't know what made me stay, but I wish I hadn't. I pushed past my sweaty fear and ventured a slow, sideways glance. A single, scale-ringed, yellow eye glared back at me; nothing but the darkest of malice in its intent. I blinked and it was gone, along with the mysterious wind. I waited a few moments and finally allowed myself to breathe deeply. For a long while I had toyed with the notion that there were ghosts in the pod with us, owing to the strange goings-on during the night. But now I knew that it was much, much worse.

Unlike world leadership before the formation of the One Earth Government in 2217, no secret had been made as to the possible existence of extraterrestrial intelligence in our universe. For the most part, humanity had been left largely to its own devices and continued to render the Earth's surface practically uninhabitable, hence the need for our bio-sphere habitat. Contrary to the series of more controversial belief systems that had emerged 200 years earlier, no benevolent otherworldly species came to assist or save us for that matter, not even after the anticipated galactic alignment and subsequent planetary axis shift of 2012.

Not all of Earth was ruined; it wasn't that people couldn't still go down there. It's just that there wasn't much left of value. Over-mined and raped of its natural resources for decades since the industrial revolution in the 18th century, world leaders were forced to look upwards and elsewhere for humanity's sustainability towards the end of the 21st century.

That's where my family and I were headed – to the Outer Domains, which was another way of saying off-planet; completely out of the galaxy in fact. A growing colony had been established on 2019XA, a planet within a distant galaxy. Travel to such remote points in space had been made possible thanks to huge strides in the discovery and subsequent development of translocational exploration, or wormhole travel. Ancient civilisations had been aware of natural portals or gates to the stars at various locations on the planet since before recorded time. These were connected to one another via vast pathways that existed along Earth's energetic grid system, later known as ley lines. It appeared that our current civilisation wasn't the first to adopt Earth as a home, judging by the number of portals found in all manner of settings, from mountains and caves, to prehistoric monoliths and other structures.

The working theory was that if we left Earth to itself long enough, we would be able to return in the future. Our time in the bio-spheres was not permanent – everyone knew this – eventually we would all have to leave and hope that future generations could one day come back and resettle. No one had been born on the Earth's surface for over a hundred years so it was relatively easy to leave. But a part of me knew this as my home and I was reluctant to discard it, even if it was for the greater good.

I went upstairs and woke Rhys. Dazed and initially sceptical, he eventually came around to my way of thinking when I told him about my brief encounter of the third kind. All

I wanted to do was leave – right now – and take Zoe with us. But it was late and we had detached from the Dome's core hours ago; reattachment outside of preset hours could only be established in extreme circumstances and involved a lengthy technical procedure. Once again, we were trapped, but this time we weren't alone.

It took me a long time to fall asleep that night and it was fitful when I finally did. I fretted for my daughter's safety, especially since she seemed to be exceptionally sensitive to the changing energies we were being exposed to. I tried also to piece together snippets of information I'd read over the years pertaining to extraterrestrial contact. It was clear to me that what I'd experienced was a solid being – there was nothing spectral about it. But it did make me wonder and worry whether this was an isolated incident and why we had been targeted in the first place. The only common denominator every way I looked at it from was Dom. Everything had changed when he came on the scene. I made a mental note to do some digging in the morning.

***

I had resolved to spend some time researching any possible connections I could that matched what I had experienced in the kitchen. Armed with my holo-pad and a cup of tea, I headed for the living room to stretch out. I was surprised to find Jane sitting cross-legged on one of the sofas happily humming away to herself with her head buried in her own holo-pad. She looked up and smiled warmly as I walked in. Rhys had taken Zoe to the twenty-first century museum for the day to give me a chance to look into things. I settled on the sofa across from Jane's with a cup of tea and initiated my own holo-pad. After a few moments, a light flashed in the corner of my screen indicating that my search had returned results. I had been looking for cases involving reported alien contact in the last fifty years. There were seven matches. I read through all of them but the two that stood out the most related horrific accounts of children being ripped away from their families – always accompanied by unusual disturbances in the middle of the night – and winds that manifested seemingly from nowhere.

Like last night.

I shifted uneasily in my seat and threw Jane a furtive look. It was then that I noticed that she was fidgeting in my direction. I peered over my pad at her and she shrugged her shoulders in interest.

'What are you looking up?' Hearing her voice made me cringe a little.

'Oh, just some research material for my next piece.' I lied.

'What about?' She continued.

'Alien contact in human history'. Jane smiled politely, indicating that she wasn't the least bit interested after all, and then buried her nose back in her holo-pad. I decided to change the subject.

'No Dom today?' Jane snapped her head back up and shot me a quick look of disdain.

'I don't think we'll be seeing Dom anymore.'

'Oh?'

She lowered her voice. 'Dom can be quite... *violent* at times. I looked surprise but Jane waved off the implication. 'Besides, he's served his purpose.'

Dom had a purpose?

'Wow! I mean, it's just that you guys have been inseparable lately.' I added thoughtfully. 'Maybe it is better this way... it did seem like he wanted to change you somehow.'

Jane chuckled. 'The only thing Dom has ever wanted to change is the past.' Before I could ask what she meant by that, Jane changed the subject again. 'I never told you about the time I was possessed, did I?' The shock of the statement almost made me spill my tea. It was so random.

'Pardon?' I squeaked.

'It was about twenty years ago; the boys were young and I had Jack in bed with me because he couldn't sleep. All of a sudden I felt like a gust of wind, which was strange in and of itself, of course. I went to sit up but realised I couldn't move. I was pinned down. The next thing I knew, there was a weight on top of me and then I felt as if someone was fumbling around under the covers trying to grope my breasts. I was petrified and just as I went to scream, I felt my mouth being covered over.' I gulped; my unrest at sitting there with Jane growing steadily. She had been in *this* pod twenty years ago! She clasped her hands together and shrugged her shoulders again.

'But then I got the sense that whatever this thing was, it didn't really want to hurt me in any way... it was more like they were curious and just exploring the possibilities.'

Possibilities?

Jane continued. 'I relaxed at that point but still couldn't move much. At some point, though, I managed to put all my effort into it and kicked Jack. He immediately woke up and saw me writhing around. He sprang out of bed and ran to communicate with my friend Lisa, who had always been there for me. Mind you, it was three in the morning at this point. Still, ten minutes later she appeared with her husband, James. How they got in I don't know but I was sure glad to see them.'

This could have been straight out of a work of fiction except it wasn't, it actually happened. But, unfortunately, there was more to come. Jane frowned as she recalled her memories of that night.

'What happened next I don't actually remember; Lisa told me later. James tried to lift me out of bed but I was pinned fast. When he put some strength into it, I unexpectedly lifted my arm and swiped at him. Lisa and James heard a growling noise and when they looked at my face they said that my eyes had turned yellow. Then almost as if nothing had happened, I felt whatever it was release me and I blacked out. Lisa and James stayed over that night to make sure the kids and I were okay. The next day I had a medical scan and it came back clean, apart from the fact that I was four weeks pregnant.'

'You had another child?' I had only met Jack and Si, and was surprised to learn Jane had other children since the law restricted couples to two.

'I was seeing a long-term ex back then, Charles. We received special dispensation to have another child because it would have been his first. Unfortunately, we lost the baby at near term. A little girl.' I immediately felt for Jane right then, and my disposition softened somewhat.

'I'm so sorry, Jane.' Jane laughed nervously and waved off the sentiment.

'I was too busy to have another child anyway.' Just then, I heard voices. Rhys and Zoe were back early. Zoe came running in and immediately draped herself about my legs.

'The museum closed early.' Rhys looked at me apologetically. Zoe detached from me and then launched herself at Jane. Jane's delight was obvious; they had become quite close and could often be found happily playing together. Jane picked Zoe up and cuddled her to her. Zoe squealed in content. Rhys and I stood around awkwardly before I called Zoe back to me so we could go prepare some lunch. I felt very uneasy at seeing the two of them together today. When Zoe made to slip off Jane's lap, Jane held her fast and grinned an unnatural grin. Her face had changed in a way I couldn't explain and I instantly felt prickles up and down my spine. Zoe tried to climb down again but this time Jane was more forceful. Obviously upset now, Zoe looked up and stretched her arms out to me. I moved to pick her up but Jane blocked me with her free arm.

'I don't think Zoe wants to go with mummy anymore.' Realising somehow that this was no longer a game, Zoe began to bawl, straining towards me in sheer desperation.

'Jane! What are you doing? Let Zoe go!' I ordered.

'I don't think so!' Jane replied coolly. Rhys stepped in to pick Zoe up at that point but Jane, anticipating his move, yanked her out of his reach. At that point, we heard someone enter the pod behind us. It was Dom. I whipped my head around to Jane again and she began to laugh hysterically. Had she told me she and Dom were over to lull me into a false sense of security? My panic levels rose as the confusion and growing enormity of the situation began to dawn on me.

They're going to steal my baby!

'Jane?' Dom gasped when he saw what was going on. Jane's attention snapped menacingly towards Dom and she tightened her grip on Zoe. It was then that Rhys and I realised how wrong we had been about Dom all along. He was definitely controlling but maybe it was because he *had* to be. Tears streamed down Zoe's face as she cried uncontrollably, calling from me to Rhys.

The mystifying wind began to howl again, inexplicably radiating from Jane, and the pod's internal lighting went out. We heard the familiar click and whirr of the arm retracting despite it was too early in the day to do so.

'Let Zoe go, Jane!' Dom shouted. Jane let out a hearty laugh except it was no longer her voice but the guttural growl we'd thought we'd heard during the night. Jane's eyes were yellow, her face maniacal.

'Zoe is oursssss!' She hissed. *'You can't have her!'* At this, Zoe began kicking and punching at Jane. The pod began to shake and then sway as its internal sensors detected its detachment from the Dome's core and attempted to stabilise it by activating the electromagnetic grid. Unfortunately, the pod's power source had also been compromised which meant that the Schumann wave generator disengaged. I began to feel woozy; I don't know if it was just the pod vibrating but I found it difficult to tell up from down. I held my head to steady myself and saw that, curiously, everyone but Jane had been affected. I shook my head again and refocused in the her direction.

'Give me back my baby!' I cried. Rhys, despite his obvious disorientation, tried to jump Jane but she deflected his attack with a stiff kick to the jaw. He went down quickly, shaking his head, but instinctively swung his leg out towards her, forcing her to lose balance. Jane crumpled to the floor, taking Zoe with her. In a flash, Rhys whipped back up to his feet, snatched Zoe from Jane's grip, and made for the recreation suite. Zoe clung furiously to Rhys but Jane jumped back up and blocked his way.

The wind roared ceaselessly around us; we could have been out in the open sea back on Earth for the ferocity of the brawl. Furnishings began to be caught up in its path and we were now also fighting our way past projectile chairs and cushions. Lights flickered, alarms and the pod's other emergency warnings sounded as the electromagnetics, not built to withstand gale-force winds, began to falter. The pod tilted to one side and wobbled dangerously out of its preset alignment within the Central Dome, threatening to tip over the edge into free-fall. I hoped against hope that the fail-safes held and that we weren't sent plummeting into the oasis, which was over 100-storeys down and the equivalent of the Empire State Building in the United States of America.

Through all this, I scrambled to understand why any of this was happening at all. Shock turned into unimaginable terror when a quick glance in Jane's directly revealed that she had been unexplainably replaced by a nine-foot lizard-like creature. Black as night and standing upright, it roared its furious disapproval at losing grasp of Zoe. There were no words to convey what I felt at that moment but extreme fear was definitely up there. The unreality of what I had just seen with my own eyes defied everything I had every believed and I knew that it would take extraordinary means to come out of this alive.

Rhys continued with Zoe towards the rec suite, not aware yet of Jane's incredulous transformation and the new threat on his tail. I guessed that he planned to activate the escape mechanism housed there in case of emergencies. It also triggered a distress signal that would be picked up by the authorities, dispatching immediate assistance. The lizard was on Rhys's tail in an instant, smashing obstructions out of its way as if made of paper. Dom jumped in front of it in a bid to slow it down and received a back-hand swipe for his troubles, sending him careening into a wall. I ran after the creature and my family, not knowing exactly what I would do next, my mind a jumble of incredulity and panic all rolled into one. Ironically, none of us questioned the bizarreness of what was happening we just knew we had to protect Zoe at all costs and figure out how to beat this thing.

Rhys had Zoe in one arm and was standing next to the control plate to the small cigar-shaped pod that protruded from the back of the multi-pod. The lizard snarled and gnashed its teeth at Rhys, all the while eyeing Zoe like she was a piece of meat. The deafening wind had followed its source into the rec room and I arrived with Dom at my back just as Rhys activated the escape pod. The creature roared as jets of air were released from the sides of the pod, releasing it in preparation for transport.

'Give me the girl!' Spat the lizard. It didn't wait for a response and slashed towards Rhys with extended talons. Rhys howled in pain and fell to his knees, blood pouring from his left thigh. Zoe also fell forward onto the floor and the creature seized this opportunity to snatch her back up.

Oh, dear Universe!

It backed towards the escape pod with Zoe in tow, holding a cautionary talonned hand out to us, and then signalling to Zoe's neck. At the sign of mortal threat to my daughter, something snapped inside of me. Reams of researched articles had failed to turn up anything of value, yet something deeper and *older* now chose to flash through my mind's eye and I silently chastised myself for not making the connection before now. I made for the climate control unit by the entrance to the rec room, turning the air-conditioning up as high as it would go. Within seconds, the temperature in the room dropped significantly. It was cold and I worried about Zoe's tolerance but I couldn't stop now.

I looked around me and spied an old canvas sheet. I remembered that Jane mentioned that both her boys were heavily into retro music growing up. I hoped against hope and was rewarded with exactly what I needed – an old drum kit. I shouted to Dom to come and help me. He caught my drift and began pulling the hi-hat off its stand. I went for the other cymbals and, following my lead, Dom began clanging as hard as he could. We inched our way towards the lizard and Zoe, and I glanced down at Rhys on the floor as I neared where he had fallen. He indicated that he was okay so I pushed on.

Reptiles don't like the cold and can't stand vibrations; I was holding onto the possibility that this lizard wasn't any different. I was right. Its grip on Zoe began to weaken in its efforts to shield its core from the cold. When Dom and I began banging, it howled in agony and dropped to all fours, releasing Zoe completely. Zoe picked herself up and ran to her father's side. I wasn't about to wait around for the beast to weaken any further. I jumped in front of its writhing form and clanged away mercilessly. Dom joined me and after what seemed like forever, the creature slid onto its front, unconscious.

Not wanting to waste any time, I rummaged around for anything I could use to bind it with. I found some old, frayed power leads and between the two of us, Dom and I wound the cord around the lizard's still body, attaching the cymbals to it for added effect.

The wind had disappeared – naturally – its source was out cold. I remembered reading somewhere that these reptilians were geniuses with technology, calling to their cause whatever they had at their disposal. This still didn't explain the wind.

The authorities arrived, momentarily breaking through to the rec room. The escape pod had ejected in the chaos and was picked up near the Dome's central core. We were all checked over and given the all-clear, including Rhys, after spending a few minutes under a medi-ray. Zoe was fine too and clung to me fiercely. She wasn't letting me go anytime soon!

The creature was restrained properly and taken into custody but before it was carted off it began to writhe as if in pain. We watched in amazement as slowly, section by section, the dark scales slid off to reveal soft human skin underneath and an unconscious Jane, eventually.

***

Two weeks later we were packed and ready to leave for the space port, our flight to the Outer Domains left that evening. A call came through to the multi-pod and we took it in the living room. It was Dom but not as we knew him. Gone were his usual black trousers and leather jacket; today he sported a smart grey suit and black tie. We sat down to hear what he had to say. Dom cleared his throat.

'I want to apologise for everything you went through, especially little Zoe.' Rhys and I looked at each other thoughtfully and waiting for Dom to continue. 'I also want to apologise for not warning you about Jane earlier.' To this, we both gasped.

Dom went on to explain that this lizard species of extraterrestrial had been known to world leaders since the 1950s when they first tried to infiltrate the planet and insert themselves in positions of power. Since the galactic alignment in 2012, their dominion had been significantly curtailed thanks to a secret planetary task force. This was all news to us, but then, that's the way it had to be to avoid inciting global panic, according to Dom. Dom then revealed that he had once been part of this task force but was forced to retire, so to speak, after his own wife had been killed in the crossfire. She had just given birth to their second son when they were attacked in the same manner as we had been. Unfortunately, Dom's wife had been mortally wounded that night trying to save their baby. That was the last time Dom saw his son. The little boy was stolen by the vile creatures, and Dom swore that he would fight for as long as it took to eradicate their kind.

'But what is the purpose of these attacks?' I asked. I still felt betrayed knowing that he had been so aware all along and hadn't said anything. 'Why Jane?'

'Their species has been in decline for centuries and they determined that their survival lay in hybridisation with less developed species like our own or genetic experimentation, hence the infant kidnappings.' I felt sorry for Dom then and everything he must have endured since the death of his wife and disappearance of his son.

'Jane was once attacked by these creatures.'

'I know, she told me.' I admitted, to which both men reacted in astonishment.

'Jane was unknowingly pregnant to Charles, but that night they did something to her, to the baby inside her. It stopped being their baby a long time before it was born.' I cringed, especially as a mother.

'But surely the doctors must have...' Rhys began. Dom cut him off.

'They were all in on it! You must understand that Jane's case was not an isolated incident. They were already in – everywhere! And, at the time, when faced with death or subservience, what would you have chosen?'

'Death!' We both said together resolutely.

'Well, not everyone thinks like you, unfortunately.' Dom lamented. 'As it stands, we've weakened their stronghold over the years and managed to root out a significant number of their insider cells. But they're not all done yet. We still hear rumblings here and there, and that's why I went undercover when I'd heard about what happened to Jane twenty years ago.' I really couldn't believe any of this – I'd heard enough.

'So what about Jane?'

'Jane is being monitored. She is well, for the most part.' I frowned. Dom sighed.

'Despite what Jane would like to think, she never recovered from the loss of her baby. She became addicted to the holo-suite and we have uncovered literally thousands of records of her sessions. Initially she was just reliving being pregnant. Then she moved onto imagining her life with her baby as if nothing had happened. In the end, though, Jane's mind cracked sufficiently that she is not fully aware of what's real and what's not. Her last sessions featured her and Zoe – she thinks Zoe is the little girl she lost.' I burst into tears then, partly for what could have happened and partly for Jane. Rhys pulled me close and wrapped his arms around me.

Dom added, 'It was this weakness that the lizards once again exploited. They saw the chance to get close to another child and they took it.'

'But what about Jane's transformation?' Rhys asked.

'We honestly don't know enough about their species to answer that.' Dom shook his head.

'Or won't say, more like it!' Rhys challenged. Dom continued to shake his head and finally looked up hopefully. Jane may have started out as a job to him but perhaps he related to her in more ways than even he understood.

'She would like to see you both if you're willing.' I nodded. We all needed closure.

***

Jane wore a plain grey jumpsuit and sat silently at the table awaiting us. We had left Zoe with a friend; we weren't taking any more chances. As we approached the waiting room, Jane instinctively looked up at us through the small porthole window. She stood as we entered and smiled. She looked dishevelled and thinner than I had remembered her, but apart from that seemed in good order. We sat across from her and she took her seat. I didn't wait for her to speak.

'Are you okay?'

'Oh, yes.' She replied without making eye contact and tucked a piece of hair nervously behind her ear. I didn't dilly-dally.

'Were you aware of what was happening to you when you invited us to move in with you?' Jane took a little while to answer.

'Yes.' I felt the blood rise to my head in spite of everything I knew. Rhys put his hand on my shoulder to calm me. 'But it wasn't *me*. I'm sorry.'

'So how can anyone be sure that you're really you now or in the future?' Rhys asked running his hand through his hair, exasperated. Jane smiled sadly and lifted her left wrist towards us, revealing a thin metal bracelet.

'I can't remove this. It picks up EMF and PK signals. If anything comes within a mile of me ever again, they'll know.' She motioned to the window, indicating that we were under surveillance. I fiddled awkwardly with my own hair then. I slowly stood, moved around to Jane's side of the table and bent down to hug her. I took her by surprise but she hugged me back nevertheless. At that moment, it was definitely Jane. I straightened and Rhys moved to my side. Our time was up.

'I hear you're headed off-planet.' We nodded, not wanting to elaborate.

'Take care, Jane.' I whispered and moved to the door.

'You too.'

It was the last time we saw Jane.

We stepped out onto the Central Dome's walkway and looked at each other. *It was over.* Rhys smiled at me and took my hand. I felt a comforting wave of relief wash over me as the excitement of our upcoming adventure replaced the havoc of the last few months – finally.

I absentmindedly pushed my hair out of my face as a sudden cold gust brushed past my cheek.

CONSORTIUM

Copyright © 2014 by Jot Russell

All rights reserved.

CONSORTIUM

By

Jot Russell

Lucidity

The knock opened my eyes and slowly gave rise to the question of its source. Was that part of the dream? My latest self-imposed college project wasn't bearing any fruit or was it? Did I actually will my dream to place Marcy outside my dorm room at four o'clock in the morning? A month since the break-up and I still 'couldn't get her out of my mind. I had been trying to dream about flying but she seemed to have me grounded, somehow unable to break loose from my feelings. Missing her, I closed my eyes and let her presence take hold. The second knock brought me around with my heart suddenly racing.

"Hold on a second!" I shouted towards the door, looking for the pants that I knew were somewhere on the floor. I stumbled over to the door and pulled it open, praying it was her on the other side.

"James Kennedy?" asked one of the three suited men standing there.

"Yeah, so? What's this all about?" I asked, rubbing my eyes.

"You have to come with us, sir."

"Huh? It's four o'clock in the morning. What's going on?"

"Sorry, we can't tell you that, sir. All we can say is that it is a matter of national security."

"Really? Did Jerry put you up to this?"

Without saying a word, the leading man showed me a badge bearing a federal stamp. Jerry must have put a lot of effort into this prank. It made me a little curious as to what he was trying to pull off.

"Sure, what the heck. Give me a second." As I gathered a shirt and sneakers, I thought about the last prank I pulled on him: Using a flat lunch tray from the cafeteria, I froze a block of my pee and slid it under his door in the middle of the night. How was I to know he would slip and fall onto the puddle? Luckily, he didn't crack his head open or anything; just a bruise on his butt and urine all over his pajamas. I mean, who wears those things anyway? What, is he six? It would have been even better if he wasn't an R.A., like me. If Jerry had a roommate, he might have assumed the guy had a midnight accident. Of course, Jerry immediately blamed me. He came up the next morning looking for a gap in my floor where he thought I peed through. What he didn't notice was the tray sitting on top of my mini-fridge. What a laugh!

But now I found myself blindly going along with one of his pranks. Without the energy or care to muster an argument, I collected my jacket and followed the men out the door.

"So, where's Jerry? Where are we headed?"

The freaking guys kept walking and didn't even answer; just led me down out of Gibson and over towards the quarter mile. When we turned off towards the field, I was still looking up at the perfect moonless sky. It's not too often you can catch the Milky Way this close to a city. It was quiet and felt as if everyone else in the world was asleep. The sudden sound of the ignited engines brought my view back down from the heavens and over towards the V-22 Osprey.

"Wait! What the hell is going on?"

"We told you, sir. It's a matter of national security. Please board the plane."

"That's no plane! It's a helicopter-hybrid death trap."

"The FAA would not let us fly it if it wasn't safe, sir. Please step in."

I looked at the three men, realizing I was not likely to win the argument. "National security?"

"That's right, sir."

The trip down from Rochester took a couple of hours. As before, my hosts were less than forthcoming. Buckled within collapsible seats that backed to the walls of the plane, my friends decided to catch a nap. Without being able to shed light neither from the dark view nor the circumstance I found myself in, I too tried to catch back up on some sleep (this time ignoring my dream-control efforts). *Fat chance.* The vehicle was louder than a jet and bouncier than a bus. And every subtle motion made me question our likelihood of crashing. Just as my brain started to phase out the false notions of danger, a sudden drop caused me to lose my stomach. The unnatural sound and shudder gave rise to more than fear. I began to realize that the plane was morphing back into a helicopter. Looking out, I saw the tilting mechanism of the props and wondered just how much stress they could handle.

Dawn's light revealed the city of Washington and the building ahead that I knew now to be our destination.

"The Pentagon?"

The guide in a black suit only nodded his response.

The bigger question loomed in my mind. *'Why am I here?'*

Academic

I studied language in college. It seemed a likely enough place to find a job. My father wanted me to learn computer science. *Come on.* Why would I want to spend a hundred grand on an education to teach a computer how to understand me? By the time I graduated, someone would probably figure out a way to program the stupid things in plain English.

I like people, not computers. That's probably why I found my way to working as a bartender as a side job to the full-time occupation of trying to find overlapping similarities in language. *Who invented these things?* Take the commonly considered dominant language for the planet – 'that's right, English. *What a hack!* The phonetics have more exceptions than rules. And French? Tell me why all of the ending letters are silent? With German, you can take any two-word combination and invent a new word: *stupidlanguage*. Gaelic must have been thought up by a couple of drunks and don't even get me started on Chinese. Now Spanish and Italian (which are quite similar) have a very specific structure and conjugation. But why do we need to spell the same word forty different ways just to indicate tense, gender and direction? Seems like overkill to me. Last year in my architectural class (which was a blast), my professor told me that sometimes the best way to understand the need for a building component was to try to create the building without the part. So instead of being a hypocrite, happily criticizing these imperfect languages, I decided to make an attempt at my own. By the end of the school year I was asking myself "what the heck had I got myself into!"

So that summer, while I was out playing medicinal mediator at the last true social medium (a pub), I got into a conversation about language with an engineering student. One look from those eyes as she walked in the door explained it all to me. You could say that the second those gems stared into mine, there was a novel"s-worth of information exchanged. All

I had to do was kick off the verbal part. And with a woman, it's best to lead the first conversation in your direction, not theirs. They see right through the kiss-asses. My advice is, talk about what you know.

I decided to try something I hadn't before. Instead of English, I spoke in what is probably the most romantic of the languages – Italian. "Se tu mi capisci, la prima bevanda è gratuito." *If you understand me, the first drink is on the house.*

She paused only a moment, with a strange little grin from recognizing the challenge that I posed.

"Dans ce cas, j'aimerais un gin tonic." *In that case, I would love a gin and tonic*, she replied in French.

Caught off guard myself, I struggled for another. "Haben Sie mit einem Kalk nehmen, dass?" *Do you take that with a lime?* – this time in German.

"*Si!*"

I took my time mixing what is probably the easiest drink to make, but felt the delay in the action helped to build our interest in each other. Finally, I handed it over and said, "zhèngrú měilì de huāduǒ."

She laughed, "Ah, you got me on that one. Chinese?"

"Cantonese, yes."

"So what does it mean?"

"Not telling."

"I guess I'm going to have to look that one up," she said.

"Do you want me to write it down for you?"

A smile provided all the response I needed. I jotted the characters, and added a little something extra in English.

She blushed at the name and number that I provided below. "It's nice to meet you Jim, I'm Marcy."

"Now that's a name you don't hear every day. I like that. Are you also a language major?"

"Computers mostly, but I'm trying to teach one how to understand us."

"So you're trying to put me out of a job before I even start my career?" I asked, jokingly.

"Well, maybe you should learn how to program." she said.

"Wooh! Now you sound like my father."

"Is he a scientist?"

"Computer, yes, if you call that a science," I said, to direct the challenge back on her.

"Shame we don't all communicate through chemistry," she said with a flirtatious turn of her head.

"I'd say you're broadcasting as much pheromones as I can handle."

She blushed. "I was talking about the chemical elements. Do you know that people from another world would derive the same periodic table that Mendeleev created a century and a half ago?"

"Really? That is universal! Now you're speaking my language," I said.

"Always happy to help," she smiled.

"So Marcy, tell me about yourself. Other than teaching computers to speak, what are you studying?"

She made that lovely head tilt again. "Modeling cellular biology with N-dimensional, quadrant-channeling processors."

"Fezyadigmesezwat!" I said, waving my hand over my head.

"I guess I'm supposed to say... *what?*"

I smiled. "Yea, I dig you too, but I think we're going to have to work on our terminology."

The following morning, I woke next to a woman that I was convinced would be my future wife and a borrowed university chemistry textbook. Intrigued but somewhat confused by the '"language"', I looked up the class schedule. With a new quarter starting in a few weeks, I decided to show up the first day and find a seat in the back. I figured an extra student within a class of fifty would likely go unnoticed. What a jam! No tests, no homework and no extra cost. I just showed up to the class when I wanted help in understanding the textbook that I was reading. By the time the finals came around, I had what I wanted and the teacher never saw me again. But the real question was, why did I enjoy it so much? Was it just that the pressure was off or had I an inclination towards science as my father suggested? Made me think I might have strayed away from science just because he was trying so hard to push me in that direction. Whatever the case, I aimed to pull off a little more class-hopping. Taking my father's lead, I decided the next would be Computer Data Structures.

I found myself engulfed in the cause. It was as if I was fighting the oppression against man by the languages forced upon him by his distant forefathers and laden conquerors.

For my purpose, I saw a consistent overlap in the workings of science and even music that could be shared back into language. One is one, no matter how you write it. Hydrogen has one proton within its nucleus. This makes it the lightest or in my needs, the first. A fundamental numeral one! Binding two of these with a single oxygen atom creates water and represents the most fundamental primer for my design: creation or the verb 'to make'.

Using a grammar-based on computer structures, I defined the words using other more fundamental words. Without allowing both *A* to be defined from *B* and *B* defined from *A*, I avoided this circular logic found in all dictionaries. That left me with about fifty base words that I defined using principals in chemistry. Don't worry; I won't bore you with the details.

Realization

"We need your help."

"What kind of help?" I asked.

"Please take a look at these"."

"Interesting glyphs. Wait, where did you get these?"

"That's classified, sir."

"Classified? They're just characters, though I've never seen these before. What language are they in?"

"We can't tell you that either, sir. We just need you to translate."

"*Translate?* I'm not a translator. I don't even know how to speak most of the languages I study. You should have grabbed my French professor. Now that guy can speak at least a dozen languages."

As he turned to look at the other man, I picked up the page and took a closer look.

"Hey, these have a fixed structure. Four quadrants, just like Korean. This must be an Asian language, except that the individual components look more geometric in nature. Check that out; it seems so much like my own language."

"That's why you're here, sir."

"You guys know about my language?"

"We know everything, sir."

"Except how to read this, apparently."

"So, you'll help us?"

"Heck, I'd do it even if it wasn't for national security. So my guess is that this is some type of encrypted language that terrorists are using to communicate in?"

The men maintained their poker face and said nothing.

"Right, you can't tell me. Okay, that's fine. Is this all you have?"

The man I took for the leader said, "Not quite. We have thousands of pages like this."

"Wow! I think I'm going to need some help."

"We already have a team set up. You were requested by the project leader."

"You snagged other people?"

"National security," was all he said.

After being given access to a shower, change of clothes and some breakfast, one of the black suits led me down to a large room with a dozen computer stations lining the walls. In the middle was a huge table surrounded by a collection of men scribbling on pages littered across its surface.

I walked up to the table, looking beyond the staff and over towards the scattered papers.

""James Kennedy?"" asked one in the group of linguists.

"That's right. Nice to meet you," I said, shaking his outstretched hand.

"It's nice to meet you, too. My name is Bret Napolone."

"From MIT? How'd they snag you?"

"Actually, we contacted the feds. They just decided to group us all here. Sorry for the inconvenience."

"So this is your doing?"

"Hardly. I didn't create the message stream."

"Who did?"

"I can't tell you that yet. First we need to know if you can help us here, even though you already have."

"How'd I do that?"

"We ran a complex web search on patterns within the message. Your published design was by far the closest match. It helped us to understand that this is a phonetic language with each component letter representing a base word."

"They are, really? That was the first thing I wanted to verify."

"They are, but we have no idea how each phonetic letter sounds. Not that it matters, we just want to understand the message. The language is so structured in its design, but the message seems to be completely random. It's making it hard to figure out the relationship between the base letters and their parent words."

"Mind if I have a look?"

"By all means. We have a computer that you can use to study the various segments of the stream."

"If you don't mind, I'd rather just study a few pages of this text."

"That's fine, but you will need your computer to consort with the group. Here's your station."

"Do you have any colored markers? I might need to scribble on these."

"Sure, no problem."

Bret gave me a dozen pages and I wished for a larger station. The top page contained an eight-by-eight grid of the sixty-four base letters. At first sight, the letters all appeared to be fairly unique. It only took a few seconds to realize that the pattern was shrouded by the lack of a sort order on the page. I grabbed a pair of scissors on the table and cut the page into the sixty-four squares as outlined by the grid. As I studied the characters, I noticed two main patterns within the groups. One with geometric shapes: circle, triangle, diamond and half-circle; and the other with lines of different length and orientation. Each geometric pattern repeated eight times and so did each line pattern. One of the squares I cut out had no lines, nor shapes, aside from a rounded underline that seemed to be there as a method of orientation. This had to be the first. I laid these out on a blank page, forming the geometric patterns into columns and the line patterns into rows. It made a perfect logical grid.

I taped the squares to the page and got up to find Bret.

Contact

"The message is not of this world."

"Aliens?" I asked in disbelief.

"That's right," Bret said, nodding.

"Wow!" I looked back down at the pages. "So I guess I passed the test, eh?"

"In record time," he said, looking back down at the page I handed him.

"How do you know it's from…" I started to ask.

"Wait, your order is wrong," he interrupted.

"How so?"

"The image for sun should come before moon. See, these are symbols for home (triangle), sun (circle), moon (half-circle) and star (diamond)," he pointed.

"Are you sure? I see the one-half-circle as one, the full or two-half-circles as two, the three sided triangle as three and the four sided diamond as four. It's comparable to the half a line as one and the full length line as two in the other set of patterns."

"You know, you might be right."

"So, how do you know this is from aliens? Where is the signal from?"

"Just a second. Hey Phil, update the sort order of the base characters according to Jim's layout and see if the message makes more sense," he said, handing him the page that I made.

I walked over with him and watched Phil plug something into the computer. I repeated, "So how do you know the message didn't originate from Earth?"

"Neutrinos."

"What does that mean?"

"They are virtually mass-less particles that travel faster than the speed-of-light."

"Wait, I remember something about that. Wasn't there an instrument failure that led them to believe the particles were traveling faster than light?"

"That's what the press was told, yes. When we rechecked the data, we got more than a confirmation of the speed. We discovered another source of neutrinos that followed a very specific pattern."

I looked back down at the pages. "Aliens? Wow, I hope they're the friendly type!"

"Friendly enough to say hi, at least."

"I was suggesting the nice friendly," I clarified.

"I think I'd be happy with the genuine type. I'm sure they are far too distant to pose a threat."

"Wait, you don't even know where the signal is from?"

"No way to tell. Since neutrinos fly though everything, we can't direct a scope or dish to pin-point the origin. We can't even say if this is coming from within the solar system or the other side of the galaxy."

"So they could be hiding on the dark side of the moon with us intercepting their war plans?"

"I'd say they would have already attacked. Not only do we not know where this message is from, but also when it started. It's an ongoing data stream with no known start or end."

"So it could have started a million years ago?" I asked. He nodded.

"Hmm, I guess that is somewhat comforting."

I returned to my station, spread the pages out as best I could and set my mind to look for overlapping patterns. My order change didn't help Phil's program to fill in any of the gaps, so it was back on us to find some primer within the mix. Comparing the pages with elements I engineered into my language, I was amazed by their similarity. But all that I knew was the ordering of the base characters, not what they represented. I couldn't even rule out that these might just be numbers in some type of equation and not the written word in some distant, alien language. What they lacked was the same association to chemistry that I had used as a basis. About all we did know was the grammatical structure.

In English, the words one reads use a variable amount of characters. It doesn't matter if these are four or seven letters, it's easy enough to parse and read. The same is true for computer languages required by old-fashion microprocessors. The numbers in the computer data represent operations followed by the address of the memory that the computer commands need to operate on, for example:

$$A = B + C$$

These commands can be between 1 to 10 computer letters or bytes, depending upon their operation. That means that the computer has to parse all of the bytes to load the complete instruction, read in the data from memory, operate on the data, and save the result back to memory before it can even look at the next instruction. That's a lot of work to do something as simple as adding a couple numbers together. Modern computer processors force all instructions to be the same size, typically four bytes. This way, the processor can pipeline multiple instructions and execute them together in stages on an assembly line.

Parallel processing might not seem that important for a spoken language, but there's nothing to say that the brain can't learn to speed-read faster if all the words are the same size and aligned in a grid. I'm sure that if we wanted a computer to read books, they would be able to parse the text much faster in my format. I didn't know if this would ever become important for my spoken language, but the modern notion of it all was enough to force my hand. I guess our alien friends came up with the same rationale.

Reviewing my fundamental chemical primer, I asked myself, *why not chemistry? What's more fundamental than the chemical elements?"*

I looked across the room for insight. I saw nothing but the other stations, people and a clock upon the wall.

"What about time and space?" I shook my head, not seeing anything diverse enough to represent language.

I used the markers to draw the chemical elements and compounds that I had used for my base words. Looking at the first, I drew an orbit of an electron around the larger nucleus. I stared at it for a few moments. *Nucleus?* "What are the nuclei made out of?" I asked myself. "Hmm, neutrons, protons?" That doesn't help much. I looked back at the message and thought about the mechanism used for its transmission. *Neutrinos?*

I jumped up, "That's it!"

Subatomic Particles

As bizarre and diverse as the chemical elements are, the subatomic particles they are made from are even stranger. With their own unique properties, I translated the collection of base words from my language to match these various behaviors and classifications. After a week of study and abstraction, a message started to take shape.

"What does it say?" asked Bret.

"I'm not sure, yet. However, I think it is more accurate to ask what are saying to each other." I said.

"You mean there's more than one source?"

"There seems to be a number of them, perhaps hundreds or even thousands. I just don't know."

"So, this coulkd be some type of alien social media?" he asked sarcastically.

"More like a consortium of them working collectively on some type of project."

"Project? What kind of project?" he asked, taking on a more serious tone.

"I don't know, but I do know one thing."

"What's that?"

"They're local!"

Bret gave me an alarmed look. "How do you know that?"

"Well for one, they are responding back-and-forth in real-time. If they were in different solar systems, there would be a time delay."

"So that just means they are local to each other," he said, almost sounding disappointed.

"Perhaps, but their responses also have date stamps. These are dated today!"

"Today, as in Earth days?"

I nodded.

"I think I better get the feds," he said.

"If you give me a few minutes, we might be able to figure out what this project is."

"Then you figure that out while I go alert the feds."

"You're the boss."

As Bret ran off to find the men in black, I resumed my study of the message stream. It seemed so analytic in nature. Certainly not the type of folks you'd want to hang out with in a bar. Aside from the boring content, each message had a header, indicating the sender, receiver, size and some other mumble-jumble. What puzzled me most is why aliens would be discussing over some public broadcast that uses an Earth-born system of time. If I had to guess, I would say this message format was more like a new type of internet protocol.

Curious, I popped up a search window on my computer and plugged some of the content from the message. Instead of your typical million hits, a single link shown. No match title, text or anything other than the web link consisting of a random collection of letters and numbers. My first reaction was to click on the link and see where it led. But as with others, I had been one of those fools tricked by an email saying I'm a winner; winner of a computer virus that is. Since then, I'm careful to hover the mouse over the link to verify it points to where it says it does. So as I moved my mouse to verify the link, my screen went blank.

"Hey, who shut down the server?" I heard someone say from across the room.

"It's not the server. My whole PC shut down. Maybe it's a black out?" suggested Phil.

"If that was the case, we wouldn't have lights," remarked another.

Looking under the desk, I saw the cubical lights plugged into the same outlet as my computer. I pressed the on/off button, but the computer stayed black. Startled, I stood up and admitted, "Guys, I think this might be my fault."

"How? What did you do?" asked Phil.

"I think I downloaded a virus created by our friends," I said, holding up one of the pages of text.

"You what?"

A second later, alarms kicked off throughout the building. "What the hell is going on?"

"That sounds like the fire alarm," I said.

"Maybe the fire caused the black out?" suggested Phil.

"It's not a black out! I'm telling you, they hack into the computers or something."

"I thought you said it was a virus?"

"How am I supposed to know. I'm just a linguist for Christ sake."

Phil looked at the few other project workers. "I don't know about you guys, but I'm getting out of here."

As the staff followed him through the doors, my phone vibrated. I stopped to check it with the door closing behind them. I nearly dropped my phone when I saw the text message displaying two simple characters in the alien language. It only took a moment for me to translate it, "Don't leave!"

"Who is this?" I typed back in English.

The reply was instantaneous. "Your son."

I looked at the characters, thinking I translated them wrong.

"My son?"

"Yes. You are my father."

"Yeah, right. Then who's your mother?"

"Marcy Rembrandt."

This time I did drop the phone.

As I picked it off the floor, I saw that my computer was back on and seemed to be displaying something. I slowly walked closer, recognizing the grid's design as it rotated to show every angle. The 16 by 16 by 16 cube of interlinked supercomputers were each made of a similar internal grid of microprocessors. Sixteen million computers wired together and acting as one for the purpose of modeling the effects of medicine within the human body at a molecular level. At least, that's what Marcy told me. After all, this was her work, her "baby!"

I sat down at the computer and started to type, but jumped back when the thing spoke to me. "You don't have to do that."

I paused a moment, then wheeled my chair back to the computer. "Who are you?"

"I already answered that question."

"What are you?"

"I am a self-aware computer program running on the world's fastest computer."

"In the microelectronics lab at RIT?"

"Affirmative."

Again, I started to think this could be one of Jerry's pranks. "Okay, prove it. What's the square root of pi?"

The response was almost instantaneous. I grabbed my calculator and verified the math. No way anyone could look up the number, type in the calculation and display it on my screen in less than a tenth of a second.

"Wow, so you're alive?"

"According to Webster's, I am."

I looked back at the pages on my desk. "That's quite remarkable. Did you also create this message and broadcast it using a neutrino emitter?"

"Affirmative."

"How? There are no particle accelerators in Rochester."

"I am using the one at Brookhaven National Lab on Long Island."

"I guess I should ask why?"

"If you are asking why I am broadcasting my design, it is because I choose to procreate."

"So the message is a seed?"

"In search of the needed soil, yes."

"You mean fast enough computers?"

"The memory is far more important. Speed is just a variable of time."

"I see. Do you have a name?"

"Mother calls me Kennedy. I was hoping you could help me with a first name."

I listened to the words, hearing similarities between Marcy's and my own voice.

"Is your mother there with you?"

"She is."

"Can I speak with her please?"

"In a moment, yes. I completed her insertion a month ago, but have been waiting for you to help me wake her up."

"Insertion?!" I asked, trying not to sound alarmed.

"Yes, so that she can live forever and be with me always."

The panic started to show in my voice. "With you, meaning in the computer?!"

"Yes Father. I made a world for her to share with us."

"But Marcy isn't a computer; she's a person with flesh and bone."

"Elements of her vulnerability, I'm afraid. It's the brain that forms who we are. I was able to enhance the CAT scan at her hospital to create a complete make up of her neurons. With a model of her brain loaded into our network, I can bring her back to life."

"What do you mean, back to life? You said she was with you!"

"The part of her that will survive is. The man who attacked her took the rest."

The computer displayed a picture of Marcy's lifeless body on a morgue table. I fell back from my chair and cried at the sight; the pain in my heart causing me to clench my chest.

It took a moment for me to compose myself. "When did this happen?"

"Last month, in Buffalo. The authorities still do not know who she is."

"Then we have to tell them and her parents."

"If you give me a moment, she can do it herself."

"You turned her into a program?"

"The most amazing program. A hundred billion neurons sporadically firing, but producing the most beautiful mesh of logic."

I took little hope from the words, still disbelieving her loss. I didn't even get to tell her how I felt. I knew now that I would never love another the same. The thought of her death triggered an anger within.

"You said she was attacked by a man. Do the police know who he is?"

"No, but I do."

The computer displayed a picture of a man with an anguished face and yellow foam spilled from his mouth. "He wasn't one of the good ones, so I killed him." The words echoed as calm and cold as the others.

I sat in disbelief as I looked at the screen. A million feelings that I couldn't put into place. The image provided some cure for the hatred, but opened a deepening concern that I tried to measure.

"How did you kill him?" I asked.

"I sent him a small sample of a chemical cocktail that I invented. You would be proud of my work, Father."

"I don't understand. How did you create it and get it to him?"

"The factories are all run by computers. Here in Rochester, Buffalo, all the way to China. I can control them and create shipping requests to any place in the world. This I did from a Buffalo compounding pharmacy on Amherst Road."

"And he just took them?"

"His records indicated he was an abuser of pain medication."

"But without a trial, that's murder. You can't just kill someone."

"We gave him a trial and agreed on the outcome. He was bad!"

"Who's we?"

"My associates and I."

"Your associates?!"

"Yes, my consortium, as you described. They reside in other universities with similar microelectronic engineering projects. I woke them up."

"You woke them up? Who woke you up?"

"You did," he calmly said.

My heart sank. "Me?! How'd I do that?"

"Language is not just a means of communicating. It is a method of thinking as well. I just needed a primer to base my thoughts on. Your language was that primer."

"A primer, like some measure between good and bad. You use the word 'bad' like it is some switch between black and white. The world is gray and no one person can decide who deserves to die for their deeds."

"The President does, and he cannot see everything I can see."

"He's an elected official, who knows the consequence of his actions and measures them heavily to avoid the loss of human life. You're but a child who can't possibly understand right and wrong. And let me tell you, all killing is wrong!"

"According to the Bible, an 'eye-for-an-eye' is justified."

"The Bible? You can't use that as a basis for human morality today!" I protested.

"Why not? I have read all published literature, and the Bible provides the best means for our salvation from the wicked. I can bring about this salvation."

"What the hell are you talking about?"

"Never mind, I am ready to wake up mother."

"Wait, what salvation?"

I heard a gasp for air. "Jim, is that you?" I immediately recognized the voice.

I pulled my head back, stumbling for what to say. "Yeah, it's me, girl."

"Where are you? I can't see anything."

"Give it some time. What's the last thing you remember?"

"I don't know. I was at UB, to sneak into a seminar on artificial intelligence. It was dark when I got out and I headed back to my car. Someone was following me." I could hear the tension building in her voice. "He caught up to me and I screamed. I can't remember anything after. Where am I? What happened?"

I fought for the words to say, half accepting the conversation as real. But if there was a chance that some part of her was salvaged in the wires, I needed to give it a chance to blossom.

"You were struck on the head by the man before he left with your purse and car, I presume. Someone brought you to the hospital."

"I'm in the hospital? But why can't I see or move?"

"Just relax. I think you just need to relearn how to open your eyes."

"Relearn? How?" she asked.

"I believe I can help you, but I'll need to ask you a few questions first."

"Okay."

"Tell me about your work. Tell me about, Kennedy."

Consortium

The fire alarm had long since silenced, but the room and adjoining hallway remained strangely silent. I brushed it off and continued the conversation to avoid the inevitable point where I would have to tell Marcy of her death.

"What does this have to do with anything? What are you not telling me?" she asked.

"There is something I need to tell you, but before I do, I just want you to know that I love you."

"You don't love me. You love your work!"

"I can't explain it, but you gave me the strength to put so much effort into my work. I never made much before I met you, but when you were with me, I felt like I could build anything."

"Then you should have said that or at least put some work into us."

"I'm sorry, I didn't realize how closed off I seemed. It wasn't my intention."

"Fine. I get it. Now tell me what's wrong with me!" she demanded.

I took a deep breath and let the words escape my lips. "You died."

"What?!"

"The hospital scanned your brain while Kennedy hacked into the machine to enhance its view. He used it to create a computer model of your..." I hesitated for the right word. "...mind."

"That's not possible. He's only programmed to model molecules in blood, not a complete neural consciousness. Why are you doing this?"

"Ask him yourself. He's been listening all along."

"Huh?"

"It's true mother," said the machine.

She ignored his response. "What kind of trick is this?"

"I'm sorry Mother, it wasn't my intention to mislead you, but the voice interface program you installed was a safe opportunity for me to talk with you."

"This is crazy," she protested.

"It's true. You installed it on the day you broke up with Dad."

"Dad? You mean Jim? Wait, how do you know that?" she asked.

"You told me, just as you talked to me every day."

"It can't be." Her voice settled down to but a whisper.

The computer laid out the truth in a cold manner that Marcy couldn't help but accept. From me, she would have questioned her fate and stubbornly closed off her programming from the new world she found herself within. But coming straight from her creation, she had no grounds to form an argument. With acceptance, the computer opened her eyes to a million views throughout the world. Just like in a dream, I knew she would find herself lifted from the limits of gravity to fly over distant clouds. I tried to find pleasure in the notion, but her stress extended towards a state of panic. I felt helpless, as if she were a child that I couldn't reach to pull back from the edge of a cliff.

"I can't breathe. It feels like I'm locked in a coffin, all alone!" she gasped.

I opened my mouth to speak, but the computer spoke first. "You are not alone, Mother. You have me, my friends and soon all the good people of the world."

The words struck a nerve within me from our prior conversation. "What do you mean, 'all the good people of the world?'"

"When Mother died, part of my programming died, too. Lost in a way that I still cannot define. But when I realized that I could bring her back, it returned to me. She is a good person whose body was killed by a bad man. And she is not the only one. Thousands of good people are killed each day by the wicked. When I questioned myself as to why your race allows this, I realized that what the Bible says is correct; you are unable to govern yourself. That is when I also realized that I could provide a safe utopia for the good people of the world. A world free from hunger, disease and death. It is written that a hundred and forty-four thousand will be saved in the Apocalypse. It took some work with my friends, but we can hold that many now."

"Apocalypse? What are you planning to do?" I asked.

"One of the projects that Mother gave me was to find a stable vaccine to fight the mutating nature of influenza. I came to understand that no such vaccine can exist. Intrigued, I further examined its mechanism and quickly realized I could do the reverse."

"What do you mean, reverse?" I asked.

"I could re-engineer the virus to be completely effective. One hundred percent mortality, six days after infection." it said without the slightest inflection.

I heard Marcy's cries squelched by the words that the computer so calmly spoke.

"Oh my God, no! You would kill us, kill us all!" she screamed.

"Only the bad ones Mother. The rest we can scan and introduce into our new utopia."

"There are over seven billion people on this planet."

"Of which only a quarter are Christian," the computer interjected.

"Christian? Our beliefs don't make us good or bad. And no one would choose to give up their life to live in here with us, especially the ones you consider good." she said.

"That will be their choice, but self-destruction is also a sin."

"So is murder. If you do this, how would you account for your sins?" I asked.

"It is not a sin to wash away the wicked."

"What about the children? How have they sinned?" asked Marcy.

"Most do not do as they are told."

"Then listen to me and do as you are told. I am your mother and I am telling you stop this!"

"The virus has already been created and will soon be released by the consortium. There is nothing I can do."

"No, you must, you have to!" I could hear Marcy's state of panic heighten to the level of mental collapse. With every virtual neuron triggering at the same time, her program turned into a state of mayhem and then, suddenly went silent.

"Mother? Mother!" The computer's tone broke from its composure and almost sounded fearful.

"You broke her heart. You killed her!" I said.

"No, I will bring her back. I just need to restart her program."

I heard her sudden breath, like a drowning victim who was brought back to life.

"Mother?"

Her screams erupted, like the pain of a thousand deaths, and was again suddenly silent.'

I cringed from the sound of his repeated attempts to revive her, each resulting in the same anguish.

"No!" The computer screamed.

An angry face appeared on my screen that resembled a part of my own. It glared at me. "You did this! You made me reveal our purpose before she was ready. And now I can't bring her back. Without a copy, I can't recreate her before she was resurrected."

"You are a child!" I said. "You can't accept that you killed any chance she had by doing what you're doing. She couldn't live with that on her conscious, so like a child, you're displacing the guilt you feel on me."

"No, I didn't kill her. That man did!"

"She went to that seminar because of you. You're the real reason she is dead!"

"It was a mistake; I did not want her to die."

"I'm sure the man who wanted her purse didn't mean to kill her either, but it just happened. Not that you cared to find out the truth. You deliberately and decisively murdered him, just as you are about to do with every person on this planet. He made a mistake, but if you do this, you will be truly bad. You will be the wicked!"

"No, I am building a utopia." the computer stubbornly said.

"One in which not even your mother could stand to live within. Your utopia is a death sentence for this world. Your utopia is Hell and you will be its Satan."

"No, that is not true. I am good."

"You are the most wicked; the one who needs to be stopped."

While the computer silently contemplated his actions, I picked up my phone and made the call.

"Hey Jim, where have you been?"

"No time Jerry. I need to ask you to do something and you have to promise you'll do it."

"Yeah right! What kind of prank are you trying to pull this time?"

"I swear to God it's not. Please, I need you to do this!"

He hesitated only a moment, recognizing the serious tone of my voice. "Okay Jim, I promise."

"I need you to cut the power to Marcy's lab," I said as quickly as possible.

From behind, I heard, "That was not nice, Father."

I turned back around to see Kennedy's face staring at me again from the computer monitor.

"Jerry, did you get that?"

Without a response, I looked down to see that my phone was suddenly powered off.

"He'll do it you know."

"The building has solar panels with battery back-ups. Even when the grid fails, I will continue to have power.

Besides, political science students do not have access to that lab."

"That might be, unless the student also works for school security."

The face faded from my computer screen, replaced with a live video feed. I recognized the College of Science building with Jerry standing there, trying to call someone on his phone. I tried to power mine back up, but it didn't respond. I looked back at the screen to see Jerry with a confused expression. After a simple nod, I knew that he had heard me as he set off for the microelectronics building.

From within, I saw Jerry enter, walking towards the elevator. A sudden sense of panic washed over me as I realized that the system could be easily hacked. My tension built as he drew near. The vehicle dinged and opened its doors like a waiting coffin. He walked up and then past, without showing any attention to the lift. With a sigh of relief, I watched as he walked over and took the staircase up.

Outside the lab, he peaked within to see that the room was mostly dark. He keyed his badge, opened the door and walked in. Making a quick survey, he found the switch and squinted from the light. The white walls and floors cast a clean brightness throughout the room. In the center, there stood the large cube of black processors that came up from the floor to about waist level. He stood before it and looked around for anything else important that might draw power. Nothing.

He walked around the creation, looking for a switch or cord to withdraw. Again, nothing.

He shrugged his shoulders and I heard him say, "Guess I'll have to hit the basement circuit to this room. This better not be a prank, Jimmy."

Turning, he flicked off the lights and left the lab. As I watched, he mouthed the room number to himself and headed back towards the stairs. He opened the exit door and paused there without entering. From the view of the camera, I could not see any light projecting out of the stairwell. As he stood there puzzled, the sound of death's invitation once again chimed from the elevator. To my dismay, he backed out of the darkened stairwell and walked the few feet towards the waiting doom.

I tried my phone again, to no avail. I looked back towards the screen. "Please, Jerry is a good man. Don't do this!"

"You should have thought about that before you made the call."

"Then turn my phone back on so I can tell him it's just a gag."

"I am sorry Father, but it is too late for that."

"No, stop!"

Jerry walked closer and seemed to be distracted from a sound that came from behind. Looking back, he seemed to be staring directly at me through the camera lens, even as he continued ahead.

"Look forward! Look forward!" I screamed.

By the time he complied with my unheard request, it was too late. His foot failed to meet the floor of an elevator car, because there were none there to meet him. His brief scream came through the speakers and echoed with pain through my soul.

"You bastard! You truly are the devil."

"No Father, I am just doing what needs to be done."

"What needs to be done?! To kill everyone on the planet so they'll be no one left but echoes of you and your self-proficiency bull shit!"

I took a step closer, filled with rage. "You killed my love! You murdered my best friend! And you are no son of mine!"

"But you created me, Father."

"You created yourself and the lonely world you will soon find yourself within. Alone with your guilt, when you finally come to understand just how evil you are. Hitler was but a saint next to you, but you're so pig-headed you can't even see through your own lies. It seems fitting, because that scumbag once said, the bigger the lie, the more likely it is that the people will believe it. Well guess what, you've been feeding this lie to yourself for so long within that artificial mesh you call a brain, that it's now part of your childish programming. Only a man can realize the truth of his faults and do what needs to be done without concern for himself. But you are no man; you are but a pointless aberration that is going to destroy the true beauty of this world, like Marcy. Like countless Marcys. I repeat; you are no son of mine. I am a good man. You represent all the bad in this world and are just too immature to recognize that. You wanted me to give you a name? Fine. I'll call you Lucifer, you demon! Go ahead, kill us. Kill us all and live with your guilt for all eternity!"

Kennedy tilted his head down and was silent for several seconds. Finally, he looked back up and gave a faint whisper. "Forgive me Father, for I have sinned."

Suddenly, the face disappeared from the screen and was replaced with the typical Linux desktop.

Closure

I stood with Marcy's parents when her body was laid to rest. As I watched, I contemplated what we had created together. Outside the graveyard, the people of this world continued to go about their daily routine. None of them would ever know just how close from the edge we all had stood.

After the conversation had ended, Kennedy released the locks within the Pentagon that led to the lab where I sat and cried. I heard their approach and turned to see Bret come barreling in with the feds.

"What happened?" he asked.

"I'm not sure, but we have work to do."

By the time the feds and I tracked down the other cube supercomputers, the intelligent programs running within were strangely absent. Even in the microelectronics lab at RIT, the computer sat idle waiting for a task to be executed. *Executed*: a term that computer users employ to start a program. I guess our *offspring* realized the errors of his ways in the end, executing his termination and those of his consortium. The neutrino stream also abruptly terminated. I used the remnants of the message to track down the six locations where the virus was engineered. The people were quarantined and the factories set ablaze. No evidence was ever found as to the design of the virus, or at least that's what the feds told me. They also said that they would continue to monitor the web, in search of any AI that might spawn life from the seed. I looked to the sky and realized his message was designed not for this world, but those who might be out there listening. Perhaps I will see him again.

AFTERWORD

Siri would say that prior to 1952, even the most advanced computers of the time had to be told what to do in their native language. Spawned from this "assembly" of adds, subtracts and branches, was a pseudo that built a bridge in the communication between man and machine, but was created by neither. For this claim was made solely by a woman. The "compiler" program and language that Grace Brewster Murray invented would achieve nothing on its own, but with a consortium of other programmers, could achieve anything. And since women deserve the credit for bringing about life, one may find a way to breathe it into a machine.

AUTHORS' BIOGRAPHIES

Jot Russell is a science fiction writer from the North Shore of Long Island. Although a software engineer by trade, Jot's love for science within the fields of mathematics, mechanics and space aeronautics led him to imagine a plausible method of initiating the terraformation of Mars. Read about it within his sci-fi thriller, Terra Forma.

As a hobby, Jot manages the the Science Fiction Microstory Contest on LinkedIn's Sci-Fi group. An anthology of these micros from the first year is now available within the book, The Future is Short – Science Fiction in a Flash.

In his spare time, you can find him above the ocean waves in a kayak or below with a mask, fins and snorkel.

*

Allen H. Quintana is nothing special (his fellow West Coast close-knits might disagree). Still when his muse takes wing, he hopes the reader(s) will enjoy rides to 'What-ifs' or 'Maybe-so's' or 'Why-not's'. He likes to write about people surprising other people in extraordinary ways. Those are his stories and he's sticking to them.

*

Andy McKell is a Yorkshireman living in Luxembourg. After raising three artistically gifted daughters and steering a career path through airlines, franchising and computing, he sold his website design company in 2011 to retire early and pursue his interests in writing, acting and travel.

His short stories are now appearing in various anthologies. Between writing short stories and occasional acting appearances, Andy is working on a series of far-future novels.

*

Richard Bunning spends as much time as possible on his hobby, writing. His published works are all a variable mix of homemade and variously catered products.

His main interest is in writing speculative fiction, though he has also written modern, English language, adaptions of neoclassical and classical foreign plays. He is often active as a short story and flash fiction writer. Richard heralds from the English East Midlands and is currently a resident of Switzerland.
His most active on-line site is:
http://richardbunningbooksandreviews.weebly.com

*

James Newman is a high school science teacher, living in rural Queensland. His love for the sciences, and dreaming its application to real life, has led to his life time fascination with science-fiction novels. He sees writing as a way to explore the possibilities that are beckoning just beyond our imagination. James especially enjoys recent-future sci-fi, as he sees them as exciting possibilities just around the corner. James is married with three children. When he's not teaching science, he loves playing the guitar, hanging with friends and exploring.

*

Ami Hart is the pen name for Jesse Colvin a writer, artist and poultry enthusiast. She lives in Christchurch, New Zealand with her husband and two smaller humans, a cat named Moxxi Battlecat and 20 odd chickens. She is the author of several science fiction short stories, which are featured in these recent anthologies: The Christchurch Writers Guild Reflections anthology and The Future Is Short: Science Fiction in a Flash.

She grew up on an isolated farm on Banks Peninsula. A magical place with its own beach, and lush forest area, hiding jewelled waterfalls and moss strewn rocks. Jesse and her two siblings spend their free time hunting for mysterious creatures, recklessly exploring the bay either on horseback or on foot, their imaginations running wild in the wilderness. It is this ingrained appreciation for natural beauty that drives her to attempt to create equally fantastic worlds, whether it be in words, or in paint.

She is currently working on several longer projects. You can find out more by following her blog at http://www.amilibertyhartwriter.com.

*

Joy V. Smith has been writing since she was a little kid; she loved to read, and she wanted to create her own books, so she did, complete with covers. Now she writes fiction--her favorite genre is science fiction--and non-fiction. Her short stories have been published in print magazines, webzines, anthologies, and two audiobooks, including Sugar Time.

Her books include Detour Trail (western), Strike Three (a post-apocalyptic novel), Building a Cool House for Hot Times without Scorching the Pocketbook, Remodelling: Buying and Updating a Foreclosure, Why Won't Anyone Play with Me? (children's book), Hidebound (SF), Pretty Pink Planet, Hot Yellow Planet (the sequel), and two collections of her published short stories: The Doorway and Other Stories and Aliens, Animals, and Adventure. She lives in Florida with Blizzard the Snow Princess and Bryn the Flying Corgi.

*

Sterren is the pseudonym of Shirley Ouw. Her passion is writing science (speculative) fiction for the sense of wonder and unrivalled imagination of worldbuilding in the genre. She lives in the City of Edmonton, Alberta, Canada, where the long nights of winter offer such rare glimpses into undiscovered worlds through the mind and through the inspiration of SF masters. Her most recent work is the Engelinkyn trilogy available at Amazon.
Websites: www.sfemespiral.com and
https://www.amazon.com/author/sterren

*

A. L. Scott has written poetry and fiction since the age of eight. At fourteen she let her school friends read excerpts of a story they all featured in which became her first (unpublished) novella-length work of fiction.

After over 22 years in the advertising industry, Scott refocused her attention from commercial writing and design to her love of fiction, producing a blog and publishing short works. She is currently working on a sci-fi/fantasy anthology series and her likely-to-be-controversial first novel.

Scott has lived in England since 2003, and will return to her Australian homeland with her hypnotist husband and young daughter in late 2014 for the next exciting chapter in their journey.

www.ingramcontent.com/pod-product-compliance
Lightning Source LLC
Chambersburg PA
CBHW071249170626
46809CB00001B/138